CONSENSUAL HEX

CONSENSUAL HEX

AMANDA HARLOWE

GRAND CENTRAL
PUBLISHING

NEW YORK   BOSTON

Copyright © 2020 by Amanda Harlowe Miller

Jacket art and design by Tree Abraham. Jacket copyright © 2020 by Hachette Book Group, Inc.

Hachette Book Group supports the right to free expression and the value of copyright. The purpose of copyright is to encourage writers and artists to produce the creative works that enrich our culture.

The scanning, uploading, and distribution of this book without permission is a theft of the author's intellectual property. If you would like permission to use material from the book (other than for review purposes), please contact permissions@hbgusa.com. Thank you for your support of the author's rights.

Grand Central Publishing
Hachette Book Group
1290 Avenue of the Americas, New York, NY 10104
grandcentralpublishing.com
twitter.com/grandcentralpub

First Edition: October 2020

Grand Central Publishing is a division of Hachette Book Group, Inc. The Grand Central Publishing name and logo is a trademark of Hachette Book Group, Inc.

The publisher is not responsible for websites (or their content) that are not owned by the publisher.

The Hachette Speakers Bureau provides a wide range of authors for speaking events. To find out more, go to www.hachettespeakersbureau.com or call (866) 376-6591.

Print book interior design by Abby Reilly.

Library of Congress Cataloging-in-Publication Data

Names: Harlowe, Amanda, author.
Title: Consensual hex / Amanda Harlowe.
Description: First edition. | New York : Grand Central Publishing, 2020.
Identifiers: LCCN 2020005492 | ISBN 9781538752203 (hardcover) | ISBN 9781538752210 (ebook)
Subjects: GSAFD: Occult fiction.
Classification: LCC PS3608.A7445 C66 2020 | DDC 813/.6--dc23
LC record available at https://lccn.loc.gov/2020005492

ISBNs: 978-1-5387-5220-3 (hardcover), 978-1-5387-5221-0 (ebook)

Printed in the United States of America

LSC-C

10 9 8 7 6 5 4 3 2 1

To my unconditionally loving, phenomenal parents. And to the survivors who weren't believed. I believe you. Keep going.

WINTER BREAK

THERE ARE TWO TYPES OF rapists, the corkscrew-haired receptionist at the local hotline says with an additional drag on her cigarette—she doesn't smoke often and she's going to quit any day now, probably tonight, probably after this one last smoke, it's just that she's only come back from the hospital in the past hour and now she's being questioned and she needs to take the edge off, you know?

There are two types of rapists, she repeats. Her eyes are dark underneath, shot with cracked-glass veins—she's just returned from the hospital, you see, she had to hold the hand of a three-year-old going through a rape exam after they picked her up from her stepfather's trailer at midnight. If that's not an excuse to smoke...

She takes the cigarette away from her mouth. Smoke unfurls over the monitor of her mid-aughts Dell. The phone starts to ring. She cranes her long neck over the cubicle divider.

"Georgia, can you grab that?"

She sits down. Her fingers shake, and her cigarette wilts like a half-dismembered branch after a hurricane.

The first type of rapist is stupid, she says. He openly admits to rape. The jury laughs at him in court, standing in front of the judge in his hockey jacket (not that she means to demonize athletes, but the stupid ones are often athletes), saying that, yes, he "forced" his penis into Ms. Doe's mouth, until the jury thinks about it and their lips go numb.

The other type, she says, is a snake.

He joins feminist groups. Collects signatures for Planned Parenthood. Even wears a T-shirt with THIS IS WHAT A FEMINIST LOOKS LIKE displayed across his skinny chest. The hetero girls think he's gay. Or bi, hopefully. He listens like a good ally when the girls discuss Margaret Atwood and Judith Butler. He shuts his mouth like a man should.

In three months he rapes four girls. All in his room. Because alcohol was involved, he proposes that they simply don't remember what really happened, that just because a sexual experience wasn't enjoyable doesn't mean it was rape, my God, don't victimize yourself.

At once, the receptionist with the birthday-ribbon mass of hair draws her hand over her mouth like a curtain and leans in.

This is not for the record, but that boy you've come in asking about—she knows him.

She can't say what happened, not definitively. She doesn't remember all of it. Just his Axe cologne. And the jaded yellow tile of the bathroom floor. And—well, you get the picture.

But when she took him to court—to upgrade her campus no-contact order to a civil order, the kid was stalking her after the incident and she had loads of texts, he was a little novice of a garter snake, not a viper—he shook and shook and the six-hundred-dollar-an-hour Hamptons lawyer his parents flew in started wiping his brow repeatedly with the edge of his Brooks Brothers sleeve and checking his watch.

Oh.

All right, then.

So you want information on the potential whereabouts of John Digby Whitaker III, otherwise known as Tripp, the Amherst senior who disappeared right before finals?

You think this could be connected with the vigilantes from the fall—the "witches" (obviously the boys showing up at various infirmaries with burns and broken thumbs meant to say *bitches*)?

The receptionist finishes her cigarette and laughs.

CHAPTER ONE

AMORAL FAMILISM

THE TRUTH IS, I DIDN'T want to go to college at all. Even once we're chugging gas down I-90, west to the foot of the Berkshires, the end of Massachusetts and the beginning of New York, I don't have the overwhelming desire to leave home and find myself at the bottom of a tequila bottle. I just wish home were populated with different people. I tried to tell my parents that I didn't want to go to college—I wanted to write books, or go to L.A. and live out of my car until I made it as a big-time director—several times: the drive up to Middlebury sophomore year; baccalaureate, graduation robes slung with not-enough honors; when my mom was crying in the master bedroom last night. My dad's response, lingering on the edge of Miller Lite bliss, was the same as before: I'd have to experience college before I could hate it.

He doesn't understand. My distress comes not from unawareness, but from intense, crystalline knowledge of communal shower floors and the piercing memory of my chemistry tutor's story about her cousin who died from swine flu because his roommates forgot to get him Gatorade and he got dehydrated. She had a tattoo of his face, forever young, in black ink on her left calf. Sure, I was relieved, after four years of delirious coasting (still doing better than the pissing-yourself-in-front-of-your-sophomore-soiree-date-after-too-much-vodka majority, but never as well as I could have), sneaking food into the computer lab behind the ninety-year-old nuns' backs and playing with the Adobe suite some donor paid for, to have gotten into Smith, a bona fide *very good college* that will enable me to go to a law school that I can really brag about. But my desire to do more than scrape by, to have reached some kind of summit on the cliff of my potential rather than just sunbathing on the valley floor, always rises from the dust of Zara's drawer (where we would always hide our report cards before my parents started calling the school and asking for extra copies). In the two-plus hours between home and Northampton, meditating to emo drums and drizzling window views of the remote stretches of the Mass Pike, pines craning their slender necks over the guardrails, I feel nothing but subterranean dread, on a day that's supposed to be bursting with the fresh juice of a major life milestone.

We reach Northampton—lesbian couples with strollers, hemp clothing store, yarn emporium—around three, and my father is angry. He's screaming at the car in front of us, a crimson Honda Civic with a REDDIT license plate and a driver who bears an uncanny resemblance to George R. R. Martin.

My father beats the horn as we round the traffic circle. He then interjects with "Cocksuckers!" because homophobia helps him let off steam.

The light turns green. We're about to cross the intersection when a couple with a Baby Bjorn and two French bulldogs saunter onto the street. My dad hits the brakes.

"Jesus Christ, do all the dykes in America live in Northampton?" he says, and I remember how the absolute last thing I want to discover is that I'm gay at college, because then I'd be a scarlet-lettered LUG (Lesbian Until Graduation), gay before May, a trend chaser, a sheep, not my own person. Weird. A failure. If there's one thing that would deepen my father's frown, that would make things worse than him just ignoring me every time I walk downstairs and say "Hi, Dad," like I'm a ghost, like I'm dead, it's discovering I'm gay at college. Though he mentioned once that it would be okay if I were really gay, which I wasn't, so long as I were to marry a real woman and become one half of the type of lesbian couple "men like to fantasize about," my mom added, before she also assured me that I definitely wasn't gay.

But I won't be gay at college. I've never touched a dick but I know I love them.

We cut through the maze of cars and arrive at my new residence, Chapin House, the biggest house not on the Quad. Margaret Mitchell lived here for one year before she dropped out, and her description of the staircase at Tara is said to have been inspired by Chapin's staircase, except the building got renovated ten years ago and they demolished those stairs and built something dull and dark in their place (Yankee revenge on the fictional Old South). Behind Chapin is the greenhouse, and then there's the lake, and across the lake are the woods. I don't think the woods are forbidden, but the close-crocheted amber summer pines remind me too much of Wompatuck, the huge reserve in my town where sex offenders camp out with stolen greyhounds and a year's supply of baked beans. I vow not to go hiking, at least not alone.

My roommate Rachel's mother has MS, so Rachel's family got permission from the school to move in one day early. Even though Rachel and I swore on Facebook in June we would make a floor plan for the room together, draw straws or flip coins or rock-paper-scissors, she's gone ahead and claimed the good side of the room and I can tell by the horde of overhydrated plants occupying her superior windowsill that she has no intention of drawing up a treaty or agreeing to a cease-fire. I'm not surprised. Rachel is the kind of person who doesn't get why people hate John Green, and it's often those Pumpkin Spice Latte types who can't be fully trusted, not with matters like collaborating on our room design.

My dad goes back to the car to grab my fourth suitcase.

"Are you feeling okay?" My mom puts her hands on my shoulders, and I realize I don't remember the last time she touched me.

"I'm glad I'm at school," I say. "I need a new start. And to start exercising."

"That's all a doctor would ever tell you to do," she says, kneading her fingers between my shoulder blades like I'm made of frozen dough.

I push her away and go to sit on the edge of my bed. "You still don't think I should get checked out?"

"Any doctor would just tell you to exercise, honey." She goes to open the window, starts talking about the importance of fresh air in her Snow White lilt, as if she's about to burst into song and command the little sparrows to dust the cabinetry. It's just like sophomore year, when she was sitting in the green velvet chair in the newly renovated living room with the floor-length windows and her only response was *No you don't, honey*, like I was a three-year-old ranting about Pretty Pretty Princess and not a nearly grown woman who'd just worked up the courage to say *I want to kill myself*.

My dad returns, complaining about all my stuff and how not all parents are so generous, how most parents would not let me bring four suitcases. "You're going to love college," he continues. "It's such an *intellectual* environment, you'll fit right in." Of course, *intellectual* is code for *impractical*, *useless*, *disappointing*, but I thank him anyway and promise to get perfect grades and get into Harvard Law.

He dumps the suitcase on my desk chair, brushes the dust from his hands, and reminds me that I wouldn't survive at Harvard Law, not like his friend's son who is just more that type of kid, if I catch his drift.

"Columbia Law," I say, and he reiterates that he's just trying to help, and I don't need to worry about where I go to law school; it's not about where you go to school, it's about who you know and whether or not you make Law Review. And Mom never went to graduate school, she went straight into the workforce and she hasn't exactly done badly either.

"Honey, I have a call this afternoon so we need to move it along," she says.

Once I have the mattress pad down (so Mom can sleep at night, knowing I won't be in contact with whatever has happened on the mattress before) and Dad makes sure I have a phone charger and a raincoat, my parents hug me and leave.

"Goodbye," I yell after them, watching the backs of my mom's older-than-me Eddie Bauer suede and my dad's Patagonia flash through the door.

"Love you," my mom says, feigning tears.

My dad seizes her arm and barks something about traffic.

Alone. I check my phone. Then I check to make sure I have my birth control pills. I open the package and—*shit*. I took two pills last night when I was supposed to take one. I think I put one pill in my mouth and halfway through swallowing I thought Zara texted me, so I ran in the direction of the vibration before discovering that it was just my iPhone calendar letting me know that I was leaving tomorrow.

Hormones—probably why I feel like shit. Or I feel like shit because of Zara. But I shouldn't feel like shit because of Zara, because Zara said goodbye really nicely and waved and smiled and I'm sure she's going to text me and we're still going to be friends.

Rachel comes back. She's sipping a venti mocha and won't mention where we're going to get dinner until I ask her point-blank.

She finishes watering her plants, screws her Poland Spring closed, and leans over her twin XL to crack open the window.

"I actually was going to get dinner with Katherine from next door, if that's okay," she says.

I wait for her to ask if I want to come with them.

She leaves. I rush across the room, slam the window closed, and sink my face into her pillow. I know I should get up, but I can't stop crying, even though this is Rachel's pillow and I'm going to have to replace her pillowcase with one of mine and she's going to notice. This is the same feeling I've had all summer: observing my decline into sedentary misery like a reptile-blooded surgeon standing over my own shaven-head form, ready to cut my skull open right along the hairline and scoop out the problem and replace it with what should have been my rightful human inheritance, the ability to gracefully sit in a darkened cubicle of a room and do as I am told.

Too bad what's wrong with me can't be fixed with a scalpel.

In the absence of social validation, after replaying and recontemplating Rachel's obvious hatred of me and what it could be about my skull and scent and skin that makes people loathe me as soon as they are unfortunate enough to look my way, I opt for the momentary delight of mindless consumerism—the sustainable, proto-commune type. Chapin's free bin is right at the foot of the stairs, a decrepit cardboard box underflowing with Dora pencils and Pocky boxes, and a pair of really obscene platform shoes, complete with pornographically high heels, in goldenrod yellow. The kind of shoes that belong in the attic of that great-aunt who lived in the East Village back when it was the *real* East Village, during her tenure as the free love girlfriend of an art dealer with an overgrown handlebar mustache.

I exchange Zara's Old Navy jacket (a navy blue cropped bomber I actually really like but I now hate because I hate Zara now) for the shoes, because maybe height does equal power.

After dropping the shoes off in my room, I find the will to go to the bathroom. There's a pair of feet in stiletto Oxfords in the last stall. I hear the subtle clack of thumbs on a screen, and a few sniffles, so I assume if she does come out, we'll make a silent pact to ignore each other and, if we see each other again, pretend we never met.

I'm still sobbing when I get to the sink, so I splash my face with water repeatedly, but it doesn't help, I still have the blotchy cheeks and red eyes of a social-media-induced twenty-first-century breakdown.

I'm about to turn the water off when she comes out of the stall.

She's a waifish Asian girl in Pippi Longstocking thigh socks and denim cutoffs, a dog-eared Didion crammed inside her elbow, and when she smiles and says "Hello," she's already my enemy because she's seen me all red and slathered in mucus and I'm sure she's thinking how weak and pathetic I am and how it would be better for the world as a whole if I just had the courage to hang myself with my baby blanket.

"I'm Luna," she says. She tells me she lives in the room right next to the bathroom, and she accidentally has a single because the girl who was supposed to be her roommate is taking a gap year.

She asks if I want to get dinner. She's going with her friend who lives in Lawrence House. Afterward, we could swing by Lawrence and try to see Sylvia Plath's old room. Luna knows the girl who lives there.

"I'm good," I say. "I'm already getting dinner with someone."

She smiles, like she hates me. "You sure?"

"I'm sure, thanks."

"Cool. See you around," Luna says with a wave of her vermilion nails, and part of me, suddenly, desperately, wants to join her side, compliment her hair, ask her about *Slouching Towards Bethlehem* and get bubble tea after dinner and not stop talking until we come back to the bathroom to take off our eyeliner.

"See you," I say.

"I live right next to the bathroom," she repeats with a glance over her shoulder, in a tone I expect to interpret as pity, but feels like a golden June fireside, a whole branch of marshmallows dripping onto her thighs.

CHAPTER TWO

MADWOMEN

I GO TO ALL THE required Orientation events, the auditorium speeches about the honor code and diversity and sexual misconduct that you have to attend in order to get your registration code, but otherwise I sit in my room and try to pay attention to *Orphan Black*, or, when I figure I should go outside, sit cross-legged on the lawn with a book in my lap, watching people learning and flirting and smoking weed with confidence and the adventurous, toothy ruggedness that accompanies a self-image that isn't constantly sifting through your fingers and expanding into an ever-greater pile of quicksand.

People try to talk to me, try to get me to come and join the icebreakers in Chapin's common room (they assure me they won't do the viral one from Swarthmore, where everyone has to line up in descending order of oppression).

I always have an excuse: migraine, cramps, all the graphic period issues you're not supposed to talk about in the big wide polite world of not-women's-colleges, where you must say you're *under the weather* to seem dainty and appealing to hypothetical male listeners.

"We're *totally* understanding of that here," one of the Orientation leaders assures me. "Let me know if you need any Midol."

Way back when—junior year, when Zara and I would go to Starbucks and loudly discuss Gramsci and Gloria Steinem, until she fell out of fashion for being a TERF (trans-exclusionary radical feminist)—I had this idea that I was going to be a Campus Activist, and when the Smith course catalog arrived with a list of clubs, I vowed to go to the first meeting of every "political" student organization. But by the time Orientation week rounds up on a rainy Friday, I only feel okay enough to go to Smithies Against Sexual Violence, which meets once per month and doesn't require members to attend every meeting.

They meet in an empty lecture hall basement decorated with a solitary poster explaining that you should not speak just to speak; you should let other folks talk when the issue concerns their daily bread, not just some tragedy you saw on the news. There are a couple of guys at the meeting, male allies from the other Five College campuses. One stands out from the scruffy hipsters in his Amherst hoodie and whale-print pants (in that washing machine accident they call *Nantucket red*), sand-hewn Sperry topsiders on his feet. But he's carrying a copy of Judith Butler, which washes him clean like a bucket of holy water. He's the sort of guy I suppose I should like, who might play a round of golf with my brother and spontaneously whip out a bouquet when he's got his arm around me on top of a Ferris wheel, overlooking the shore fading to dark Atlantic, the end of the cotton-candy seersucker world.

I wonder if it will play out like Zara promised me over flatbreads and carrot hummus at the deli where she worked. That day she *didn't* tell me that no guy could ever be attracted to me (unlike that other time, with Gianna in my room, where we all confessed we'd touched ourselves without ever using the word *masturbated*, and Zara assured me I was safe from sexual harassment because, in her words, *No offense, no one is ever going to look at you as a sex object*, and Gianna objected because she's nice). At the deli, Zara assured me *it* would happen, with a friend, after we got to know each other over common interests and *that sort of thing* just arises out of getting coffee and exchanging DVDs and eventually making out. Only I didn't have any male friends. Zara then criticized me for intentionally attending a women's college and started telling me about her friend with a pineapple allergy who had to go to the hospital the other night because she was hanging out with her boyfriend, and then, you know, she started to go down on him and all of a sudden she was like, "*Cade! You know I'm allergic to pineapple!*"

I didn't want to blow any male friends, I said. I wasn't sure I wanted to blow anyone, especially if blowjobs land girls in the emergency room.

Zara rolled her eyes and assured me she hadn't gone down on that guy she was seeing, who worked at the café at Barnes & Noble and desperately wanted to unlock the Zara Karen

Khoury Pussy™, especially after he kept paying for dinner. It must be great to have so many guys into you, I said, watching her lick the dripping white feta from the webbed skin between her fingers.

Before the meeting starts, I learn the Amherst guy's name is Tripp—which we almost started calling my brother before my mom objected—and he's from Greenwich. Great, I'm from Fairfield, originally, before we had to move for my mom's job. We talk about Connecticut and dogwood trees, Metro-North, and the Blue Man Group. Oh, I'm a freshman— sorry, *first-year*? Intending to be a history major? We have something in common. "Great shoes," he adds, pointing to my feet wobbling in the platforms, his hand accidentally brushing mine.

He says he's a sophomore and he just thinks it's so critical that *male allies* work together with women activists to fight sexual assault. Like how in Sweden, they did that big campaign encouraging men to stick up to their buddies trying to steal disoriented women from bars, and it cut rates of sexual assault by a huge margin. We should all be like Scandinavia.

I'm asking him why he's at the Smith group, instead of the one at Amherst, when a girl trips over his outstretched legs. Her hundred-calorie bag of Doritos catapults into the air and spills over his lap.

"Go to hell," Tripp says with a smirk, brushing the crumbs off his pants. Then: "Sorry, I didn't mean—are you all right?"

He helps her up, his knee a ladder, his hair shining like the helmet of a knight.

16

"Are you all right?" he repeats.

The girl doesn't respond, and as she's walking away she looks me in the eye.

It's *her* again, the Chapin bathroom girl with the thigh socks—Luna—but this time, instead of staring at me with Fourth of July–seaside-barbecue, serape-blanket expectation, she's seething. Her brown eyes are muddy, her glasses fogged up with tears.

So *he* broke up with *her*.

Tripp and I sit next to each other during the meeting, which is moderated by a blue-haired senior with rainbow feathers dangling from her ears and her shorter, Justin Bieber–lesbian roommate. They want us to make T-shirts about sexual assault, which they will use for a protest art exhibition on the Quad, with all the T-shirts arranged in a big circle. But they want us to turn the shirts inside out during the day, so as not to trigger anyone.

They're just about to discuss the budget when heavy feet in sneakers crash down the stairs.

It's a petite girl, and she's halfway between sobbing and cackling. She reaches the last step, careens out of the shadows, and turns to the messy rectangular assortment of tables and chairs, student limbs sprawled everywhere. But her eyes, red and shot with veins, aren't looking at the confused congregation—she's staring up at the high fluorescence of the ceiling, as if she's been blinded.

' The girl grips her middle and chokes back a sob. She's swaddled in athletic gear, running shorts and an Amherst sweatshirt, blue k-tape wrapped in a thick layer around her knee, but she's frail, with small wasted muscles and ankles so delicate they look ready to snap at a vigorous gust of wind. She is barefoot (there's a tattoo clenching her ankle, the red string of fate). Her hair is wet, her face pocked with acne.

She reaches into the fleece pocket of her hoodie and removes a long plastic object that I realize too late is a vibrator.

The girl cries out and flings the vibrator at the group, knocking over the slim white vase holding a sprig of white daisies, just as more feet pound down the stairs: Campus Police, mumbling into radios, followed by a pair of paramedics bearing a slim white stretcher.

I stare at the vibrator on the floor, the mess of flowers and water and ceramic shards, as the girl screams over the radio fizzle and the paramedics wrestle her onto the stretcher.

"You know who you are," the girl is screaming. "I have your texts, I have the sweatshirt, I have evidence—"

The paramedics start hoisting her up the stairs, one officer bounding up the steps to hold the door open—but I can still hear her, "*I have proof, it's not just my word.*"

The stretcher disappears, the door creaks and shuts, the screams roll away, and all that's left are the girl's muddy footprints.

We stare at the moderator, who doesn't know what to do.

"Uh, can people help us clean this up?" she says, indicating the flowers and the vibrator.

No one wants to touch the vibrator, but I pick up a daisy and the Bieber lookalike finds paper towels in an abandoned cabinet.

"Are you all right?" says Tripp, hand on my back, as I spin the daisy and try to look busy.

"What? Yes—" I drop the flower.

He picks it up.

"For you," he says, handing it back to me.

Someone else is sobbing.

Actually, two people, but Luna—who has since removed her glasses, wiping them on her cardigan—is walking toward me, and I wonder if she's going to throw something at me, if she's a part of this.

She passes me, and I hold the flower out to her; she doesn't take it.

"Excuse me," says Luna.

I'm blocking her way. "Sorry."

"It's fine." She passes the vibrator, stepping over it clumsily, so her heel twists the long pink object sideways and the rounded end points at Tripp's golf-tanned feet.

Luna goes upstairs; the group starts to disassemble.

Tripp puts his hand on my back again.

"Leisl," he says. "Has anyone ever told you you look like Taylor Swift?"

Tripp walks me out. We go to the PVTA stop and wait for the bus. The rain has stopped, but the concrete is damp and mosquitoes keep pricking my arms.

"You sure you'll get back to your room okay?" Tripp asks, opening his wallet to remove a bus token, his plastic Amherst ID reflecting the streetlight (CLASS OF 2014).

"Chapin is like two hundred feet away," I say, craning my chin toward the postcard red-brick exterior of the house. "And I thought you were a sophomore?"

He ignores my question, starts to smoke; he asks me if I want one.

"My grandfather died from lung cancer," I say.

Tripp exhales, smoky tendrils reaching out to smack my cheeks and eyes. I start to cough.

"My dad was a smoker," says Tripp. "But he stopped when I was seven. He was supposed to be on the plane that flew into the Twin Towers, would you believe it? But something went wrong with his luggage. He got delayed."

"My mom almost died in 9/11," I say. "She was supposed to be at a meeting at the World Trade Center that morning. But she was late. She's never late for anything in her life. That's why I believe in God."

"But how could God have let all those other people die?" Tripp says, hazel eyes hooded and bloodshot. "Is God still good if he only saves you?"

"God doesn't always make sense." I pause, hoping he won't think I'm an idiot for repeating my sophomore-year nun teacher's explanation for why evil exists if God only creates good things. "So when are you going to stop smoking? What terrorist event or natural disaster will you have to narrowly avoid to convince yourself to quit?"

He laughs, and, like all nicotine-dependent twenty-year-olds asked to defend their habit, doesn't provide an answer. I remember sitting in my house with Zara after I tried to get her to stop smoking, that time she got a splinter from the new wood floors and sat in my mom's velvet chair while she removed it, caught her blood on a single tissue; when I pointed out *the statistics* she just insisted she was going to die young. I hope Tripp isn't planning to die young. I hope he's planning to stop being a mild asshole so he can ask me to the Hamptons next summer and his dad can introduce me to the dean of Columbia Law so I can coast by on a three-point-seven and not a four-point-oh because I've got *connections*.

A bike hitched to the fence rattles in the wind, but not long enough. Tripp's chapped mouth is sealed and it's up to me to fix the silence.

"I wonder what happened to that girl," I say.

"What girl?" He raises an eyebrow, my chest ballooning with inadequacy. "Oh, *that* girl."

Silence. Closed mouth. I gulp and feel like I always do when I send a text that is accidentally unanswerable and I spend the next five hours with my phone against my hip, ready to climb into a hole and seal myself underground forever. "I mean, I hope they're able to take care of her at the hospital—"

Tripp puts his hand on my shoulder.

"You're a freshman," he says. "Sorry—*first-year*. You don't know."

I gulp. "I don't know what?"

He takes his hand away. "You don't know her."

"No?"

"Her name is Clara. She goes to Amherst."

"What happened to her?"

"She obviously just had a mental breakdown. She was, well, it's hard to say without sounding insensitive. One of *those* girls. The type who goes around accusing every man

21

she encounters of some serious crime just because they were both drunk one night and something happened she doesn't remember. God, it's not like she didn't have someone with her when she went to get the morning-after pill. And he *paid*. Anyway, what I'm saying is—"

"What?"

"I slept with her," he admits, hands shoved deep in his pockets; with his admission, he turns from a silver knight to gold, solid gold, a prize at the end of the race, a medal to hang over the mantel and dust. "And she's just, like, this *insane* girl. I really hope she's able to get the help she needs."

The PVTA bus halts at the light and Tripp slings his backpack over his shoulder.

He touches me, again.

"Leisl," he says, and I'm amazed he remembers my name. "I've got my own TV in my room. Why don't you come back to Amherst?"

His skin collects the yellow streetlight and spits it back gilded; he's that hazel-cat-eye, upturned-nose, sharp-jaw phenotype of Burberry fragrance and rolled-up white shirts, the kind of guy I *should* want, desperately. I feel like if I could just get a picture of us making out and post it where Zara would see it, that would be enough. Proving that an objectively hot guy was into me, that's all I need.

"I have an Orientation thing early," I say, "and you look tired."

The PVTA careens toward the curb.

"Oh, I'm so sorry," Tripp says, his voice ringing like an auriscope shining deeper and deeper into my ear canal. "Another time?"

The bus headlights swing into view; he grins, cups the back of my neck, and kisses me. He smells like dish soap, the lavender kind, a strangely clinical, dental-mask-latex sort of scent that makes me wonder if carnal passion is like swallowing bland toast and warm orange juice, something you only eat because breakfast is the most important meal of the day. He's messing up my hair and I don't know what to do with my hands. I'm glad he's being clear with his intentions, but I feel something in me twist, and it's not until he quits sucking my bottom lip that I realize the feeling is unpleasant. I don't want him close to my body, even though he's a man, he's attractive, he goes to Amherst, and he probably has a house in the Hamptons.

Tripp stops kissing me and I feel better. Why don't we go to dinner, he asks as he inches toward the bus. What do I like? Sushi? All girls like sushi. I assure him I'm the real sort of sushi lover, I like everything raw, but I won't eat sea urchin two hours from the coast because it's supposed to be alive when you consume it and I don't trust seafood delivery trucks, not after my Vermont food poisoning incident.

He'll text me.

ʊ

Saturday, he texts *good morning*, and my heart swims—men are always better in retrospect, I realize—but then the texts stop, even after I ask him, for the *second* time, if we're going to get sushi.

23

Saturday night, I'm alone. By Sunday, I'm subsisting on diet soda and energy bars in the comfort of my twin XL. Convocation—the ringing in of the academic year, a tremendous celebration in the main auditorium where all the seniors are naked and the first-years swear they'll never be naked and the bare-breasted Head Residents are taking swigs of vodka and recalling that they felt the same way *when I was your age*—is tonight, but I ignore the false invitations of my floor's RA, and Rachel's guilty last-minute attempt at including me in her group of intramural volleyball *Bachelorette* friends.

Tripp texts me after sunset, and invites me to meet him at SooRa, which closes in an hour. I wear the shoes he likes, and run, not walk, past the auditorium booming with laughter, past the Northamptonites ushering their dogs through the melted-butter air, my throat tight from moving so fast. Tripp texting me late doesn't mean anything, aside from that he's busy, which is a good thing, he doesn't just play video games, and not texting me back immediately doesn't mean he thinks I'm ugly.

And, even though it's super essentialist, it's like my mom always says: *Boys will be boys.*

SooRa—nestled at the bottom of a hill, next to a parking lot and the Peter Pan bus station, marquee sign and neon-nailed hostess, a table by the window—is the restaurant my mom took me to when we first visited Northampton, when I decided to go to Smith because the tour guide and a bunch of her friends had all gotten into top-fourteen law schools, there were no triple rooms, and Northampton had good restaurants. (Though, looking out the window, up the hill, past the used bookstore and the witch shop, not much else.)

I order a sparkling water and wait. They bring out the free kimchi and chilled potato appetizers, and I'm still waiting. I take out my book (*Cold Mountain*) and then I'm like, *Fuck it*, I don't know anyone here and I'm sick of pretending I can focus on any block of text for more than thirty seconds without my own inner experience dripping down my eyes.

The waitress comes back with a second Pellegrino. I wonder what Zara would say if she saw me eating kimchi alone, the first weekend of college. I search my backpack for the wrong-prescription glasses I have for lectures and crying in public and hope the staff doesn't think I'm looking for a homemade bomb.

The waitress returns. "May I please take your order?" The back end of her pen tangles a long string of Mardi Gras rainbow beads. She must go to my school; she's probably planning to hit the Convocation after-party once she gets off work.

"I'm still waiting for someone," I say.

"The kitchen is closing in thirty minutes," says the waitress as she scribbles down my order, and it's not a second after her denim-skirted back turns and I shove the Warby Parkers onto my face that I sink my mouth into my hands and start to cry.

The hostess swings by, and the next table fills up with a young man who has the sort of greasy split-down-the-middle haircut typical of libertarian fans of Lars von Trier, his gooey secularist heart encased in an ironic Darwinist T-shirt from CafePress. He's followed by an older woman, perhaps not his mother but a relative, putting her weight on a walker.

He stares at me, longer than could be justified by my hair

sticking straight up or a piece of seaweed obscuring my two front teeth. I start to think of Zara and how I'm so unfuckable, of my dad and how last spring when I tried biking to school to lose weight he swerved his head underneath the kitchen table to get a good look at my thighs and frowned wordlessly. *He's still staring at me.* Greasy film guy is exactly the sort of man Zara predicted I would be fucking in college, because who else would want access to my unappetizing pussy, even if his gaze vibrates like a hornet, the whole restaurant smells like fish but it smelled fresh until he got here.

Salmon donburi arrives. I call the waitress back to the table and ask her to bring me chopsticks instead of cutlery, because I can't stop staring at the knife and thinking about the serrated edge sawing through fingers or leg or stomach.

I eat and don't feel better, just less angry.

The guy at the next table is still staring at me.

I grab my purse and decide to go to the restroom, to see if he'll forget about me if I'm not in his sight.

I brush past his table and he grabs my arm.

"The fuck?" I tug my hand away, with enough force that he knocks into the table and his glass of water tips over, soaking the tablecloth and the lap of the older woman.

The staff rush over.

I hear the front door slam, and my name: "Leisl?"

Tripp rushes over like a nineties fairy tale knight, saving me because I'm genuinely in danger and not because I'm incompetent and need to be saved. He's red across the forehead and down his nose, fist stretching toward the middle-part guy, but I get between them.

"It's fine," I say. "He wasn't—"

Tripp seizes my shoulders. "Are you okay?" He's loud, perhaps too loud, and I sense the eyes of the staff and other patrons on the cutout back of my cheap linen tank top, on his square sun-bruised fingers digging into my skin.

Tripp waves to the hostess. "Can we get another table?"

We move to a table in the very back, halfway behind a shoji screen. I can't see the hostess or the door. Tripp sits down across from me.

"Sorry I'm late," he says. He stares at my mostly empty bowl, chopsticks laid across the rim. "Did you eat?"

"Yeah, I did," I say.

Tripp orders a tuna roll and two cups of hot sake, flashing his fake.

"No, just one," I tell the waitress.

Tripp shakes his head. "Make it two."

"I'm kind of sensitive to alcohol," I tell Tripp after the waitress departs.

"Sake is not that alcoholic."

The food arrives, with the drinks. Tripp insists I drink the sake.

I sip it; my nose crinkles. "I don't like it."

"You need to try something more than once to see if you like it," he says, mouth full of rice and fish.

He starts looking at his phone, and all my doubts return.

"I'm going to the bathroom," I say, standing.

He slips his phone into his pocket. "Don't worry, I'll watch your drink."

I lurch past the central tables, through the bamboo curtains to the bathroom. When I return, Tripp still isn't done eating.

"I think the restaurant closes soon," I remind him.

"I know," he says. "You should finish your drink."

I go to grab my drink, then stop. "What if I don't want to finish it?"

He frowns. "You know, I bought it for you. It's only polite to drink some of it."

"I don't think so."

Tripp seizes my hand.

"I think you do," he says, and even though my mind says *pull away pull away pull away*, I can't.

I look at his chest—there's a crystal point hanging from the black cord around his neck—and at his napkin, where my name is written in faint red ink, *LEISL DAVIS*.

"I think you should finish your drink," says Tripp, and, like I'm attached to someone else's limbs, my spare hand grabs the sake and brings it to my lips. I swallow the entire cup.

Tripp lets go of my hand and calls for the check. He pays.

"I'll walk you back," he says, helping me to my feet, his touch gentle again.

I feel like I'm watching myself from an observatory, my body leaning into Tripp, moving with him through the door, up the shallow hill and onto Northampton's Main Street, the humid night speckled with blinking red lamps and giggling throngs of college girls.

"I'll get you home," Tripp assures me. Every movement I make is a surprise; I should feel terror, but there's this strange, dreamy calm within me, indifferent to the fact that I'm basically a puppet.

Tripp turns us in the opposite direction of Chapin. That terror, the *no no no*, returns to my gut like a crack of lightning.

"I need to sit down," I insist, but I still can't move of my own accord; my mind is all fire, *no no no*, but he still has my body.

Tripp brings me inside Thornes, the mini mall near CVS, with benches and public restrooms.

"I'm pretty sure this place is also going to close," I'm able to say.

"Don't worry. I won't leave you here," says Tripp, reaching down to kiss my cheek, his wet lips like a slobbering dog.

There doesn't need to be a rape scene, but let me tell you, everything you've heard is true. It comes back over the course of the next few days in flashes, fragments: the song (LeAnn Rimes), the bathroom tiles (blue, green, off-white), the exact point my head hit the tiles (that little bump on the back of your skull, just above the brain stem), stumbling back to Chapin without my glasses or shoes, indifferent to the possibility of getting tetanus from walking barefoot on the sidewalk. When I go for a strep test at the infirmary because my throat aches and Rachel's already on antibiotics, the little stick they use to swab hits the back of my tongue and my whole body— chest to stomach to feet, everything—tingles like a subzero lake, head bobbing up against ice, caught under the surface, drowning, but inside there's fire, the need to vomit, immense pressure behind my sinuses. Excedrin doesn't work in these cases. This isn't a migraine—it's a memory.

The nurse rips off her gloves; instead of calling the psych ward, she touches my shoulder, tells me I'm fine, I'm safe, no one is going to hurt me.

When I tell her about *that night*, she hugs me and says the same thing happened to her.

The day after—before I started using the word *rape* to describe what happened—I argued with him over text. He insisted he asked for my consent, and when I pointed out that I was intoxicated, he said, *Well, you didn't say no.*

CHAPTER THREE

GENDER, POWER, AND WITCHCRAFT

BY THE END OF THE first week of class I've deleted his number, though my subconscious still grapples for a word to describe *what happened between us*. I keep waking up in the middle of the night with additional details filled in: the smell of toilet water, the carpet of unrolled paper towels, the flash of his great white teeth. I take Benadryl, which always dulls my senses, get dressed without looking in the mirror, and set out for my ten A.M., a history seminar called Gender, Power, and Witchcraft: Sex Work, the Body, and Blasphemy in Early Modern Europe, with Professor Sienna Weiss.

The course description was the first one I circled in the catalog that arrived in the mail way back in August; not to mention the note at the end: Only five spaces would ultimately be available in the seminar, with the students chosen according to the strength of their first paper. Cheap marketing trick or not, the course filled up before my registration time, but I'm only second on the wait list.

I cross campus to Seelye Hall and amble up the grand marble stairs, past the fray of smoky fake Parisians, the future librarians with unshaven legs peeking out from tea dresses, and a dapper young newsboy-capped person trying to rebrand the fanny pack, reaching the classroom just as virtually all the seats are taken. I grab the remaining chair, clear my throat, and try to squeeze between two girls crammed around the long wooden seminar table.

"Sorry, would you mind if I put my laptop down?"

The girls turn. One is an über-lanky Asian girl in a tennis skirt and knee socks, paging through some art/fashion/culture website I haven't heard of, and the other brushes her bangs aside to reveal an undercut, smudged red lipstick, and a smile I recognize.

Luna grins, seemingly forgetting our interaction at Smithies Against Sexual Violence. "Leisl, right? Don't you live on the second floor of Chapin?" She looks me up and down. "I love your nineties look."

"Thank you, and I prefer to be called Lee, actually."

"Lee. I'll remember that."

I jam between them, taking out my laptop.

"Crazy what happened at SASV, right?" Luna says, folding her gum into a napkin. "I feel so bad for that girl. Doesn't surprise me that Amherst just wanted to lock her up rather than listening to her, though."

My stomach drops. "Crazy, right."

I'm still trying to think of some kind of small-talk topic that won't feel like a punch to a vital organ when Professor

Sienna Weiss enters. She's a willowy black woman in a fluttery dark ensemble, a sort of Angela Davis/Stevie Nicks hybrid, complete with clogs and a crown of dyed-gold coiled hair. She places her beat-up rucksack at the head of the seminar table and goes to the blackboard.

I leave my laptop and rush to meet her.

"Hello, Professor Weiss? My name is Leisl Davis, I was second on the wait list as of nine forty-five this morning. I'm really, really enthusiastic about this subject matter. Is there anything I can do to have a better chance of getting into the course?"

Sienna Weiss's nails are painted a gooey crimson, and her hands are stacked with so many rings I can't tell if she's married. "No, there's really nothing you can do," she says, and I get the sneaking suspicion that she thinks I'm an idiot and doesn't like me at all. I don't have any evidence for this except for the way her dark red mouth curves into a wide Cheshire smile and her eyes don't move.

I sit back down, and class begins.

Professor Weiss seizes a long piece of chalk and writes on the board:

PROFESSOR Weiss
Gender, Power, and Witchcraft—course # in the syllabus
Do NOT miss class
Do NOT call me by my first name

Professor Weiss fits the chalk behind her ear. "Laptops away."

33

We scramble to obey.

She weaves her fingers together and nods, satisfied. "Any questions?"

None.

"Well, I'm sure you all know that you must do the reading," she begins, "and that your first paper is due on the seventeenth. The paper will cover the Ehrenreich and English text. And if I go a little over time, please feel free to remind me that our class has ended—I was teaching in Berlin this summer and our lectures were four hours, no break—though not before twelve fifteen, and please resist the urge to pack up your bags before class has formally ended. I can't stand the sound of all your laptops and what-ever else being crammed into your bags while I'm trying to speak."

She wipes the chalk dust from her hands. "I had the pleasure of carrying Ehrenreich and English's text with me the first time I was arrested. The historicity of their claims has been disputed, which we will review later in the semester—Goddess knows claiming that midwives were persecuted as witches to eliminate the threat to the male medical establishment would get you laughed out of any doctoral seminar faster than claiming you're a Marxist— but it's an essential part of the historiography." She clears her throat, ring-sheathed fingers curling into a resolute fist as she coughs. "And, before you ask, the third time I was arrested was not with Gloria Steinem in South Africa in 1984, though I had the pleasure of interning for *Ms.* the summer of 1973."

Professor Weiss picks up the roster and starts to call names.

"If you use a different name or pronouns, please tell me and I'll try to remember. Though I must confess I'm terrible with names."

She goes through Celia Aaron, Gabrielle Avery, Ally Babenko, and Kelly Bayers before calling a name I recognize.

"Clara Dale?"

Her pen grazes the roster, and she starts to cross the name off before realizing no one has raised her hand. Professor Weiss's eyes probe the faces around the table. "Clara?" Blink. "She's not here?"

We look around at each other. Professor Weiss's gaze flicks from door to roster and suddenly, like the ring of the tocsin heralding a cart of heads about to roll, she drops the clipboard on the heavy wood with a *clatter* and walks out of the room.

"Excuse me for a moment," we hear as the door slams.

She comes back a minute later to grab her flip phone.

A small conversation, quarantined among the seniors, breaks the silence. "Who's coming to Fetish on Saturday?"

I rip off a small end of paper and start to roll it between my fingers, enjoying a rare flash of idle mind before Professor Weiss returns. She takes the roster again and clears her throat.

"Leisl Davis?"

I can't decide which hand to raise and end up embarrassingly raising both. "I'm on the wait list, yes."

Professor Weiss doesn't look me in the eye. "Jillian Ebben?"

Karen Edgars, Sarah Fifer, Charlotte Hwang, Gracie Lacroix, Rahmah Musa...

"Lorraine Trenton?"

35

"I go by Luna."

All the names accounted for, Professor Weiss slams the roster on the table and starts pacing back and forth, but not in an addled-professor sort of way—she knows exactly where she's going, but we don't, so every change of direction sends us reeling like rabbits, with no peripheral vision or concept of the future.

"The witchcraft craze during the early modern period was influenced by a variety of factors," says Professor Weiss, "including the burgeoning development of the nation-state—especially the shift in people's identity from residents of an insular town community to members of a collective nation—as well as changes within the family structure and especially the legal status of sex workers, which we will be examining in this course as a major element of the shift in gendered power that aroused the witch craze."

She goes to the board and writes:

Summis desiderantes affectibus
(Desiring with supreme ardor)

My hand clamors for attention.

She blinks, striding back to the table to glance at the roster. "Leisl? Do you have a question?"

"Pope Innocent VIII," I spit out. "Pope Innocent VIII distributed the papal bull condemning witchcraft in 1484, *Summis desiderantes affectibus.* Forgive my Latin. It gave the Inquisition the power to condemn supposed witches, even witches practicing so-called 'white' magic that had previously been dealt with through penance and confession, but was

36

probably really issued to grant officers of the Inquisition greater control over local German jurisdictions—"

Professor Weiss stops me. "Yes, but we're not going to be discussing any of that today, especially since so many of you will regretfully not be present for the majority of the course." She goes to her rucksack. "On with the lecture, then."

She flicks back the flap and removes a large neon green Super Soaker, jostling with water.

"Power," says Professor Weiss, "is the capacity for violence—holding power is an act of violence."

She proceeds to spray the class, concentrating on the one girl who did not put her laptop away.

The girl scrambles to wipe her computer with her sheer summer clothing, tears crystallizing at the start of her cat eye's messy flick.

Professor Weiss holds the Super Soaker in silence. Then she places it on the desk and removes a miniature water gun from her bag.

"When I have power," Professor Weiss says, circling the table, ultimately handing the gun to Luna, "I choose who else can have power." She looks down at Luna. "If I told you to spray your classmates, would you?"

Luna's mouth curls as she sprays a girl across the table, right on the boob.

Professor Weiss continues to lecture about how consistent acts of violence are embedded into the social structures of power and privilege that uphold the white cisheteropatriarchy, before distributing the paper assignment and reminding us that she doesn't remember names.

She glances up at the clock.

"Class dismissed. If you have a water gun please return it to me."

I wait for Professor Weiss after class; when she ignores me and heads for the door, I block her way.

"Professor Weiss, excuse me? I just want to double check that there isn't anything else I can do to ensure entrance into the course."

She frowns. "What's your name again?"

"Leisl Davis."

"Are you German?"

"Distantly. My mom is a tremendous fan of *The Sound of Music*, though."

"Ah." Professor Weiss coughs into her elbow. "I don't like musicals."

She skirts past me and leaves without a word.

I amble into the hall, my feet lumbering and slow. I grab my sunglasses and slam them over my face, sure Professor Weiss hates me, that my paper will be terrible, that Luna was only talking to me because she's particularly charitable. The truth is no one ever wants to interact with me unless they're planning to use my body like disconnected parts of a machine, unless they want to make my throat burn, trap me under the covers, shaking, and convince me never to leave.

On the way back to my room I pass Chapin's lawn, where Smithies Against Sexual Violence are setting up the T-shirt exhibition (because they couldn't get permission to take over the entire Quad). A bunch of folks from the other night are handing out flyers. I scan the crowd, but I don't see Luna.

The Bieber-imitator moderator adjusts her snapback and

greets me. "Leisl, right?" I'm floored she remembers my name. "Do you want to make a T-shirt?"

I clench my jaw, try to hold back the lump in my throat. "Sure."

I take a blank white shirt, a couple of Sharpies—metallic, red—and wonder how I could sum up the distinct sensation of the post-traumatic ninth circle in one T-shirt-worthy phrase.

FUCK, I write, unsure whether to follow up with MEN, THE SYSTEM, JOHN DIGBY WHITAKER III, or MY LIFE.

I feel a hand on my shoulder, fingers digging into the crevice of my collarbone.

My stomach drops like I'm strapped inside a roller coaster that lied about how safe it is, that's just about to crumble to the ground.

Tripp stands over me wearing a T-shirt with NO MEANS NO handwritten in red block letters, grinning, his teeth large and bright.

"Hello, Leisl," he says, arm stretching out to seize me, and I run, I run as fast as I can, across the lawn, past Chapin, past the Quad, as far as campus goes, until my knees hit a patch of putrid yellow late-summer grass and I watch cars cruise down the road and, phone in hand, my face wet, eyes stinging and bleary, I find the number, make the call, because even though I have so little energy, no motivation, I *can't* see him again, not in hell or purgatory or on random Friday nights; there has to be something I can do, something to keep him away from me.

♀

I tell the salt-and-pepper-bearded Campus Police officer, badge tinted a blinding gold under the fluorescent lights of his office, what happened, and he responds with a gruff, fatherly "I'm sorry, miss," immediately rattling off questions: *Have you been examined at Cooley Dickinson, where they have the special sexual assault nurse?* No, this happened five days ago. *Why didn't you report it earlier?* I didn't really remember what happened to me, and I didn't know it was rape. *Can you tell me what happened?* I was raped, and the perpetrator came to Smith and met me outside my dorm. *Do you have evidence of the rape or the stalking incident?* No, sir. *Is the perpetrator part of the Smith community?* No, he's an Amherst student, and, oh, yes, I assumed you couldn't really help me with Amherst students.

You say you know him, the alleged perpetrator? You could point out his face?

"Of course I know him. Of course I know his face."

The officer, chin encased in his interlocked hands, tries to give me advice, but all I hear is *It's a shame you don't have evidence, without proof there's not much we can do.*

The worst is when he tries to get more details about the crime: the date, the time, the location. And, of course, the million-dollar question: Was it rape? Was it *really* rape?

Does he want me to say, *I'm pretty sure John Digby Whitaker III, otherwise known as Tripp, forced his dick down my throat?*

When I start to cry, the officer hands me tissues. He says he's genuinely sorry, but he can't do anything about Amherst students. He elaborates on my options, how I could get a civil no-contact order, but I'd have to go to court. If the stalking continues, I might want to do this.

When I'm ready to leave, he gives me the name of the Title IX coordinator on campus, and wishes me luck. But doesn't he understand how I woke up this morning, my stomach in yacht-tight sailor knots, how I couldn't eat, got a bunch of questions wrong in class, had diarrhea for hours? Doesn't he understand what this conversation alone has already cost?

I pace back down the urine-colored basement hall, where a young janitor mops the floor. I sidestep the soapy puddle expanding across the linoleum, keep my head down, try to keep the tears in, at least until I'm completely alone.

The janitor turns.

"Hello, Leisl," says John Digby Whitaker III, otherwise known as Tripp.

I run. He drops the mop and follows me. I sprint, as fast as I can, but the hall seems to grow longer the farther I go.

"Leisl," Tripp shouts, voice parched from running. "Leisl, can we talk?"

The fluorescent lights flicker on and off.

I start, in vain, to scream, as loud as I can, still running, still possessing the will to save myself, even in the dark.

The lights come back, steady.

He stands in front of me.

"Leisl," he says. I swear he's wearing a different shirt than when he was mopping. "Can we talk?" He steps forward. I step back, throat-to-tailbone seizing, freezing like Arctic water, like bathroom tile. "I'm sorry. I'm really, truly, *sorry*." He grins. "You know, when you don't have a lot of experience with guys, it's easy to get confused. But there's no reason to be so overdramatic and report me, just because you feel you made a mistake. Do you know how naive you sound, going to Campus Police because you went a little further than you did at Catholic high school dances? God, Leisl, I thought you were a much cooler girl than that."

I can't fucking move. He loosens his collar, revealing the same crystal necklace—one of those cheap quartz points from a quasi-Buddhist New Age store where the shopgirl talks about bangs blocking your third eye. It catches the fluorescent light, glowing.

"We were just having some fun," he says, stepping forward again. "Let me take you out again. I promise, I'll make it up to you."

Tripp steps closer, closer, and I can't move, I can't *fucking* move. His hands are outstretched and he's coming for me, I can see the whites of his eyes, I'm going to die, I absolutely swear I'm going to die, and I *want* to die, I want to go away, I want him to disappear, I need him to go away, I need to go away, whatever it takes, just make him go away, I'll die, I'll die, I'll do anything, *anything*.

I stretch my arms out—a last resort, a plea, a prayer, as if my hands are a real weapon against him and not a rotten fence easily scaled. My neck, my chest, my face is hot, sweat collects in the aching underwire of my bra, and at least I'll be asleep, at least I'm going to pass out before he can touch me, so I can pretend it never happened.

I hear a snap, a crack, like backyard fireworks.

My eyes burst open. He's not there. I turn, see him at the other end of the hall, crumpled on the floor.

He raises his head, a blue-red bruise blooming over his left eye.

He starts to speak, and I run, I run as fast as I can.

)(

I get worse, not better. Every time I close my eyes, I swear I hear his voice, his breath, feel the frigid tile, the country-pop (*I need you like waaaaaaaa-ter*), taste the sake burn my tongue, the back of my throat.

I keep waking up in the middle of the night to check the lock. Some nights I take the flashlight from under my bed and search my closet, the corridors, the stairs, before settling into Chapin's basement, where I watch infomercials and wonder how long this can go on—sleeping two, maybe three hours at a time—before I get sick, before I get hit by a car I didn't see (which would perhaps be a blessing).

When Rachel leaves one morning for an eight A.M. lab and doesn't lock the door, I send her a stream of texts so angry that our brief interactions diminish from cold daily hellos to biweekly requests to turn off the lights. I feel bad, but I also start to worry. Now that my roommate hates me, maybe she'll let him come into the room while I'm sleeping, maybe she'll hold me down for him.

Even when Rachel is out of the room, nowhere is safe; even

with the door locked, windows closed, curtains drawn, my bed feels infested with danger, and it's only sheer exhaustion that halts the suffering, never for long enough.

I try Internet suggestions, like cold showers and unusual breathing exercises. I even try running, because I remember Gianna from high school saying that running keeps her mind off that cousin who repeatedly molested her when she was eight years old. But every time I double-knot my sneakers and pound my feet on concrete, I just feel like he's chasing me.

I try to go to class, because if I survive long enough, I'm going to want to get into a top law school, which will make me a semi-worthwhile human being. But I end up asking for extensions on nearly every assignment, because every time I go to the library and open my laptop, I become convinced that he's hiding behind the vending machine, or waiting in the bathroom (*he'll lock me in, he'll knock my head against the tiles again, again, again, again*), so I run back to my bed, only I can't focus there either. I can't focus anywhere.

Most of my professors are sympathetic. My biology professor—a tiny birdlike woman with a wardrobe eerily reminiscent of that science teacher I had in high school (the one who said evolution was true but it had stopped for humans because we were God's perfect image, right here right now, school shootings and inequality and environmental destruction and all)—gives me the greatest comfort of all, at the tail end of her Thursday office hours when I ask for an extension on the lab write-up.

I haven't slept enough to care, so I come out and say it: "I'm trying to get help for a sexual assault case."

She goes quiet, interlacing her hands and drumming them on the edge of her laptop, and starts talking about sharks, how if you turn a shark over on its back (good luck with that) it goes into this state called *tonic immobility*, and you can poke it, prod it all you like, and no matter how much it wants to bite your hands off, the shark can't move, it's petrified. There's all this research about how tonic immobility affects people too, particularly women, particularly women who are assaulted, how women who don't fight back are *stunned*, sharks on their backs, victims of inconvenient evolutionary mechanisms in addition to rape culture and patriarchy. Not fighting back, in scientific terms, is evidence.

She tells me to just hand in the write-up when I can.

I do meet with the Title IX coordinator, halfway through September, who reminds me that I can't get a campus no-contact order because he doesn't go to the same school, but I could go to court and try to get a civil no-contact order. The idea of putting on a suit, bought just for the occasion, and standing before a judge, surrounded by lawyers and all sorts of people who want to know every last detail, like we're going to film it, induces me to say, against all judgment, *You know, I don't really remember what happened and whatever it was, I'm sure it wasn't that serious.*

Call me crazy, but I swear—just as the coordinator's

inoffensive pink lips are forming the words *no evidence*—the light shifts, the shadow lifts, and I see *his* face, freckles and nostrils and hazel sneer, inside the arched brown outline of her schoolmarm bob, his pointed chin jutting out over her sagging neck.

I race from the office with a desert-dry mouth, hands trembling and slippery, run to the other side of campus, where there are people around, in case he comes after me and I need a witness. It's sunset, light stretched over the low point of the horizon like rope. I sit down on a bench, wipe my tears with my sleeve, and call my mom. She asks me how I am, sounds surprised to hear from me; I bet she's at the golf club, or out with friends.

I try my best, my absolute best, to sound happy. "Hey, Mom, would it be okay if I came home?"

"What?" The connection sizzles. "Sorry, honey, I couldn't hear you, what was that?"

"I want to come home," I say.

She pauses. "Okay, honey, what do you need? You can use the credit card."

"No, Mom, I want to come home. Tonight. I'll take the bus, and Uber from the bus station so you don't have to pick me up."

"Your father will have a heart attack," my mom says, low and dark.

I hold the phone slightly away from my face so it doesn't get wet. "I didn't necessarily mean permanently, I just want to come home for a little while."

"Don't you have class? Honey, you know there's an adjustment period—"

"Mom, if I could come home tonight, just for tonight, I'll take the bus back tomorrow, please, just let me—"

"Honey, I think you'll be over this in a couple of hours, why don't you go find a friend—"

My tears mix with colossal tsunami rage, and I throw the phone onto the pavement.

I hear her, shouting through the receiver: "*Leisl? Honey?*"

I pick up my phone, throw it again, and again, even let myself scream, which I know is totally pointless and will only bring me negative attention, but I don't care, I just want to go away from here and not have this body, not have this life, fuck my phone, fuck my mom, fuck college, fuck me, fuck whatever Gnostic demiurge created this world and all these people but doesn't actually give a shit about their well-being.

"*Are you okay?*"

People come up to me once I'm seated, cracked phone in hand; I wave them off. I do text my mom, dismissing our chat as a poor reaction to a bad grade. My phone still works, well enough.

Night falls, and even though I haven't been outside at night since, well, *that* night, I don't feel any worse than usual, I just feel the same, which is pretty fucking intolerable.

"Hey, Lee?"

I lift my face from my arms, see thigh-highs and red lips. It's Luna.

She asks the same question: "Are you okay? I haven't seen you in class. Professor Weiss keeps asking if someone can find out where you are."

I intend to tell her that *yes, I'm fine*, but she swings

her backpack over one shoulder and sits down next to me anyway.

"You know, he technically can't go inside Chapin. The RA down the hall, she has a no-contact order," Luna says. "He's not supposed to be on Smith's campus at all, actually, but even a court order isn't going to be terribly effective, with a guy like that."

She takes out a small tin of mints, offers me one. "You know, there was a time when I didn't believe people like him existed. They tell us everyone is three-dimensional, even criminals love their mothers, have sisters, get married, but the truth is there are monsters in this world who are beyond our scope of understanding. And he's one of them."

I sob again; she leans closer.

"Can I touch you?" she says.

I nod. She puts her hand on my back, keeps it there, steady and warm.

"I hate seeing you like this," Luna continues. "I'd do anything to make sure another girl didn't go through what I did." She pauses, breath still, cheeks red, her voice as small as her worst secret. "Fucking gut him with chopsticks, you know?"

"That's a good idea," I say through the tears, and with her smile, and our mutual laugh, we become friends, and the night feels a bit more welcoming.

"I wanted to stop you, as soon as I saw you with him," Luna confesses as we're walking back to Chapin. "When I saw you and him at SASV. I wanted to tell you the truth. But I figured you're an adult, you can make your own choices. Maybe after he went to court a couple of times, he wouldn't try again. But I was wrong. If you can't forgive me, I get it."

"I forgive you," I assure her. "It's not your fault. We didn't know each other. And I could have just been having a conversation with him, that one time."

"That's what I thought. Which was naive."

We go back to her room, spend the night talking and drinking chrysanthemum tea from Chinatown. She sits under her moon phase chart, explains that her real name is Lorraine, that she started going by Luna during her freshman year of high school, when she got really obsessed with the moon. I glow with the ultimate awe, realizing her moon chart probably comes from an authentic Seattle thrift store, that she's the type of tastemaker who inspires Urban Outfitters to start selling moon charts in the first place. Until midnight, we keep the conversation light; she talks about missing her ex, a five-foot-ten dishwater blonde with tiny spritelike hands, and she fantasizes about red-blooded, Route 66 twenty-four-hour diners—mediocre burgers, soggy fries, milkshakes from a packet. "I want to wash up in a big booth at two A.M. after a show and stay there all night."

Only after the seniors upstairs stop playing ABBA do we talk about John Digby Whitaker III, otherwise known as Tripp. Luna met him when she was a first-year (she's a sophomore). Same thing: Orientation week, faux-feminist act, took her for sushi.

"You know, I read once that bi girls are assaulted at this ridiculously high rate," she says while we're on her bed, her black camisole barely covering her nipples, and I don't correct her assumption, don't assure her that I'm totally straight.

49

She clutches me as I cry; her shoulder is perfectly smooth, with only a faint citrus soap scent, clean and inoffensive, yet nostalgic and welcoming, like your grandmother's downstairs bathroom or that ancient little breakfast place just off the highway with the lace curtains and strawberry butter.

"I get it," she assures me, "I get it. I used to dream, you know, about some kind of magic potion that could make me forget him—some sci-fi dystopian innovation that could get inside my mind and get rid of him forever, but—I promise, it gets better—*I promise.*"

CHAPTER FOUR

PARSLEY, SAGE, ROSEMARY, AND COLUMBINE

THE NEXT WEEK, LUNA INTRODUCES me to her friends. We get bubble tea on Monday with Charlotte Hwang, the tall girl from Gender, Power, and Witchcraft. Charlotte grew up in Mexico City with her Korean American expat parents, and worries she won't have anywhere to go for Christmas break now that her parents are divorced, her mother busy circling the globe for her wine import business and the lease on her father and his French boyfriend's Paris apartment up in November and she doesn't know if they'll renew it or just travel and live out of hotels. She doesn't use a phone case, she dresses in hiking boots and fairy-gauze ponchos that overwhelm and suffocate her elongated, Mannerist limbs, and her bulky iPod Classic is stuffed with the sort of Scandinavian pop that undoubtably will be featured on next year's H&M playlist, and Françoise Hardy.

"You should come visit Hubbard sometime," Charlotte tells me, slurping up the last of her taro tea and boba. "I can save us a table for pasta night."

I see Charlotte the next day, on the way to Professor Weiss's witchcraft seminar. We walk to class together, and Charlotte asks if I get stoned. I tell her not really.

"Super nervous for this first paper, right?" Charlotte says. "I don't know what else I'm going to take if I don't make the course. I think I'd rather graduate late than take a nine A.M."

Class is brief: Professor Weiss waxes for a bit about how the twenty-first century hasn't had any good, real protests where you're not quite sure what you're protesting but everyone is singing Bob Seger and you can feel, smell, taste the community around you and you feel unindividual and human for the first time in your life. Then she says she's not going to lecture because she wants to get going on grading our papers, so we turn them in and pack our bags.

On Thursday, Luna texts me and asks if I want to go vibrator shopping with her, Charlotte, and their other friend, Gabi, who apparently sat across from me the first day of Sienna's class. I'm skeptical, but considering the time I've spent with Luna has been the only time I haven't had to think about *him*, or wanting to kill myself, I accept her invitation.

I meet them on Chapin's lawn. They're laughing, Charlotte is smoking, and a head of abundantly thick russet curls rests on Luna's shoulder, Luna clutching the other girl like a raft. I'm considering putting my head down and scrambling by, removing myself from a friend group that probably never wanted anything to do with me to begin with, when Luna shouts: "LEISL ANN DAVIS!"

Luna hugs me, Charlotte and I fist-bump, and Gabi Avery—red curls reaching all the way down past her waist, a decidedly bulbous forehead, and more boob than her sports bra can contain—squeezes a cloudy dollop of hand sanitizer into her palm and says it's nice to meet me. Then Luna puts her arm around Gabi again, Luna meets Gabi's cornflower blue, Kewpie doll eyes, and I learn two things:

1. Gabi is a person who refuses to touch money (it's dirty).
2. Gabi and Luna have hung out alone.

We set out for Oh My Sensuality, the sex shop next to the taco place. It's hot as fuck and I'm wishing I'd been less vain and worn shorts instead of vintage jeans, but I didn't bring shorts to college because I hate my legs and there's no point in baring your flaws to every person who sees you on the street. I ask if we can stop for some water, so we go to Starbucks and I use up my birthday gift card on two bottles of Fiji water and "Helena" is playing, so Charlotte and I naturally start to challenge each other to name an emo band the other person hasn't heard of.

"Blood on the Dance Floor," I begin.

"Weatherbox."

"The Medic Droid."

"Cute Is What We Aim For."

"Forgive Durden."

"If you think the nether regions of the Fueled by Ramen roster are obscure—" Gabi starts, and we respond by singing "The Church of Hot Addiction" and don't stop until we're halfway down the stairs leading to the basement-level entrance of the sex shop.

Oh My Sensuality has a red velvet interior and reeks of cheap musk and roses. Round, square, cylindrical, and hexagonal vibrators dominate the shelving; corsets and a sheer curtained fitting room are in the back. The shopgirl is a limber blonde who floats on a pair of swanky little combat boots. She plays with her phone and blows blue bubblegum while we shop.

Luna, the most experienced of the group, starts showing Charlotte different kinds of vibrators, while Gabi gravitates toward the dildos and I glance at corsets.

Gabi comes up behind me, pointing to a purple corset. "Should I try this on?"

"How about the red one?" I suggest.

I'm looking at the books in the Tantra section when Luna comes into earshot.

Luna: "That's the thing, if your girlfriend buys you the wrong cereal it's over."

Charlotte compares two vibrators, a long skinny one and one shaped like an Easter bunny. "But you've never had an orgasm?"

Luna shrugs. "No."

I come up behind Luna and Charlotte. "Never?"

Luna shakes her head. Charlotte and I exchange a glance, incredulous.

Gabi bursts out of the fitting room. The corset is gapping at the back and the cranberry pleather covers her hipbones. "Do you like it?"

Luna drops the vibrator and circles Gabi. "Babe, you don't

have it on right." She starts to tighten the cords; Gabi shudders, and I feel like I'm watching someone else's acceptance speech get cut off by a commercial break while I'm on my couch, unnominated, with sweet-and-salty popcorn and a flat bottle of cherry-flavor Sprite.

"You can't, even with a vibrator?" I say to Luna.

"I can't orgasm because of Prozac," says Gabi. "And I went on Prozac when I was fourteen, so I've never had one either."

"I had an orgasm before fourteen," Charlotte says low.

Luna frowns. "It's not uncommon for women to struggle to reach climax, you know."

My jaw drops. "Luna! The female orgasm is not some mythical entity! That women struggle to climax is a fundamentally patriarchal idea."

"Yeah, it's really not that hard," Charlotte concurs. "I don't mean to suggest this, but like...are you not doing it right?"

I whip out my phone. "Here, I'll message you on Tumblr right now."

Gabi opens her ask box. "*Touch your clit?*"

"That's how you do it!" I shout from the register, where Charlotte is checking out. She opted for the long skinny one. ("A great first vibrator," the shopgirl says.)

"I already know to touch my clit!" says Gabi.

Someone else emerges from the fitting room, swathed in a black hoodie and cork-sole clogs. (Why anyone ashamed to buy a vibrator in the twenty-first century wouldn't just do so on Amazon is beyond me.)

Charlotte is pointing to an egg-shaped rosy stone on the back shelf.

"It's a yoni egg," says the shopgirl, gum smacking her lips. "You put it inside your vagina for, like, pelvic floor Kegels or something."

"I'm getting it," Charlotte says, sprinting back to the register.

Luna poses a question: "Who would you fuck if you could fuck anyone?"

"Frigg," says Gabi. "The wife of Odin."

"Adèle Exarchopoulos," Charlotte shouts.

"Alexander Hamilton," I say.

"Professor Weiss?"

My eyes snap to Luna, and I see that she was not confessing any latent attraction to our professor but greeting Professor Sienna Weiss in the flesh. Hood down, hair out, Professor Weiss's steely brown gaze flits from yoni egg to me to Gabi, then back to Luna.

"Good afternoon," says Professor Weiss, and I think I'm the first to realize she isn't going to offer a comfortable excuse for why she's visiting Oh My Sensuality.

"So nice to see you," Luna continues as Charlotte desperately pockets her change and Gabi starts unthreading the corset. "We were just going. See you in class."

"Yes, see you in class," says Professor Weiss, and again her eyes round the circle of Charlotte to Gabi to Luna to me, and I think she's making a mistake looking at me because I obviously did not make her class.

As soon as we're back on the street Luna breaks down.

"Holy fuck," she starts, and we all mimic her, a flock of fake-septum parrots going "Holy fuck fuck fuck fuck fuck fuck *fuck*!"

"I feel like Sienna's had a lot of sex in her life," Charlotte says as we pass the town hall. "I know you probably don't want that image, but just saying."

"Sienna was totally hot in her youth, I can tell," says Gabi.

"*Professor* Weiss is still hot," Luna offers. "I need Midol. Can we run back to CVS?"

"I'll come with you," says Gabi.

"How soon do you think we're going to be synced up, seriously," I say, and the collective laugh and estimate of *next cycle, tops* is as much confirmation of our status as a solid, impenetrable Friend Group as the experience of meeting our professor while vibrator shopping.

All I need from CVS is some floss, so I give Luna five dollars and she says she'll get it for me. Charlotte and I keep moving toward campus, reaching the lone stretch of sidewalk and plowed grounds between town's commercial lights and Smith's neoclassical huddle of classrooms and administrative buildings. Somehow, Charlotte and I get on the topic of birth and infancy and how we were born at the same hospital (Mount Sinai), in the same year, and how we both had surgery when we were babies. I was born with my skull sutures closed and had to get them torn apart so my brain could grow when I was six months old, and Charlotte was born with six toes and had to have one removed when she was six months old.

The horizon reveals an almost Western emptiness, with only the steeple of the bright teal Catholic church between us and the rusted gates that precede campus. I spot a lone biker, thirty or so feet behind us, far enough away to ignore.

"Do you think Sienna—sorry, *Professor* Weiss—was going to buy a yoni egg?" Charlotte asks.

"Not sure," I say, and, having exhausted everything clever I had rehearsed, ask: "So what are you majoring in?"

"Art, with a glassblowing concentration, and women's studies, probably."

"I'm going to major in history or government," I say, before realizing she didn't ask me.

"That's cool," says Charlotte, and I spend the next minute listening to the crack of her heels on the sidewalk and honing my memory for any hint of sarcasm in her *cool*. But Charlotte, despite her invitations to smoke pot at their friend's room, is sweet as rainbow sprinkles and fresh boxes of Crayola, and almost as young.

Rain begins to fall, clouding my sunglasses in an Impressionist haze and tickling my shoulders like an itchy moth-eaten Christmas sweater.

"*Leisl.*" Charlotte swigs my name around her mouth. "Are you German?"

"Distantly, but my mom just really likes *The Sound of Music*," I say as Charlotte twists and rams her chest into my shoulder.

"Watch out!" she shouts.

Wheels in my peripheral vision, handlebars knocking into the small of my back—my body pivots to the side and I'm clinging to Charlotte's fringed vest, then my hand is slipping and whacking the concrete, and my knee strikes the ground, skids long enough to rip the softened cotton of my jeans and cut my skin on grimy road.

Charlotte leans over me; I broke her fall. She gathers me up under the arms, her bony limbs shuddering from the effort, and rolls me back onto the sidewalk.

We watch as a pair of boys in Nantucket-red whale pants glide away from us on vintage handlebar bikes, buzz cuts and boat shoes, collars popped. Amherst kids, most likely frat. I squint, inspect them: Both are blondish redheads, big hulking football types.

The rear biker turns his stubbly large head and fixes me with a gleeful, yacht-on-the-Cape, Episcopalian-unguilty stare, as if I'm a ladybug he squashed to death under his toe.

I notice then that his basket is detached from his bike. It floats in the air, shuddering under the weight of an eighteen-pack of Bud Light.

"What dicks," says Charlotte. She helps me to stand. "Are you hurt?" She eyes my knee, frowning.

"I'm fine." I'm bleeding, but not in pain.

Another voice: "Charlotte? And, I'm sorry, your name is—*Leisl*?"

Sienna Weiss approaches us, forearms slung with groceries and a discreet brown paper bag from Oh My Sensuality.

"We're fine," Charlotte and I say in unison.

Professor Weiss frowns. "Leisl, are you injured? Do you need help?" She stares at my leg, squinting, as if she knows on some level that she should help me, but her offer to assist comes from hypothetical ethics, not emotion.

"I'm helping her," says Charlotte.

"Please do," says Professor Weiss, swerving around us with a nod.

"See you in class," I shout after her, but she doesn't hear me (or just doesn't answer, because she's one of those people who doesn't believe all talk merits a response).

Charlotte and I stay together until Gabi and Luna get

back from CVS. Luna helps me put some disinfectant and a bandage on my knee, and once we're sure I'm okay, Gabi suggests we do a sacrifice to Freya, the Norse goddess, in the woods. I don't want to be alone, especially if Luna isn't going to be in her room down the hall, so I take some Advil and agree to come along.

We go to the wine store across the street from the most remote, far-flung of the Smith houses, where a gaggle of Smithies and dreadlocked white people huddle together, speaking in hushed tones like they just saw a friendly ghost.

Charlotte finds out what's going on. "Rachel Maddow just walked out with a nice Malbec and took selfies with people."

"Oh, she lives in Amherst," says Gabi.

Luna pulls out her fake and goes inside. Charlotte goes with her because she has strong opinions on wine.

Gabi and I sit on the bench across the street. She tells me that her Aunt Kristin (early forties but retired, some kind of finance guru, Gabi lived with her throughout high school, is paying Gabi's tuition, her parents aren't mentioned and I don't dare ask about them) has a house in South Hadley where she lives in the summer and fall. Gabi's sure her aunt will take us all out to dinner sometime. Have I tried Amanouz, the Moroccan place? Good, we have the same favorite restaurant.

"I love their sardine sandwich," I say. "It's on a baguette with red onions."

Gabi's frown is on fire. "I hate fish."

"Okay." I take a deep breath, wonder if she was like this with Luna when they first met, if you acquire a taste for Gabi over time.

"We should totally get Indian food to take to the sacrifice," I say, pointing to the Indian restaurant next door.

"To sacrifice to Freya?"

"No, to eat—" I gulp. "Well, to eat and to sacrifice to Freya. Both, if that's allowed."

I almost ask Gabi if she's really a Norse pagan and if I should be solemn and respectful at the sacrifice because it's her religion.

"So how did you meet Luna?" I ask.

"I kissed Luna," Gabi says, perhaps accidentally, lips and fingertips blooming pink with love at first sight. Her hands twist and bend, crisscross applesauce in her lap. "Just as friends, of course. It would be cool if you wanted to kiss sometime, too. As friends."

"Yeah, that would be cool," I say, not really processing what she said until after, when her chin is bent into her neck and she stares down, silent, cheeks still pinched.

Luna and Charlotte come back with three bottles of wine. We walk through campus, crickets alive, phone screens masquerading as fireflies, empty beer cans and broken eggs and a decapitated garden snake splitting the lane.

Charlotte: "We're going to the woods, right?"

Gabi starts talking about how it's so great that Smith has a ton of nature where you can do sacrifices to the gods. If she had gone to Columbia, where she would have gone if she had gotten in, it would have been super hard to worship.

We move down the hilly road behind Chapin, lake and woods in sight. I'm not really listening and all of a sudden they're rattling off dates—"2009," "sophomore year," "when I met Grace," and then I'm being included.

"When was it for you?" says Luna.

"When was what?"

"When you came out?"

"Oh," I say, hands up, caught in the headlights. "I'm not out—" Their mouths are shut. "I'm not out *yet*."

Charlotte pats my shoulder. "My parents didn't believe me until they found lesbian porn on my iPad, and even then, my mom referenced some study about how straight women get sexually aroused from watching other women too."

"Wait, where are we?" Gabi asks.

Luna, the only sophomore, pretends to know. "We're still on the main trail. Does anyone have a flashlight?"

Charlotte has a new-enough (even though it's case-less) iPhone that has a flashlight. She lights up the young blue night and we plow deeper into the woods, our feet disrupting beds of newly fallen leaves.

"Converse have no soles," Gabi complains.

"Have you tried Birkenstocks?" Luna suggests.

"I don't want to break in new sandals in the fall," Gabi says.

Luna puts her arm around Gabi again. "It's really important, you know, to try new things. I started using a menstrual cup two months ago and thought I would hate it, but I absolutely love it."

"I'm satisfied with pads," says Charlotte.

"Not a fan of anything up my vag," I add.

We reach the edge of the lake, where the seniors say you can go skating when it freezes, though they warn that *high* skating is stupid as fuck, you could fall through the thin film of ice and drown. Which happened to a girl about five years ago and she survived, the police showed up with ropes and dogs and sirens and stretchers, but you might not.

Gabi is combing the shore. Charlotte argues with Luna about which wine to sacrifice and which to drink.

"Is this good?" I shout to Gabi. "Is this good enough for Freya?"

Then, like God decided to scrap his drawing and turn over a new page, we fall into the dark and the only indications that we're still flesh and blood are the untainted rural stars above.

"Shit, guys, I don't have any battery," says Charlotte.

Luna grumbles: "Wait, I've got it."

The world flicks back, bathing the lakeside in a harsh celluloid glow.

Charlotte's toes edge the lake, her arms stretched out in front of her for balance. "Luna, come check this out."

"Can I open the pinot?" Luna asks.

Charlotte frowns. "Come over here, there's something in the lake."

Luna goes to the lake, shines her phone flashlight across the surface.

Charlotte: "Is that—"

Luna: "OH MY FUCKING GOD—"

Charlotte drops her backpack, the laptop inside crunching like crackling flames.

Gabi starts hurtling down the trail, back toward Chapin— probably because whatever she saw at the lake was really unsanitary—and Luna rushes after her. I'm trying to get close enough to the lake to see what's going on, and Charlotte is running toward me, but both of us sidestep in the same direction and she slams into me.

"Watch the fuck out!" I cry, stumbling forward. It's pitch-black without Luna's phone and my legs aren't holding up and I'm falling. My knees hit the ground; it's wet, the shore of the lake. I stretch my arms out for balance, try to stand, but I can't see anything and the water is really fucking cold and again I'm falling, deeper, seized by the lake, my head is underwater and it's *cold*, cold and deep and I fear no one's coming to get me.

I surface, gobbling down a large mouthful of air.

Charlotte's voice: "Lee!"

"Charlotte?" I splash around, planting my feet in the gelatinous mud of the lake floor. "Charlotte, are you in the water?"

"Lee!" Charlotte again.

I stretch my arms out and my right hand brushes a set of fingers.

"Charlotte?" I scream.

I grab the hand, keeping my feet firmly on the bottom of the lake.

"Charlotte?" I squeeze the hand.

Her voice echoes from the opposite direction. "Lee!"

I let go of the hand. The arm *thuds* back into the water.

I start to scream. "Charlotte?"

Feet shaking the water.

"Lee?" Charlotte's voice. "Lee, that's you, right?"

Two arms, moving, warm, surround me, bring me out of the water.

"One of them is in the water," I tell Charlotte's chest. "Gabi or Luna."

"Gabi and Luna are back on the path already," says Charlotte in the dark.

Luna's flashlight appears in a blaze.

"Leisl!" She's shrieking, cat-eye leaking down her face, but her eyes aren't on mine. "Were you in the water? Oh God."

"Where's Gabi?" I ask.

"She's out of the woods by now," says Luna.

"That's impossible. There's someone in the water," I say.

Luna, gulping, points her flashlight at the lake.

Charlotte leaps back. "*Fuck!*"

I've never seen a dead person before. And it takes me a moment to distinguish between a beating red-blood victim of an accident whose lungs need a tank, and the lost cause on the water: sucked-dry-by-a-vampire pores, toothy gape framed by Gatorade-blue lips, willowy halo of mermaid hair floating just under the surface.

The body is wearing an Amherst sweatshirt. One knee bobs up from the depths, swaddled in blue k-tape.

Luna puts her arm around me and Charlotte. "Gabi? *Gabi?*"

We keep shouting, until we see the white face of Chapin in the paper-lantern moonlight, advancing toward us like a lighthouse.

CHAPTER FIVE

SEVEN SISTERS

WE FIND GABI AT THE boathouse, knees to chest, fetal position, inside one of the kayaks you can rent on nice days if you get on the wait list early enough in August. Even though we're coming up from the woods as sirens are rounding the drive and German shepherds are sticking their damp noses in the pine needles, the police don't notice us.

We wind our way back to Chapin. Everyone is sprawled over the couches in the common room, screaming.

"A literal dead body in the woods? Are you fucking kidding me?" a senior with purple lipstick says to the Head Resident.

"Of course the dead body is behind *our* house," she replies.

I get my phone. There's an official notification from Smith, coming as a text: ALERT: DEAD BODY FOUND IN WOODS BEHIND CHAPIN...

"No one saved the wine?" Charlotte asks.

Gabi, crying, asks if someone will take her back to Cutter Ziskind, she really wants to be in her own room.

I expect Luna to offer, and my heart drops, but Charlotte puts her arm around Gabi instead. "I'll take her back."

"Be careful," Luna shouts after Charlotte, ushering Gabi through the door.

My room is closer, so we go there. I flip on the lights. Rachel is at her seven-to-nine P.M. econ lecture—her bed is made. Mine isn't.

"*I'd rather be at the Cape?*" Luna reads from the poster over Rachel's bed. She scans the rest of the wall: the Walk for Farm Animals flyer, the framed photos of grandparents and friends, the grow-your-own-mushrooms kit, still in its box. "Your roommate seems so aggressively wholesome."

She nods approvingly at my prints of Cranach's *Judith with the Head of Holofernes* and Waterhouse's *Ophelia*, tacked directly above my set of four pillows.

We make sure we have each other's correct numbers, and we repeat back to each other that we can call or text at any time of the night if we need anything, and if we don't want to go into the shower alone tomorrow morning we could each stand in the part of the shower where you're behind the first curtain but the second curtain is still closed to give the actual showering person privacy (the strange features of communal college showers).

Luna approaches me, and I fall into her, scarlet nails digging into the flimsy fabric of my ill-fitting Breton stripe, and we stay there for some time.

"Hey," Luna says, still holding me, "do you think Gabi could like me?"

"Of course Gabi likes you—" I pause. "Oh, you mean, *like* you, like you?"

We break.

"I'm not saying it's romantic," says Luna, face flushed like she's just downed two shots of the vodka lingering under Rachel's desk. "I just think she might like me. But I don't know if I want a relationship right now."

"Do you like her?"

"I just broke up with my ex," Luna says, sighing. "Gabi— she's so *cool*, you know? She's just really cool."

"Sure," I say. "Well, it's up to you. If you feel like you're ready for a relationship." My voice cracks, and I'm not sure why.

"Are you seeing anyone?" Luna says.

"Me?" I'm shocked she thinks anyone would want to be with me. "I've never been in a relationship."

I'm not sure why I said that. Luna nods, then her lips part in confusion. "Never? Are you ace?" She pauses. "Sorry, that was inappropriate—"

"It's fine," I say.

"I was a virgin," says Luna. "I mean, still a virgin. Virginity is a stupid construct, of course, but I haven't been with anyone I love, you know?"

"You believe in love?"

"You think cynicism is the only way to demonstrate your intelligence?"

We laugh, hug again, and she goes to bed. I pick up my phone to call my mom, waiting until the voicemail message starts before giving up and climbing into bed, keeping the lights on.

☽

At midnight, on my laptop, failing to sleep, watching local news coverage about the case against this multiple-rapist television producer and the newscaster speaking out against him (she's crying during the interview, red lipstick staining the overhang of her twin incisors), I receive an email. Subject line: "Office hours tomorrow."

> *Leisl/*Sound of Music,
> *Meet me at my office (in the library) tomorrow at 1 PM.*
> *Yours, SW*

I make a vow to sign all my emails "Yours, LD" for the rest of my life, then toss my laptop under my pillow and fall asleep.

The student receptionists have no idea where Professor Weiss's office is. She doesn't have a library mailbox, and her office isn't listed on the website. I'm about to give up when the janitor appears and offers to take me up through the special elevator that visits the fifth floor, which none of the receptionists have ever been to.

I step out of the elevator into an attic bursting with dusty encyclopedias and a cardboard box stacked with Roman busts. I step over marble heads and shoulders, taking long enough that the elevator has the chance to descend to the lobby and creep back up to the attic, shuddering open with a *thud* and depositing a purple-lipsticked Smithie, arms weighed down by books about Greeks she's yet to check out.

Luna sneezes. "Lee! Did Professor Weiss tell you to come to her office too?" She gathers me into a hug. "I don't know if my paper was terrible or what."

"Same," I say, pulling out my phone. "It's just past one."

"We should probably find her office, yeah." Luna wades with me over boxes of manila folders with old thesis papers until we stumble upon a door that looks like it hasn't been opened in forty years.

PROFESSOR SIENNA WEISS, the engraving reads.

I knock. No response.

"Are you sure this is it?" Luna frowns.

I knock again—this time the door bursts open, and Professor Weiss looks us up and down. "Leisl, Luna." The corners of her smile are sharp and bright. "Come in, please."

Professor Weiss's office looks like the duplex everyone aspires to rent once their sugar baby careers really kick off: a ballroom-sized Alexandrian maze of bookshelves and medieval tapestries, a precarious helix of spiral stairs in the center of the room, leading up to a second balcony-floor with more books, more tapestries, and a neat arrangement of midcentury sofas upon which a number of cats are resting. Light travels down from a massive skylight, lending a circular planetarium view of pine tree tops and cornflower sky and the daytime quarter moon in black-and-white-cookie glory.

We pass tables stacked with aging papers and empty golden birdcages before Professor Weiss throws aside a set of velvet curtains to reveal her desk, and four chairs surrounding it—two of which are filled by Charlotte and Gabi.

"Would you like some tea?" Professor Weiss asks, already in the process of filling five cups of a cobalt-and-white Chinese tea set.

"Sure," we say in unison.

She gives us each a cup and takes a seat behind her desk, downing her tea in one gulp. "I want to say first that I'm so pleased the four of you will be joining me for the seminar this semester. I am looking forward to working with all of you. I'm going to send out an email this weekend so we can decide on a proper time for the extra lectures. *But*—" she says, standing and retrieving an unopened bag of Quadratini wafer cookies from the top of the refrigerator, "I must warn you that I have decided to shift the content of the seminar. As much as the study of history is crucial to the intellectual development of young people, I feel that the current political climate mandates we make our class much more *practical* in focus."

"How so?" says Luna—who, like the rest of us, hasn't taken a single sip of tea.

Professor Weiss rips open the bag of wafer cookies, her eyes flitting to each of us. "I'm confident the four of you are the right students to take on this responsibility. It's essential that students engaged in the more practical application of the lecture are as bright, focused, passionate—and, perhaps most importantly—*close-knit* as you four are. Though, I must also compliment Leisl's wonderful paper on Catholic appropriation of pagan tradition."

71

I beam. Professor Weiss holds out the bag of wafers. "Cookies, anyone?"

Gabi and I shake our heads. Charlotte grabs a handful, and Luna takes one.

Professor Weiss closes the bag and shakes the crumbs off her hands. "I need you to complete the first assignment as soon as possible." She pauses. "You may want to write this down."

Luna takes out her phone.

"Gather together and find a wooded area where no one will disturb you. Bring the following items: Graveyard dirt, preferably harvested under a full moon, but really any moon phase will do. Day-old eggshells. Medicine, something that could alter the body or mind. And blood."

"We have to cut ourselves?" I ask.

"Any blood. How you obtain it is up to you. Now, I cannot legally encourage you to perform the next step, but this exercise will be most effective if you are without clothes. Try to expose as much skin as possible to the moonlight. Then join hands and say the following."

She dictates a rhyme that sounds like it was lifted from the Wiccan underbelly of Tumblr.

Charlotte finishes her wafer cookies and wipes her mouth on the back of her vegan leather jacket sleeve. "And?"

"That's it." Professor Weiss smiles with her mouth closed. "We'll meet again after you finish the first assignment."

I swallow, trying to coat my throat in something other than shriveled-up dread. "Professor Weiss, what about the fifth person?"

Professor Weiss cocks her head to the side. "Fifth person?"

"Aren't there five spaces in your class?"

She nods. "Yes, I did say that originally."

I take a deep breath. "Is there going to be another person in the class?"

"No, I don't think so," she says.

We wait for Luna to finish her tea, then file out of the office.

"Oh, girls. One more thing," Professor Weiss calls, poking her head through the curtains. "You're welcome to call me Sienna."

We go to the woods behind Chapin around midnight, with the graveyard dirt (harvested under a waxing moon), eggshells we found in Hubbard's ant-infested kitchen that must be at least a day old, Gabi's Lorazepam, and a used pad, courtesy of Charlotte.

We take off our clothes and join hands.

Charlotte: "Does anyone remember what we're supposed to say?"

Luna wrote it down on her phone. "Okay, this is really convoluted but first: *After placing the dirt, eggshells, medicine, and blood in the center of the circle*"—Luna squints, sneezes—"*donate an additional item, that is unmistakably personal, to the circle as well. DO NOT TOUCH ANYTHING IN THE CIRCLE UNTIL THE OBVIOUS END OF THE CEREMONY.*"

I raise an eyebrow, frowning. "The *obvious* end?"

"Sienna's like an IKEA customer service representative who assumes you actually know how to use a screwdriver," Charlotte affirms, nodding.

We open our bags, filter through our pockets. Gabi, sulking, throws her phone into the circle ("I would do my wallet but money isn't really personal, is it?"). Luna chooses her stubby oversharpened NARS Train Bleu lip pencil ("Lee, would you come to Sephora in Holyoke with me next weekend? I need to replace this anyway."). Charlotte, the once-used menstrual cup she tried last month at Luna's behest.

"It's personal," Charlotte argues.

Sifting through my backpack, my hand keeps coming back to my scissors, the crap drugstore kind (the same pair I used to slice Zara's eighth-grade bob into a jagged 2008-cool pixie that inspired every boy on the bus to ask if she had become a lesbian). I start to twist my claddagh ring off my middle finger, but I'm too paranoid to leave my gold in the woods, so I toss the scissors into the circle.

Luna picks up Sienna's directions again.

"Okay, repeat after me. 'GODDESS, WE SUMMON THEE. WRONGED WE SHALL CEASE TO BE. CURSED BY US THREE'—*okay, I think this was written for Sienna's coven*—'CURSED BY US *FOUR* HE SHALL BE. FROM HIS SUFFERING HE WILL NEVER FLEE. UNTIL HIS COFFIN CAN HE SEE.'" She squints. "Wait, I might have gotten some of it wrong."

"Did Sienna write that?" Gabi says as the trees start to shake, leaves fly off the ground, an unidentifiable animal howls, and three bolts of lightning crackle and snap.

I smell heat (ever since Luna quit shampoo, that's all she

smells like, *heat*, the primal whiff of baby-soaped skin right under your nostrils, the aroma of getting really close). And sizzling pine needles and wood, and Gabi's screaming about her phone and Luna's eyes burrow into mine, this is the first time I've seen her *terrified*—

The moon ducks behind the clouds, the sky spitting hail and sleet. I seize Luna's and Charlotte's hands as the ground yawns, the earth cracks open, and red-gold lava bubbles over the open sliver of crust.

I scream, the wind twisting my hair. Shadows of wild things prowl the forest, bears and coyotes and a slim blue heron, leaping into flight and grazing our heads before disappearing into the pines.

I hold tight to Luna's pinkie finger, locked into mine, my only tether to the world.

As suddenly as it started, the moon returns, the night clears, and Charlotte is on her knees in the center of the circle, throwing up.

"Char?" says Luna.

Gabi is sprinting away, grabbing her galaxy-print jeans from the ground and trying to put them on as she runs.

"Gabi!" Luna cries, shaking her head. To Charlotte and me: "She has trypanophobia. Fear of needles, but because her panic is so bad, every time she sees someone getting sick at all, she thinks they might be contagious and she might get sick and she might have to go to the hospital and get a shot or an IV."

Gabi shouts from behind a tree: "I'll wait over here."

Charlotte stands, with Luna's help. I rush to Charlotte's other side.

"That was fucking insane," Charlotte exclaims, wiping her mouth and making sure her nipple ring is still intact. "Should we try again?"

Luna: "You saw it too?"

"The moon disappearing?" I whisper.

"There was hail," Gabi adds.

"Sleet," says Luna. "And wind, and black clouds—"

"An actual earthquake," Charlotte continues. "And some kind of forest fire? And—"

"Look at this." I point to the center of the circle, next to Charlotte's vomit. The dirt, eggshells, pills, and period blood are all gone, though Gabi's phone, Luna's lip pencil, Charlotte's menstrual cup, and my scissors remain, just the same as before.

The only addition is a slim black notebook, cracked open.

I reach down and snatch the notebook, narrowly avoiding Gabi swooping down to seize her phone.

"*Contract for the Formation of a New Coven of the Order of the Seven Sisters*," I read aloud from the open page.

"What else does it say?" says Luna.

I flip through the rest of the notebook. "Nothing. It's blank."

As soon as Gabi types in her passcode, it starts to rain.

Luna: "Sienna's probably still in her office."

"I bet she lives there," says Charlotte. "All those cats."

CHAPTER SIX

MOUNTAIN DAY

WE FIND SIENNA IN HER office, in a billowing silk robe printed with clouds and cherubs, one of her cats in her lap. She sits us down, pours more tea, offers wafer cookies. "I also have curry tofu."

None of us are in the mood to eat.

The notebook lies open on Sienna's desk. "I imagine you're all quite surprised at the moment. I can't sympathize. My own practice was passed down through my family. My mother used her gift as a healer at several Panther clinics. And my paternal grandmother was a talented diviner who saved herself and my teenage father from *Kristallnacht*."

"So magic is hereditary?" I say. "I don't think my family—"

"No," says Sienna. "Magic is an ancient tool all women possess. All women are magical. They just have to become aware of their magic."

"So, like, the Salem witch trials," says Luna. "They were actually witches?"

Sienna shakes her head. "The Salem trials primarily targeted vulnerable women on the fringes of society who offended the Puritan establishment. Any real Puritan witches—and there were few—had gone to Rhode Island by the last decade of the seventeenth century. There was only one witch in Salem, and that was Tituba, the slave, who used her powers to escape execution. Though some of my contemporaries argue that Sarah Good, one of the victims, came to knowledge of her power just before her execution, and used her fledgling magic to cast a curse on the Reverend Nicholas Noyes that would, in her words, cause him to 'drink his own blood'— and he indeed died from internal bleeding twenty-five years later. For the most part, women are ignorant of their true power, and those who discover their magic go to great lengths to prevent society from learning of their abilities. The Seven Sisters colleges, in fact, were originally established not only to encourage higher learning among women, but to act as safe spaces where covens could practice and preserve the craft."

"Are there other witches at Smith?" says Charlotte.

"No. There's a colleague of mine at Wellesley who still practices, but coven leadership of the last generation was paranoid about discovery, so the practice has mostly died out." Sienna toys with the crystal pendant around her neck. She twists the point between her fingers, and a question strikes me.

"Professor—sorry, *Sienna*—men can't use magic?"

She pauses, laying her ring-heavy hands on her desk. "You

did remove your personal objects from the circle at the end of the ceremony?"

We nod.

"Take them out, please."

As soon as Charlotte removes her menstrual cup from her so-small-her-thirteen-inch-Pro-only-fits-two-thirds-of-the-way-in backpack, it starts to levitate.

Gabi grips the arms of her seat, cheeks an anaerobic purple.

Sienna seizes the menstrual cup from midair and hands it back to Charlotte. "In my experience—in the experience of every witch who has ever documented a coven formation ceremony—it is the magical power of women that infuses your chosen objects, your *talismans*, with magic. So we think. It's one of those mysteries it's easier to accept than to uncover. Your magic is entirely dependent upon your possession of your talisman."

"So men can't use magic?" I repeat. "If a man was to steal a witch's talisman, what would happen?"

"Leisl, I already answered your question," Sienna says.

Mucus leaks from Gabi's nose. "But my talisman is my fucking *phone*. I was supposed to get the 5C when I got home for Thanksgiving break. Now what do I do?" She looks to Sienna. "What's your talisman?"

Sienna doesn't answer; Charlotte immediately chimes in with "Can we use magic to become stupidly rich?"

"Good luck evading prison on embezzlement charges," says Sienna.

Luna puts up a hand. "And we can't kill people?"

Sienna shrugs. "You can do anything necessary to protect yourself and your sisters."

I look from Gabi, to Charlotte, to Luna, whose hand still cloaks mine, and in her clammy, lukewarm touch, I feel almost safe.

"Let's block out some time next week to start training," says Sienna.

Ø

On Tuesday, half past eleven P.M., Sienna's black Mini rolls into Chapin's driveway, and Luna, Gabi, and I dart from the common room to the cream leather expanse of the back seat. I insist we buckle up, and thank Sienna for the ride.

"Oh, it's nothing," Sienna assures me. She wears a bell-sleeved blood-of-enemies-red blouse, a more conspicuous silver nose ring than I've seen her wear during the day, and the same safe's worth of rings on each hand. "The PVTA doesn't stop anywhere near where we're going. And I wouldn't expect you to walk alone so late at night. You're still novice witches."

Sienna turns up the music (Enya's "Orinoco Flow"). "My dear, we forgot Charlotte," she says. "Shall I swing by her house? She lives in Hubbard, right?"

Luna pulls out her phone, which lights up the back of the car like a low-budget horror film. "She texted me. She says *can't come yonight.*"

"*Yonight?* Like, *yonic* tonight?" says Gabi.

Gabi and Luna holler with laughter, Luna rocking back and forth so hard that the seat belt snaps her back against the seat at the next stoplight. She struggles against the buckle, mumbling and raising her exquisite feathered brows.

"Charlotte can't come later?" Sienna asks. "I'll pay for a cab."

"I'll text her," says Luna, texting with one thumb as she devotes her left hand to unbuckling her seat belt.

Luna: "She's coming."

Charlotte meets us outside the Vietnamese restaurant by the bridge, stoned and stumbling. Sienna, if she notices, doesn't react. "Thank you for joining us, Charlotte."

The restaurant closed an hour ago, but Sienna has a key. The hostess nods to us from the kitchen, where dismembered chicken legs swarm, alive and well.

"*Aww*, my mom used to take us for hot pot when we lived in New York," Charlotte exclaims, tugging Luna by the arm.

"Are you telling me there's something you actually like eating?" says Luna, nose nuzzled into the generous hollow where Charlotte's shoulder meets her collarbone.

It's not until Sienna leads us up a flight of stairs, past the massage studio entrance, and into a dark third-floor apartment that I start to question if I should have called the cops or my parents or just blocked everyone's numbers and dropped Sienna's lecture as soon as she started calling us *witches*.

The apartment is furnished, barely, with some eighties-grandmother touches like the brocade couch and doily curtains and a pebbled-glass coffee table catching the unobscured rural moonlight, peeking through a sliver of drape.

Sienna places a small, slim hourglass on the coffee table.

"Professor—" I call out, just as a radiant ball of light flashes into Sienna's palm.

"I want to make it clear: This isn't an all-you-can-heal essential oil extravaganza," says Sienna. "This is real magic. Walking on water, spinning gold from lead, raising the dead. The only limits are your mind and skill. And the strength of your relationship with your sisters."

"Are they witches?" I blurt out. "The owners of this restaurant."

"The sisters are part of a coven, yes," says Sienna. "They've kindly agreed to let us use their apartment for training. It's best not to practice in my office all the time. To avoid attention from the administration."

The room sinks into darkness. "Magic, girls," Sienna continues, "is all about intention. With your talismans, you can infuse anything—crystals, pendulums, cards, yes, but also rubber bands, socks, vodka"—Charlotte's face lights up—"with magical potential, with power, with purpose. But you must remember that intention multiplied by four witches is the most powerful force of all. You must not doubt yourselves."

Sienna conjures up a second source of light in her opposite hand, then reaches out and gifts the light to several bulbless lamps thick with dust.

"Leisl." She beckons me forward. "You try."

I take my scissors in my fist, shut my eyes, exhale.

At first, nothing, because my mind is empty of everything but the four pairs of eyes secured on my body, how shitty my thighs look rubbing together in these jeans, whether Sienna hates me, whether Luna hates me, my feet bare on the gravel that early morning walking home from Thornes, the voice of LeAnn Rimes. Expectations, wishes, regrets—the weight, the stones, the boulder between my ribs that curls my shoulders in and tugs my head down. How much I hate myself.

I open my eyes and look to the yellow-cream floral lamp-shade on the side table. I breathe in, breathe out, again, until all I see is the pattern, the tiny daisies, both soothing and maddening in its repetition, and even though I can't hold the magic for long, even though my gaze darts to Luna to assess what she thinks of me, if she thinks I look totally dumb, I have a handle on it now, the electricity, the fire, the light.

At once, the lamp explodes into ceiling-high flames.

Sienna seizes the scissors from me, and the room returns to equilibrium.

"I've been practicing," I say.

Sienna frowns at me. "You must remember that you are novices," she says. "Every time we practice, you will improve substantially, but you must take care to use magic at a distance, and never to reveal yourselves. Now, take off your shoes. We're going to levitate."

I have the same dream for several nights: I'm on a broom-stick, hurtling through a stormy troposphere, rain slapping my face like a hose and making my hands slip off the broom, but I can't stop because *he's* always behind me. Sometimes I get far enough away that I can't see him, but when I emerge into a patch of fine weather, he always reappears, shouting, "Hello, Leisl," when I'm on the cusp of waking in a frigid sweat.

One night, I let him catch up to me, and then, just as he reaches out to touch me, I whip out a gun and strike a bullet through his head. He slides off the broomstick, falling, plunging to the distant ground. I hear his bones crack, his flesh splatter, but I look to the broom and he's there, all flesh and grin, and he's chasing me again.

Sienna reminds me, when I question her before training, that broomstick flying is much too conspicuous, not to mention horribly uncomfortable and dangerous. Back in her day broomsticks were a real craze—there was a particular incident around 1970 with a Smith coven flying around Hampshire County, flinging burning bras onto streets and rooftops, which Sienna posits may have been the actual origin of the bra-burning myth of the seventies feminist movement. Anyway, flying is a gimmick and really not that efficient of a way to get around. She advises that if I want to arrive in style I should just transfigure my used sedan into an Audi, which is what most witches do.

September ends like this: normal classes, normal hours in the library (mostly studying, sometimes talking to girls from my intro poli sci class, who tell me about frat parties and how everything you've heard is true, they really do rate the girls as soon as they arrive at Amherst and roofie the eights, nines, and tens), normal avoidance of the roommate who hates my guts, magic practice, bubble tea and banh mi with the coven, Charlotte and I increasingly the third and fourth wheels lagging behind Luna and Gabi, who mention, on the first night of October, boots crunching early foliage, that they are dating. Not that Charlotte or I needed confirmation beyond the fierce stone grip of their hands, the little jokes they keep whispering to each other that we only catch the first or last words of.

Perhaps, by October, life is too normal. In mere weeks we've fallen into magic like it's brushing your teeth, an old exercise routine. Gabi (eventually) gets sick of talking to her aunt on speaker while her phone is levitating; I grip my scissors and conjure up flames to light the rough shards of palo lingering in Luna's incense dish, and feel nothing. The rest of the coven marvels at my working of spells we haven't learned from Sienna yet; Charlotte tries to repeat them but gives up, red-cheeked and frowning. "Damn, I didn't expect magic to be some kind of fucking Stoic meditation hyperdiscipline jam." It's incredible, how easy it is to take things for granted. Perhaps the truth is that we came to school so apathetic, so exhausted, that despite spending most of our time splayed across each other's beds, we don't have the capacity to experience anything as life-altering, epic, or grand.

Charlotte, upon hearing of my ennui, offers to share some weed; I say no, because I don't want brain damage on the off-chance that my brain is precious and will contribute to humanity in some meaningful way (and I'm already damaged enough). I do agree to meet her at the Quad on Friday night. I go to the party with my skin red, smacked with whiteheads, just-got-my-period, my face wants everyone to know I'm not fertile and I have nothing to offer. I wait for Charlotte five minutes, ten minutes, half an hour, until I finally scoop myself a Solo cup of punch and settle into one of those window-propped silk striped antique chaises just off the common room, where I can inconspicuously stare at this girl surrounded by an army of friends and admirers, a queen among knee-length retro dresses and pixie cuts and unshaven legs, a contacts-wearing Hepburn, hair shimmering and black like a Viviscal-addicted Rapunzel-Cher, eyes larger and more tawny and star-powered than Zara's ever were. The kind of beauty you can't pay for. When she comes up to me, when I go for my third round of punch, she oh-so-professionally shakes my hand, introduces herself as Varana Patel, asks my last name so she can friend me on Facebook, informs me like a presidential candidate at my doorstep that she hopes to see me again, because she's so impressed by me and would love to get to know me better.

We agree to drink our punch outside on the Quad and already I'm getting visions of heart emojis and words of support, Varana becoming a friend, a good friend (the kind of friend who might even sleep in my bed during finals week, when we're both so sleep-deprived neither of us will remember what exactly happened, only that we both have needs and her hair got wound around my neck and almost choked me). Once I finish my drink, we start to make out. It's just like that one time with Zara, nothing sexual or romantic about it, just two drunk girls feeding the male gaze even within the Amazonian fortress of the stately four Quad houses, two people who don't know each other bonding over their shared desperation for the kind of intimacy you don't have to work for, the connection that flashes bright enough to dent your isolation then dissipates the very next morning. Only, I'm not happy at all, especially when her long fingers glide over my bra strap. I'm not here, I'm not with her, all I can think is, *I can't let her get to know me* because what would she say if I told her what happened—"*Why didn't you just fight back? You just* let *him do that to you?*"—and how I would want to say, when that happens to you, you fucking freeze, you're a floppy fish, a blow-up doll, you've lost all your bullets and you're toothless, but I would probably just say, you know what, you're right, *you're right* and I'm making it up and I must have wanted it because everything that happens I do to myself, of course, see, I'm an adult and I'm taking responsibility, the truth is I just wanted him to approve of me, I wanted him to think I was pretty, I wanted him to want me and I did this to myself, I should have gone back to his room the first time he asked, I should have sucked his dick then so he wouldn't have had to drug me, I should I should I should I *should* have never been born a girl with fat thighs and bad luck and RAPE ME written on my low-self-esteem forehead in Times Square giant neon letters.

I break from her, amble around for the closest trash can, sink my face deep enough to smell the boozy tin and gum wrappers, and vomit.

"Leisl?" Varana calls, but I'm already on the gravel path, advancing back to Chapin and my bed and the nightmare I can't seem to overcome.

People walk past me, heading to the Quad, their faces hazy in the sun-just-set charcoal evening. I know my face is red and shiny and ashamed and I just want to curl under my covers and take out my phone and research how to turn Blankie into a real-deal noose.

I nearly bump into one of the rare guys going to the Quad, and whisper a vague apology.

His hand grips my arm.

"Sorry, Leisl?"

It's him.

"What an absolutely *magical* coincidence, seeing you here—how are you?"

I scream, I scream so loud he has to let go of me, I scream so loud the concrete cradles me, I scream and scream and all sorts of people can hear me, they're all surrounding and pointing like spectators with rocks in their fists, ready to bury me in stone, they're everywhere and then I hear her voice, Varana.

She puts her arms around me and the rest of them dissipate like foliage escaping a leaf blower.

I wipe my face; she helps me stand; I push her away.

"Don't come near me," then: "No, I mean, it's not you, I can explain—"

"What happened?" she says, and I just stare, not-yet-words lodged in my chest, the truth etched in my trembling and goose bumps and the nausea crowning at the back of my throat. "Leisl, do you need me to call 911? Are you all right? What happened?"

"I'm fine," I say, finally; I'm not gay, I suppose. She's compelling like a painting or a photograph, 2-D, static, beauty without a heartbeat, great design that uplifts you, raises you, guides you, but can't inspire you in *that* way.

Varana says she's going to walk me home, and she would prefer if I had a friend come and stay with me. She'll stay with me, if no one else is available. I search her face as she brings me home, arm locked into mine, and I know she's lying and she hates me and this is all a sick joke and she's probably in league with him, maybe she *is* him, in magical disguise.

We get back to Chapin and I claim that Luna is going to come and stay with me. Varana types her number into my phone. I vow to text her, instead of giving her mine.

She makes sure I don't need anything, shuts the door, and I vow, in my deepest of hearts, never to see her again.

ʊ

Even as the coven obeys Sienna like a pack of huskies lugging a sled across the tundra, I find myself pushing for more. Refusal to exercise power, when you have it, strikes me as a waste, ungrateful. But perhaps it isn't their fault, or mine. For so long we had no way of fighting back. Now, everything is possible. I can't let this slip through my fingers and end up dead, gone, potpourri.

The next night in the apartment over the Vietnamese restaurant, Sienna implies we are proficient enough to try magical combat. I zone out while Sienna hands us fragments of citrine, carnelian, apatite, demonstrates basic attack spells:

how to knock someone out (Gabi), freeze them (Luna), and choke them (done to herself, briefly). She says the crystals amplify our power, but the root of any attack spell is *rage*, harnessed, seized, directed.

Now, our turn.

The root is rage.

I grip the crystal and my scissors and immediately set half the apartment on fire, forcing Charlotte (my dueling partner) to jump on top of the kitchen countertop.

Sienna extinguishes the flames. "Leisl, I will need to see another spell to assess your progress as a witch. Summoning flames is extremely showy, likely to attract nonmagic attention, and excessively damaging to the surrounding environment, no matter how skilled you are at magical cleanup." She indicates the slightly singed edges of the lace curtains.

"I was just going off instinct," I insist. "I can try again—"

"Yeah, it would be cool to see you do something with magic aside from acting out your *Avatar* fantasies," Gabi quips. "You're not a one-spell witch, are you?"

On impulse I walk right up to Gabi, break my scissors apart, and slam the blades together.

She bends forward, clenching her fists, face contorted.

"*Fuck* you," she croaks as I open the scissors, slower than I should. As soon as I release her, she races to the bathroom. I hear her knees hit the floor; she retches several times.

Luna glares at me. "Lee—"

I dig my nails into my palms, dreading Sienna's reaction. But when I look to her, her face is lit up by something close to pride.

"Very good," says Sienna. Something in her voice is strange, like she's speaking into my own personal set of headphones. "But you must never attack a sister—or, at least, she must never remember it."

Sienna grabs my scissors out of my fist, slams her hand over my eyes.

When she takes her hand away, Gabi is back, Charlotte is still on the counter, and the apartment is again on fire.

"Charlotte, put out the fire," Sienna shouts. "Now!"

Charlotte does—but she's too slow, and the curtains burn to a crisp.

Sienna ignores me completely, turning to Gabi and Luna. I watch Gabi struggle to light a single candle; Luna refuses to choose a target from among the coven, instead immobilizing herself in midair, giving Gabi (with heavy assistance from Sienna) the chance to rescue her girlfriend from her own spell.

On the ride home, Sienna finally acknowledges me, making a vague comment—not quite a compliment—about my "talent," wondering if it extends beyond combat magic. But I can see from her expression in the rearview mirror that what I did was *very good*. I can't help but settle my head back against the leather seat and feel capable, effective—like I finally have a talent that can do something for me. Back at Chapin, I wake up around four A.M. and go for a walk, headphones in, *Danse macabre*, grinning and spinning and knowing that I have the power, I have the solution to all my problems, I have something to live for; I can make things right, I can be my own justice. Regardless of the ice in my bones, the terror I can't digest—no matter how helpless

I feel, I *can* do something about it, I'm fucking magic and that's enough.

Friday is Mountain Day, a surprise day off the college president announces via chiming chapel bells at eight A.M., when all classes are canceled so we can go forest bathing in tangerine foliage and swallow apples from the branch and not sit inside floral-wallpapered psychiatrists' offices or study for exams, which is what most of us do.

After I have cake for lunch, I go to the library to work on a paper for intro poli sci, which I can't focus on, because, even though I have a pocket full of sage-infused pepper spray and three witch-sisters sworn to protect me, I can't stop hearing *Hello, Leisl,* and the girl on the couch next to me is playing Martina McBride Christmas carols out of her Beats headphones (yes, in October), which I initially mistake for LeAnn Rimes. I see my poli sci professor at the vending machine; she alludes to my *talent for argument* and expresses vague gratitude for *a student like you in class,* but she hasn't read my paper yet, and I'm sure it's terrible. I'm eager to get away, but she wants to know what else I'm taking, what I'm thinking of majoring in, how I like Sienna's seminar. "Her course at Amherst last year got some rave reviews," she says.

I manage to escape, but I'm hardly past the soda machine when I hear a familiar voice shouting my name.

"Lee?"

Luna darts down the hall, settling on the couch and throwing her arms around me. (Even since she started officially dating Gabi, her shows of physical affection are frequent, intimate, long-lasting.) She yawns. "Did you get my texts?"

I scroll through my phone; an hour ago, she wanted to get lunch. "Sorry, I texted Charlotte around noon and she said you two had already eaten."

"Charlotte never eats lunch," Luna says flippantly, then: "I was just meeting with Sienna."

"About what?" I ask, glancing around at anyone who might overhear us (mostly upperclasswomen, each staking out their own couch, shoes off, feet curled under thighs).

Luna's hands fold in her lap like a claddagh ring, fingers braiding together, palms curling. "Nothing important." She pauses. "Well, actually, I was with Gabi, then Sienna emailed me back, said she had a few minutes."

"Were you meeting about the paper?"

"I just lost my virginity," she says. Then: "I mean, it was the first time...with someone I care about."

"Congratulations?"

We laugh, then she starts to cry. I put my arms around her—loose, noncommittal, like hugging a relative. Luna doesn't pull away, and the longer her body meshes against mine, the longer I smell her hair, the more I start to appreciate that in some other multiverse, on a planet next to Mars, I might have been honest and everything might have been different.

Luna tugs me away from the library to go apple picking with the rest of Chapin House for Mountain Day. She texts

Charlotte and Gabi, telling them to come with us instead of their own houses. We meet them on the lawn, climb into one of the pickup trucks in Chapin's driveway stocked with girls and boots, "Blurred Lines" on the radio (which half the girls are complaining about).

We look for seats; there's only room for Charlotte, Gabi, and Luna.

"You'll have to sit on my lap," Luna says to me, and after one glance at Gabi's indifference I sling my arms around her neck and endure the bumpy ride on top of her knees.

We get to the orchard and have an hour to pick all the apples we want. I'm not sure if there are pesticides, but I'm hungry and I start eating the first apple I can reach that isn't surrounded by swarming bees.

Charlotte leads the coven to an abandoned section of the orchard by a barbed-wire fence, next to the whizzing highway, where most of the apples are new and green, and we sit in a circle and suck meat from apple cores, and Gabi starts talking about Sienna and how she's kind of problematic. "Sienna's whole seventies Earth Mother matriarchal-prehistory spiel is kind of essentialist and a bit transphobic," says Gabi. "I bet Sienna's the type to still say *men and women*, you know? At all the fundraisers I did in high school, we always opened with telling everyone how *folks* was a good, neutral, non-gendered term that you should use, because *people* sounds weirdly Communist if you use it over and over again and *individuals* or *guests* just don't really work either. When I met Paris Hilton at the Trevor Project fundraiser—you know how I was invited along with only like four other high school kids because of my activism—I remember she kept saying *ladies and gentlemen* and it drove me absolutely up the wall. It was *very disrespect.*"

Gabi takes out her phone and shows us the picture of her with Paris Hilton, which we've all seen before.

"*Such impress,*" I say under my breath, masking my disregard in the language of doge, which we're all certain will survive 2013.

"Forgive Sienna. She's elderly," says Charlotte, diverting her eyes from the screen to toss her apple core through the fence. A pickup truck runs over the apple, splattering its seeds across the highway. "And Gloria Steinem and all those seventies radfems apologized for being transphobic, so I'm sure Sienna isn't some kind of terrible TERF."

"Seriously, do you think Sienna's queer?" says Luna. "I know she mentioned she had a boyfriend while she was at Smith at our last practice—"

"Yeah, that doesn't mean anything," Gabi agrees. "I mean, my ex was still the president of the GSA her senior year even after she left me for a guy. It was the *worst.*"

"Why is that the worst?" says Luna.

"I'm just saying, that position should have gone to someone who has to deal with presenting as queer in a toxic cisheteronormative society on a daily basis. You know, not the kind of queerness you can take on and off as it suits you."

Roaring engines and distant cheers fill the silence. Luna fixes Gabi with a stare, stands, turns, and disappears into the ripe center of the orchard.

Charlotte runs after her.

Gabi frowns. "She left her bag."

I take Luna's bag. I'm all hot inside, back of my throat tight with tears. "Gabi, what the fuck?"

Gabi starts crying, says she didn't mean it like that, and takes another Xanax before setting off with me to find Luna and Charlotte. We find them at the center of the orchard, faces stamped with shadows of branches and leaves, Charlotte's mantis arms curled around Luna, Luna's face in Charlotte's chest.

Gabi puts her hand on Luna's shoulder, digging her short nails into Luna's bare skin. "Please, I didn't mean—"

Luna swerves out of Gabi's way. "Don't touch me like that—"

"Luna, I love you—"

I am nothing but an inanimate observer as Charlotte moves between Luna and Gabi, Gabi staggers back, the wind whips the trees, and a humming fastball of an apple ricochets out of nowhere and smacks Gabi square in the head.

Gabi tumbles to the ground.

Luna rushes to Gabi's side.

"Lee!" Luna shouts.

I emerge from the position of spectator to grab a sweating bottle of water from Luna's backpack. Luna has Gabi's head in her lap; Gabi blinks, her hand suctioned to the site of the injury.

"Char, get some help," I shout. I glance around our section of orchard: no source for the apple. "Where did that come from?"

Charlotte rushes into the clearing. I take Gabi's pulse under her neck. She's panting, shaking, but conscious. I unscrew the bottle, encourage her to drink; she refuses.

Luna leans down: "Gabi? *Gabi?*"

Gabi takes her hand away to reveal a new magenta bruise crowning her forehead.

"I'm a second-degree black belt," says Gabi, eyes fluttering.

"How does that impact this situation?" I say.

"I got hit in the head before," she says, breathing fast. "Concussion. I'm not supposed to do contact sports anymore."

"You don't have a concussion," I insist, bringing the bottle of water to her lips again. The water spills over her neck and *Death Note* shirt, and she yells at me.

"Gabi, let's see if you can stand," says Luna. She helps Gabi up, clutching her like a ladder; Gabi is fine, until she lets go of Luna and crashes back to the ground.

"Okay, maybe we do need an ambulance," I say.

Gabi is crying again, Luna on the ground with her.

"Call my aunt first," Gabi is saying.

Luna tells Gabi her phone is dead (even magic devices need to be charged). "Does Charlotte have my phone? I think I gave her my phone."

Charlotte still isn't back. "Why did you give your phone to Charlotte?" Gabi whines.

"She lost hers," says Luna, then: "Lee! Go find Charlotte."

I pass several rows of trees before I see the back of Charlotte: black undamaged roots, knee socks, gaunt shoulder blades. I'm about to call her name when someone else— a boy—careens out from behind a tree, shaking off the last drops of urine and zipping up his pants, followed by a taller, huskier friend in an Amherst tennis sweater and dingy red sweatpants, LAX printed down the leg. The bigger boy holds a lacrosse stick with a sickly green, glowing apple caught in the net. The smaller, khakied friend points to Charlotte's back; the lax player aims the apple—which I pray is not magic, just unripe—straight at Charlotte's head.

I sprint into the clearing. "Charlotte!"

The boys turn and spot me, aim the apple at me—the khaki one saying, "That's her! The blonde"—just as Rachel and a group of her New Balance friends round a corner and start picking the remaining apples, filling their baskets like hoarders on Black Friday. The lax boy tucks his stick under his arm; khakis throws his hands in his pockets and walks off.

I grab Charlotte. "Why were you taking so long—"

She wipes a string of vomit from her mouth before popping a mint from her back pocket. "Sorry."

I frown. "Are you sick?"

"No, I just had to throw up. I'm fine now." She pauses to spit.

"You sure?"

In rare form, Charlotte's mouth hardens into an uncompromising line. "I'm sure. Why don't you text Luna, okay?"

I text Luna, then I remember Luna doesn't have a phone, so I group text everyone I know from Chapin. Rachel's chemistry friend replies, says Luna and a group of Chapin girls are bringing Gabi to the parking lot for the ambulance; we can meet them there. Charlotte and I arrive on the pavement while the lot is still deserted, the pickup trucks settled in a tight shady corner. The only other car is a bright blue Rolls-Royce, parked crooked in the center of the lot.

Bronzed arm hanging out the window, long fingers secured

over the wheel, is John Digby Whitaker III, otherwise known as Tripp, honking the horn at me.

I freeze. He revs the engine.

Charlotte looks to me, puzzled. "Lee? What's up?"

I hear laughing, cawing from above, and glance up to see the two Amherst guys from before, khakis and the lax player, straddling a pair of plastic broomsticks, circling overhead. They reach into their pockets, start pummeling the ground with the same green apples, narrowly missing our heads.

"Lee!" Charlotte seizes my arm, drags me back toward the orchard. "Lee, *move*—"

Tripp shifts gears, the car swerving in our direction, closer, closer, his face moving closer, I can see the color of his eyes.

"Lee!"

Charlotte's hands around my waist, dragging my feet onto grass.

"Lee!"

Out of the untroubled blue sky, a single bolt of lightning emerges, striking the ground between us and the Rolls-Royce. Tripp backs up, blood drained from his face. Charlotte takes a green apple in her hand and flings it at Tripp's windshield.

My back on the grass, I watch as Charlotte ignites a small fire at the edge of the pavement, sends it reeling toward the Rolls-Royce. Tripp speeds out of the parking lot. The flying warlocks follow him, ascending farther and farther until their images are the diameter of fruit flies against the backdrop of latte-foam clouds.

"Fuck off!" I yell after them, clenching my stomach, doing everything I can not to cry.

♀

We all go in the ambulance with Gabi, then wait with her at the ER, where the nurse repeatedly tells her she's going to be fine. Once she's in a bed waiting for the doctor, Luna holds up Gabi's phone while it's charging so Gabi can FaceTime with her aunt (Gabi says her arms are too weak). They talk for an hour; at one point, Luna asks to switch arms because she's getting tired. Gabi doesn't respond, just keeps asking her aunt to Google if she's going to need any drugs administered by IV.

The whole time, I'm numb as flames; my brain is flesh poutine; my vision is a fish tank; I'm dead but I must be living because this is a hospital and if I were dying I would be hooked up, plugged in, the essence of Leisl represented in a glaring red squiggly line on a monitor. I wonder if this is where I'll end up, when Tripp comes after me. I'm sure he'll remove any evidence with magic, so they won't find anything during the rape exam, and then I'll climb to the top floor of Chapin and get out onto the roof and jump and not-quite-die, and since Tripp is a witch—no, a *warlock*—he'll sniff my insecurity like sharks can smell a four-hour-old tampon dangling out of your bikini bottom, he'll find me anywhere, everywhere, he's probably in the waiting room right now.

Gabi's aunt says she's coming to the hospital and hangs up. Luna goes to the bathroom. Charlotte goes to the vending machine. Gabi and I are alone.

I glance at the soulless school-and-hospital analog clock tacked over Gabi's bed. "Do you want some dinner?" I pick up the menu. "They have stir-fry, some kind of vegetable korma, a veggie burger with pico and guac."

Gabi's frown is on fire. "Lee, can you Google if acetaminophen is administered intravenously?"

"Gabi, it's generic Tylenol."

"Is there a concussion treatment that's delivered intravenously?"

"I don't think so."

Gabi shuts her eyes and scrunches up her face like an American Girl doll shoved in hot embers. "Is Luna back?"

"No."

"I hope she doesn't go out this weekend. When she's without me."

"Okay."

"I can't have her drinking. I'm worried she won't think of me."

"What?"

"I don't want her getting sick. Like, I'm just worried. That she won't think of me. That she won't consider her girlfriend in every decision she makes."

"Why can't she go out?"

"She could get alcohol poisoning and go to the hospital and I'd have to see the IV in her arm. She can't do that, she has to consider my trypanophobia," Gabi whispers, words low in her throat, half swallowed, like a confession that you broke the new digital camera or backed into your own house (when, in reality, Zara backed into the house, but you'd just gotten your license and Zara was such a *good driver* so it didn't really make sense that *she* would have backed into the house considering she visited the house almost every night unless she was on one of those orchestra trips to Chicago that her parents paradoxically paid for even though they wouldn't buy enough rice noodles for both of you when you ate dinner at her house because *we don't have all the money in the world*).

"Luna is an adult," I say. "She can do what she wants. If she gets sick, it won't be in front of you."

Across the hospital wing, a nurse walks across the heavenly white linoleum floor, and when she halts beside an elderly man's bed I see she's going to give him a shot.

I try to shield Gabi from view of the nurse, but it's too late. Gabi's face turns very red, her breath starting to race.

"Gabi, don't look," I say, putting my arms around her and offering my shoulder as a mask.

Gabi is shifting and shaking, rocking the bed, a raft on thin unsteady wheels; I move to hold down the bed, and Gabi starts to kick and lodges her elbow in my face and I stagger back, swallowing warm-sterling blood and any indication that Gabi recognizes me as a mirror, a reflection, an equal image of God and not just a set of arms.

The bed tips over. Gabi slides to the floor, her legs tangled in sheets and hospital gown. I close my hand over my lip, try to stop the bleeding.

Luna and Gabi's aunt burst into the wing.

Aunt Kristin sinks to the floor and handles Gabi with an ephemeral touch. "Gabi? What happened?"

Gabi flails, swatting her aunt away, but Aunt Kristin is practiced enough to avoid the sting.

Gabi: "You didn't get here soon enough—you fucking—*fuck* you—you don't care about me, you didn't get here in time, you didn't get here—"

The lone nurse, eye on the mess of Gabi's bed, syringe in hand, shouts for assistance. Luna is at Gabi's side. I catch her wiping her tears with the flimsy hospital blanket.

Aunt Kristin takes a bottle of Xanax from her purse. "Gabi, darling, if you would just take your medicine and—*thank you, Luna*—drink some water, you'll feel better soon—remember, this is *momentary*—"

CHAPTER SEVEN

WHITE BOY MAGIC

Gabi's aunt is postponing her fall retreat and staying in South Hadley until the end of November (it used to be the beginning of November, but after the apple and the ER and the panic attack, she's going to stay until Thanksgiving), and she takes Gabi back to the house for a few days. Luna and I, at Aunt Kristin's behest, take care of getting all of Gabi's notes and emailing each of her professors every morning to remind them that Gabi has a head injury and is unable to attend class right now. "Thank you so much for this *small favor*," Aunt Kristin says over the phone to Luna, promising to take us all out for Moroccan at Amanouz once Gabi recovers.

"Don't order sardines," Luna reminds me. "Gabi hates fish."

Life goes on. Charlotte starts carrying her cracked-mosaic

MacBook Pro in a medium-large straw basket because she traded her backpack (some Korean minimalist design you can only get knock-offs of on eBay) for weed. When I try to talk to her about the incident in the parking lot, she's high, and her only response is that I should ask Sienna about it. "She'll know what to do." Sienna doesn't notice until halfway through our Thursday magic practice that Gabi is gone, which briefly floods the ditch in my chest with something I think might be *happiness*, but all my progress disintegrates when Luna repeats how much she misses Gabi, what Gabi told her over FaceTime an hour ago, whether or not we should make a care package for Gabi, even though Gabi is literally being waited on by her aunt at home as we speak.

At the end of practice, Sienna drives us all home. She drops Charlotte off at Hubbard before arriving in Chapin's parking lot.

"I'll email all of you tomorrow," Sienna says, shifting gears and glancing at the clock, "but we're going to have to start having practice earlier in the evening, with my other commitments."

"Do you still teach at Amherst in the morning?" I ask.

Sienna pauses. "I never taught at Amherst."

"Professor Meyer mentioned you taught a seminar at Amherst last year."

Sienna shakes her head. "She's confusing me with Patricia, who teaches a Five College twentieth-century women's history course."

Luna gets out of the car; I don't follow her.

"Professor," I say, "I want to talk with you about my paper."

"I'll see you upstairs," Luna calls to me over her shoulder. I shut the car door.

"Your paper?" Sienna asks.

She doesn't look at me.

What exactly I had rehearsed, memorized, I don't remember, so I blurt out, with a fresh tide of tears I wish were fake: "Professor Weiss—*Sienna*—you said men couldn't use magic."

"Is this about your paper, Leisl? Would you prefer to schedule a meeting for office hours?"

"I don't think so. I want to talk about men using magic. If it's possible. If there have been any known occurrences."

"Is this a research question?"

"Of sorts." I take a deep breath. "I just want to know, if, say, magic ever got into the hands of men, in the local community, if you would know about it. If they would have contacted you, or *attacked* you—"

"Magic is the province of women," Sienna replies.

"Yes, but are there unusual circumstances in which—"

"You know, Leisl," Sienna says, rapping her rings on the steering wheel, "you remind me of myself, when I was younger."

"How so?"

"You're ruthless."

I try to frown. "You're saying I'm a bad person?"

"Your power doesn't come from doing the right thing," says Sienna wryly, with a hint of approval. "You're good at magic precisely because you care nothing for rules or tradition. You're a gambler, and you just so happen to win on a regular basis."

106

I gulp. "Sienna, I just want to know if it's possible for men to use magic, if there have been any examples."

Sienna turns to face me, weaves her hands together, sighs. "You know, you never see it coming. Your coven breaking up. Small conflicts, tiny disagreements can fester and turn into deadly arguments. You must ensure that the peace between you girls is genuine. That you confront any conflicts immediately."

"We're not breaking up. I don't know what you're talking about."

"Then where is Gabi?"

"Gabi just got out of the hospital. She was injured while we were apple picking." I twist my fingers together, strain to keep my voice steady. "Someone hit her in the head, with an apple, and I think it was enchanted."

Sienna smirks. "And who would have enchanted the apple? You?"

"No! I—"

She shakes her head. "You and your sisters must act as a team. Always. You must agree on every spell you put out into the world. You must be united. One. You check each other's excesses. The others will benefit from your boldness, but you need their caution, perhaps even more than they need you. And it's late. Your friends will be wondering what's taking you so long."

"Sienna, you never answered my question."

"Leisl, I've done my best to explain the basics of magic to you on multiple occasions. If you are so interested in the idea of men using magic, do your own research. Be my guest."

"I'll take you up on that." I crack open the door and exit the car.

)(

We're sitting in Luna's room—Luna polishing her record player and rearranging her bookshelf (all works of Capital-L Literature, but nothing basic like *Gatsby* or Dickens; she's all Martin Amis and A. S. Byatt and Rimbaud and *Wolf Hall*— and *The Host*, because she has a sense of humor); Charlotte slathering her inflamed ankle tattoo in hemp-store antibacterial cream; and I at Luna's desk, trying to finish a French listening assignment—when Luna complains about what bad luck Gabi has, getting struck in the head with a falling apple.

"It wasn't a coincidence," I say. Even if Sienna is going to lie to my face, I know the truth.

"Yeah, I know, Jung and synchronicity and everything," Luna says.

"The Amherst guys showed up in the parking lot," Charlotte admits. The same pit returns to my stomach. "Tripp and two others from Amherst. They tried to attack us."

I look at Charlotte pointedly. "You saw it? Last time I talked to you—"

"I didn't want to believe it. I thought Sienna would be able to offer some comforting explanation," Charlotte admits.

I swallow hard. "Charlotte scared them off. Lightning, fire, broke the windshield on his Rolls-Royce. It was great magic."

"You brought down the lightning," says Charlotte, quizzical.

Luna gulps. "So they're magic and they know we're witches. Great."

"They know we have magic, *and* they have magic too." My declaration catches me off-guard. My chest seizes, like the wind has been snatched from me, but I can see in Charlotte and Luna that what I've said is the truth, even if it's inconvenient as fuck.

We recap: The Amherst boys saw us using magic, the frat boys *have* magic, they attacked Gabi with some kind of enchanted lacrosse stick and an apple that was either poisoned or unripe, it was hard to tell in the afternoon light.

"Shit," says Luna, throwing down the paper towels and Clorox, perhaps accepting that her record player will always be caked in dust, and joining Charlotte on the bed.

"Fuck," Charlotte agrees.

"We should attack them," I suggest. "Make it even."

"No way. No fucking way." Luna shakes her head vigorously.

I shut my laptop, accept that I'm not going to finish watching next week's batch of eighties instructional videos about Pierre who likes to *faire du vélo* in Paris and talk about what color *cheveux* he has at *chez* Jeanne.

"Luna, *Tripp* has magic," I say.

Charlotte: "I think smashing his windshield counts as a counterattack—"

"They'll come after us," I say. "If we don't intimidate them, they'll think we're weak. We need to prove otherwise."

"I'm not comfortable making any sort of decision without Gabi," says Luna unhelpfully.

"We don't need Gabi," I insist. "You know, majority rule."

I read online that the best way to get a raise, a big one, is to state your amount and just *stare* at the person doing the money-giving, and wait for them to suddenly realize that, because you are quiet and staring unblinkingly ahead, you radiate authority and competence and deserve all the money in the world.

Luna, however, is stingy. "That's not fair," she says. "Gabi's part of the coven."

"And my rapist is a warlock who's going to come after me unless he knows we could fight him off, injure him, *kill* him, if need be."

Luna is silent for a long moment. "He would come after us anyway."

Charlotte suggests we at least *text* Gabi, so she's included in our discussion.

Luna goes to grab her phone. "I'll tell her—"

I seize her arm. "We'll let her know after."

Luna's gaze flicks between my hand and my eyes like her arm has a gaping flesh wound, deep as bone. "Let go of me."

I release her. "Don't text Gabi."

"Don't tell me what to do."

She grabs her phone, types in her passcode.

"Luna, seriously?" I shake my head. "You don't want Gabi to have another panic attack, do you? After all the stress she's been under?"

Luna considers me. "She's part of the coven."

"And we'll tell her when it won't disrupt her health. But you and I both know what he could do with magic. What he's already done."

"We should ask Sienna," says Luna. "Also, if there are warlocks at *Amherst*, seven fucking miles away, why wouldn't she have told us?"

"I tried to ask her about it. She just kept repeating that only women can use magic."

"Maybe the warlocks are hiding themselves with magic, so she doesn't know either." Luna frowns. "I trust Sienna. And we're new to magic. We can't just strike out on our own, we need her guidance."

I sink my nails into my palms. "I'm going to Amherst tonight, to demonstrate to the warlocks who they're dealing with. We need to give them the impression our coven is bigger, more of a threat—"

Luna takes a long moment to respond. "You're absolutely determined to go? Tonight?"

"Yes."

Luna presses her phone to her ear.

"Hello, Sienna? This is Luna. Thank you so much for picking up. Yes, this is an emergency. A Seven Sisters emergency. Yes, we'll be at Neilson in five."

Sienna: "You asked me if men could use magic hypothetically, and if there were historical examples. There are no historical examples, and no, men should not be able to use magic."

She's in a handprinted-looking silk robe, confirming our suspicions that she indeed lives in her office, and this time she didn't bother going through the Quadratini, leftover curry, jasmine loose leaf routine, she just shut and locked the door with a single swipe of her hand and waited for Luna to start crying.

I say: "*Should* not doesn't mean—"

She cuts me off. "I suppose, in retrospect, it was naive to assume magical potential was connected to the owner-ship of a uterus. Transphobic, too. Historical witches went to tremendous lengths to prevent men from learning about magic, and, over time, we in the magical community came to believe that men were incapable of magic, rather than just ignorant of its existence. Yes, there is indeed a coven of war-locks at Amherst, who operate out of the Sigma Beta Zeta fraternity house."

"How did they acquire magic?" I ask. "Do they have a talisman?"

"They have something even more dangerous." Sienna goes to her bookshelf, pulls out a thick black scrapbook, and brings it to her desk. "This," she says, dark nails punctur-ing the leather binding, "is my grimoire, which originally belonged to my grandmother. Witches frown upon using your grimoire as your talisman. I believe a Sigma fraternity member came upon one, last fall, and the brothers have since become well-versed in magical practice."

"So you knew about this." I gulp. "You knew about this the whole time."

"This is an issue for an experienced witch," Sienna says.

"If they've had the grimoire since last year, perhaps ex-perienced witches aren't doing a particularly good job of handling these warlocks."

Luna grips my hand. "Lee—"

"John Digby Whitaker III has a grimoire—he's a fucking *warlock*—and you *didn't tell us*," I spit out, tearing my hand away from Luna. "And you expect me to just go back to my room and take a sleeping pill and—"

I stand, reach down for my bag, but my knees give out and I'm on the floor. The heels of my hands press into my face. My own tears and mucus flood my mouth, swimming, I can't breathe and I'm positive I'm going to die.

Sienna: "Leisl, sit back down."

"No."

"Leisl, I want to help you," she assures me.

"You could have helped me by warning us that a rogue group of Amherst frat boys, including my rapist, have super-natural powers."

Hands on my shoulders.

"Lee," says Luna, thumbs hitting my shoulder blades, "Sienna couldn't have known who Tripp is."

"She could have taken it away immediately! Besides, how did a group of frat boys happen to come across a real grimoire to begin with? Some witch must have given it to them—"

"No witch would *ever* allow a group of frat boys to possess her grimoire. Not by choice," Sienna snaps. She is stern, impenetrable, a thick sheet of ice. "It's one of my sisters' grimoires, from the seventies. It must have been entered in the Five College library system somehow—or perhaps it's been collecting dust in a Hubbard or Cutter Ziskind closet and a girl showed it to her boyfriend. We'll never know. But I can tell you, I'm not able to retrieve the grimoire from the warlocks. There's a spell preventing me from recognizing any of my coven's grimoires—it's a long story, but sisters don't always see eye-to-eye." She stares at me, unblinking. "I didn't want to involve you, endanger you, but considering you are so advanced yourself—all of you, really, despite a mere month of magical practice—perhaps I could ask you to assist me."

I look at her. "That's why we have magic. So you could train us to retrieve the grimoire."

Sienna frowns, her crimson lip pencil smudged at the outer corners like a pair of bloody wounds. "My priority is preserving the craft through the education of young witches. Yes, I did intend to include you in my search for the grimoire, *if* and when you were ready. I never expected you to be ready so early."

She hands me a box of tissues and finally grabs the wafer cookies, passing them around. "Perhaps," she says as soon as our mouths are stuffed to the point of being unable to respond, "we keep our little mission from our darling friend Gabi, for the time being. So she can recover fully."

I swallow fast. "That's very considerate, Professor. I mean, Sienna."

☽

Luna doesn't press the issue when it comes to Gabi; she permits her girlfriend to dwell in a periwinkle haze of her latest benzodiazepines and ignorance sweet-syrupy enough to swallow, enlisting our help only to come up with solid excuses for why none of us can hang out the nights of our extra magic practice with Sienna. ("We're getting our flu shots together and Lee is even considering volunteering at the clinic.") Sienna encourages us to be cautious, to gather information on the frat through social media, not the sort of magic the warlocks can detect; but every day we don't act, I wither, crumble, all my leaves falling off.

October climbs to a precipice and our concerns again turn mundane: midterms, adviser meetings, Chapin's Halloween party. We agree to deal with the grimoire once our midterm papers are handed in, though I still place a double lock charm on my bedroom door every night, accidentally barring Rachel from entering one Saturday when she's out drinking.

We all skip Hampshire Halloween to sit in Luna's room and resurrect a legendary Tumblr known as *smithboobs*, where anonymous Smithies, recognizable only to the friends who have joined them for topless parties, send in pictures of their bare breasts, captions optional.

"This is like, the reason I came to Smith," Luna reveals, as the chief moderator of the new *smithboobs*. "I think it's really important for prospective first-years to be able to find this page and see the kind of campus we are, you know?"

Boob submissions roll in, Luna going through them ("Can I really reject anyone's boobs? Wouldn't that be, like, the worst kind of white sex-positive feminism?") while Gabi endures a Hulu ad about male-oriented yogurt and I'm doing another French listening assignment, feeling like I'm about to cry.

Luna pulls a blanket over me. "It's okay," she assures me.

"Wasn't Sienna going to help you get a scholarship to that Middlebury summer immersion program where everyone else also doesn't speak French?"

"But I need to be *fluent* if I'm going to be a historian, and what if the program doesn't work for me? I don't *know* if I even want to be a historian."

"I didn't know you wanted to be a historian. I thought you wanted to go to law school," says Luna.

"Well I really want to be a filmmaker but I need a backup that's impressive, you know? And I'd much rather be a historian than a lawyer." I wipe my tears with Luna's blanket. "Sienna says if I want to go to the sort of grad school where I will actually have a job after, I need to write about colonialism, which means I'm going to have to actually read French to look at sources instead of reading translated sources that everyone has already used. Gender and the French Revolution is so nineties. I'll probably write about Saint-Domingue. But am I replicating a colonial dynamic by writing about Haiti as a white person? I don't even know if I want to be a historian." I look at Luna, her newly pink undercut, her poker smile. "What do *you* want to be?"

"I want to teach English," says Luna.

"I want to be an activist," says Gabi.

"I used to want to go to L.A. and live out of my car until I made it," I say, and this is the first time I notice a change, an erosion, the sort of transformation that you can't see with the naked eye but that raises and shatters mountains in a fleeting blink of ecological time. When I used to talk about my hypothetical Hollywood career, penning screenplays and maybe directing a feature or two, big historical pictures like

I used to watch with my father, *Spartacus* and *Ben-Hur*, movies that made you momentarily believe in God and greatness and the love of your father, I felt like living. But now, *used to want to go to L.A.* really refers to the past. That place inside me, where yearning used to linger, feels dull and dead. Like, beyond having a roof over my head, and the fancier kind of Cup Noodles, I just don't care about dreams or goals or wonders of the world. I don't want to go anywhere and I don't want to do anything, but not because I'm at peace. I'm fucking terrified of going too far, of meeting new people, people who could tear me apart from the inside, people who could haunt the space beneath my bed for the rest of my life.

"Do you think," I start, "we'll still be doing this? In grad school?"

Luna: "What?"

"Magic."

She shrugs. "You could probably use magic to get into grad school."

Gabi has to study for her archaeology midterm, so she goes back to her room. Luna confesses she has a D in English.

"How?" I demand.

Luna says she has a D in every class. She hasn't gone to class in three weeks and there's this policy about how missing more than three classes means your grade drops a certain percentage every time you miss class after, and she's missed so many, she's on the cusp of really failing. The reason she missed so many classes is she has to take care of Gabi, of course.

She laughs at my horror. "Lee, you're incapable of failure," and that makes me want to cry, because little does she know. "I don't think you could ever get an F. Like, your body would combust, or something."

She asks about my grades, assumes I have the magic four-point-oh, even though I've only gotten my early midterms back in two classes and thus don't really have a GPA yet.

"At least you've gotten an A on every assignment so far. My parents are going to take me out of Smith if I continue to get Ds," says Luna.

I hug her. She smells like vanilla and licorice, a bit like Charlotte, but I think she uses an actual bottled perfume and not just essential oils haphazardly rubbed all over her body.

Luna is thinking of majoring in history with a focus on the fourteenth-century Avignon Papacy. I start telling her about all-girls' Catholic school, how one would expect there to be a lot of gay antics going on in the locker room, all that cooped-up estrogen and uniforms and absolutely no men aside from the youngish math teacher and the priest, but the only queer incident I know of in my year was when my friend Gianna offered to give me kissing lessons so I wouldn't go to college a kiss-virgin.

Luna asks me if I've kissed anyone since then. I tell her not any girls. I mean, there was that one time with Zara, but it hardly counts. It was the first time I had champagne, and we were best friends. We did that sort of thing.

"Making out is easy," says Luna. "You just ask a friend. Someone you trust."

I reach out to brush a stray thread of hair from her face as Charlotte bolts through the door.

"Luna, Lee," she says, fumbling with the lock, her face encased in shadow. "Did either of you pay attention to Sienna's lecture on potion antidotes?"

She steps into the light. Luna's hand grips mine.

"Charlotte, you look like you have smallpox," I inform her. Red welts cover her face, her neck, her hands, even the sliver of ankle peeking out from between her legging and sock.

"Thanks," she says, grimacing.

Luna breaks out the small kit of antidote ingredients we've stockpiled—full moon water, ground-up chicken bones ("I'm thrilled none of you are vegan," Sienna said when we reviewed potions), sprigs of lavender and thyme, a cluster of amethyst. She stirs everything into her SMITH: A WOMEN'S COLLEGE WITH NO BOYS mug, then drops the crystal into the mixture.

Charlotte was at a Quad party drinking some kind of mystery punch when she started to get really itchy, and the girl she was with started commenting on her skin, so she went to the bathroom and, lo and behold, there was a tiny cauldron filled with potion that looked an awful lot like passion fruit punch, and someone's Amherst ID, which she grabbed for us.

Luna reads the name aloud. "Brett Mackenzie, DOB *1988*. How is he class of 2014?"

"Hockey," I explain.

"Lee," says Luna, calling me to the floor. We join hands and chant over the mug:

"POWERS OF GOODNESS AND LIGHT, BANISH FROM CHARLOTTE THIS WICKED SPITE; KNOW THAT HER SUFFERING IS TRUE, AND WITH OUR

HUMBLE OFFERING, MAKE HER NEW." (Sienna invited us to write our own spells but, considering I'm not a poet and Luna works more in free verse, we decided to stick with the originals.)

The concoction swirls of its own accord, powered by an internal tornado, before smoke rises from the mug.

Charlotte drinks the antidote; her face starts to clear, each welt making a *pop* as it bursts and disappears.

"This is actually really painful," Charlotte confirms, nose shriveled up.

Once Charlotte's skin is simply irritated rather than cursed, and she is calm enough to scroll through Facebook and judge people from IB school, we lay her down on Luna's bed and brew her some chrysanthemum tea with honey. Luna sits on top of her desk, debating whether to call Gabi while she's studying.

I pace the room, knowing what must be done.

"Ready or not," I announce, watching Luna put her phone down, "this means war."

"We should keep searching for the grimoire," Luna says. "Once we have that, we have the main source of their power. We can erase their magic. Then we won't have to see them ever again."

"Only in our dreams," I say.

Luna's head sinks into her hands. "That's why I can't see him, you know. If I see him, if I look into his eyes, everything I've done to help myself, all that work, all that time and effort, it's meaningless."

"I'll never stop seeing him." I sit on Luna's nonexistent roommate's bed and try to keep my voice down. "I'll never forget. So I might as well try to help someone else. Get rid of him so he can't do it again."

"I thought this was about the grimoire," says Luna.

"I need revenge." I bunch a fistful of blanket in my hand. "I need to get even. I need to make sure he can't do it again. To anyone."

"What about helping yourself? Helping Leisl?" says Luna. "Are you not worthy of feeling better? Shouldn't you offer all that care to *you*, too?" She pauses. "You'd have to kill him, if you wanted to stop that from happening. Rape is a pattern. Part of someone's character." She pauses, gulps. "You know, when I saw what happened to you, I wanted him dead too. But when it happened to me? I couldn't help but wonder, what happened to him to make him do that? I felt bad for him. I really did."

"We have magic," I say. "We can stop him. And it would be a huge fucking shame not to make a massive difference in the world, with all the power in the world."

"Or maybe we'll just make the world into more of a mess than it was before."

I stare her down; she's space-age stunning, wide eyes and scarlet lips, shining everywhere, absurdly succulent, but nonetheless incapable of convincing me to bow to the sort of victim-cynicism that *comfortable* people wearing fuzzy socks, feet propped up on warm knit ottomans, Audis toasty in the new garage, use to justify their *comfortable* lives as the poles sink and bears drown and college girls across the nation remain ignorant of the key blades and pepper spray lurking within them, dormant, comatose, but never dead.

"We won't get any closer to the grimoire without going on the offense," I plead. "Let's start small. This Brett who left his ID—even if he's not a warlock, he knows something. We'll start with him. See if he leads to the grimoire, see if he's been a participant in any of the warlocks' other activities."

Luna joins me on the bed. "I need to sleep on it."

She turns off the light; I don't remove her arm from my waist.

CHAPTER EIGHT

DRAGON GIRL

I DON'T EAT BREAKFAST THAT Saturday; still, I have diarrhea all morning, even though I didn't eat dinner either.

We meet behind Chapin, in front of the greenhouse with our talismans. In addition, Charlotte has Brett Mackenzie's ID, powdered Valium, and a hammer; Luna has crystals, a Fiji bottle full of potion, and rope.

Friday night in Amherst, it was easy to find out more about Brett. One girl we met, an Amherst sophomore, said that last year at a party, her boyfriend of three weeks decided to date-rape her, but then got tired, so he just left her, unconscious, in the middle of the frat house, and Brett found her and finished the job. One word that came out of my mouth, regrettably, as soon as I heard the story, was *unbelievable*, but therein lies the truth—monsters are everywhere, but they don't have the courtesy to stay under your bed, they get right between your sheets, so you're unable to distinguish between nightmares and reality, because reality is a nightmare.

Her head on my shoulder, Patagonia mopping up her tears, she said something about how *the punch was fucking hallucinatory, ayahuasca shit, and my skirt, we couldn't find it after, literally it vanished*. My eyes meet Luna's and Charlotte's and we all know what we have to do.

"Lee, we're a coven, not a vigilante gang," Luna reminded me in her room that night. "We don't *need* to attack Brett to retrieve the grimoire."

"We're going to Amherst tomorrow," I repeated, huddled between her pillows and scratchy clearance-aisle wool throw.

Sometime around three A.M., with the aid of a mild persuasive charm I develop, I convince them.

Amherst is barren in the morning; we pass closed storefronts and restaurants, lone residents walking their dogs. Charlotte is commenting on Luna's interest in papal history. "TBH though, Christianity is a mess. There's one God, but also three? And Jesus is God, but also not God? And the Holy Spirit is also God, and what about the saints?"

"But wouldn't you get scared, being all alone in the galaxy?" Luna throws out the remainder of her coffee at the next trash can.

I chime in. "I believe in God. My mom was supposed to be at the World Trade Center on 9/11, but her alarm didn't go off and she was late. Everyone who made the meeting died, and my mom has never been late for anything in her life. That's why I believe in God."

"I thought you didn't like your mom," says Charlotte.

I slow down, not sure how to respond. "Not like that."

We move onto campus, and Luna brings up how lucky we are that not all the frat brothers live in the Sigma Beta Zeta house, or we'd never be able to do this.

"*Never* is relative," I mutter.

Brett we let off easy. After tying him to his bed with the rope (his roommate, thank Goddess, is out for a morning run), we knock him out (potion and powdered Xanax dribbling down his sleeping chin), take the hammer (held aloft with magic, no traces of DNA), and smash his ankle, ending his hockey career and, hopefully, his Amherst education.

(No, the grimoire is not under his bed, nor in his closet.)

"Are you sure that wasn't too harsh?" Charlotte wonders as we walk to the PVTA stop.

I remind her of the girl last night, how she had to get an abortion, take medical leave, endanger her scholarship. "He made his choice. We just delivered the rightful consequences," I say.

Charlotte frowns. "And we definitely erased all of our DNA?"

Jeremy Hudson-Winslow IV, who goes by Hudson, lives in the Sigma house, but we get his schedule from his ex-girlfriend, who took him to court last year and got a civil no-contact order that Hudson consistently violates. She tells us that Hudson goes to the gym three days a week, Mondays, Wednesdays, and Fridays, at five A.M., and lifts weights until pretty much the start of his eight A.M. lecture.

Hudson's got his computer science midterm, so we break his thumbs and, just in case he's chummy with a classmate who would offer to help him type, give him a potent memory potion, erasing the entire fall semester from his memory.

Pierce Ellis, alleged triple rapist, lucky bastard who used magic to ensure his last victim's rape kit was destroyed months ahead of his trial, has, in the opinion of Luna, sifting through her makeup bag, a neutral-cool complexion that would be complemented by MAC Ruby Woo (this is after we've hung him from a branch by his ankles and secured his hands with rope). Charlotte, on the other hand, thinks he's got more of an olive undertone, so no Cherries in the Snow, Girl About Town, or Schiap. We eventually settle on Luna's Train Bleu pencil, as we can't resist the temptation to enchant the lipstick so that, no matter how many hours Pierce spends scrubbing with St. Ives and rubbing alcohol into his skin, a bloody blueberry-purple stain will remain. (Charlotte: "Wait, I thought that was NARS without magic.")

On his forehead, we write *1 IN 5*.

The next night, we're able to get free from Gabi again: She has a cold and miraculously doesn't insist that Luna bring her ramen and fulfill the role of Aunt Kristin, who last week left her South Hadley house to attend a White Tantric retreat out west, and she's staying in Idaho the rest of the year. It's Sunday, there's a party at the Sigma house, and Sienna sent us an email in the early hours of the morning ordering us to attend.

"Does she think the grimoire's in the frat house?" Luna asks me as we're getting ready.

I slip on a pair of Luna's vintage Calvin Klein jeans, caught in a brief reverie about us sharing an apartment postgrad, swapping clothes like two girlfriends who are miraculously the same size even though we're just friends who are miraculously the same size. "The frat house is probably a solid guess for a first look." I slam my hands into the tight front pockets to stop them from trembling.

"You look great in those," says Luna. "Keep them if you want."

We get off the PVTA in Amherst, pass the elegant French bistro my mom keeps talking about going to when she visits, a banh mi shop identical to the banh mi shop in Northampton, and the art house theater, before skirting by Amherst's spacecraft-meets-Brunelleschi white domed campus and filing down a dim, unsettlingly idyllic road of dead robber barons' bright Victorians. We reach the hedges barring the raucous Sigma Beta Zeta fraternity house from the street; Charlotte kicks aside a beer can and coughs into her elbow. A stray cat bolts out from under the hedges, scurrying across the street. Luna frowns, flinches.

"Everyone got their talismans?" I check.

We flash our NARS, menstrual cup, scissors; secure them into the deep zippered pockets of our coats.

Charlotte reaches into her pocket and removes a tiny bottle labeled INVISIBILITY, 50 ML.

"Is that from last week's practice?" I ask her.

"Yeah, remember when you were showing off your levitating skills to Sienna and Luna was on the phone lying to Gabi about where we were? I slipped this into my pocket. Thought we might need it."

"I wasn't lying to Gabi, I told her we were studying," Luna insists.

"I wasn't showing off," I chime in.

"Okay, ready or not." Charlotte unscrews the top of the vial. "Lee, can you look at my poli sci paper tomorrow if you have time? I really need a decent grade on this one."

"Haven't you already turned it in?"

"I mean, I was going to email Meyer and be like, *Professor, I need an extension because I have plans to hex rapists tonight,* but as cool as Meyer is I don't think she's going to believe in magic without seeing the evidence." Charlotte sips a minuscule amount of the potion before handing the vial off to Luna.

Charlotte coughs and grimaces. "Warning: It tastes like *shit.*"

Luna shakes her head. "Char, you're kind of klepto."

"Urban Outfitters doesn't count."

Luna takes the potion, then passes it to me. The potion indeed tastes like shit.

"If we mix this with alcohol, could we die?" Charlotte

says, just as her image disintegrates like pixels shattering into hundreds of rainbow pinpricks.

"It won't kill you," Luna assures her, head and hands floating without a neck or limbs.

Once we're all invisible, Charlotte and I join arms, hug Luna goodbye (Luna assures us, "I'll pick up my phone if there's an emergency, I actually have the ringer on and everything"), and approach the house. The open windows reveal a swath of bodies mashing together in a cloudy film of sweat and spillage from red Solo cups, a vision of a college experience I never wanted to have: constant purging of the contents of your stomach, hazing, a herpes diagnosis at the end of your first semester because abstinence education fails in the real world.

"Why are they all wearing ski goggles?" I ask Charlotte, eyeing the assortment of faces obscured by neon plastic.

"It's an eighties Aspen theme party. You have to dress up to get inside," says Charlotte.

"Um, what about when this potion wears off?" I say, pointing my unseen finger to my invisible head.

Charlotte's voice: "I got you covered."

The garage door shudders and starts to rise. We leap back into the overgrown vines and watch a sparkling blue Rolls-Royce—with a baseball-sized hole in the windshield, cracks circling outward like a multithreaded crater—hobble into the empty left space under a precarious string of mountain bikes, no helmets.

We duck under the garage doors just as they start to close again.

The driver exits the car, fists balled, lush mouth directed

down in a sneer. "Dammit!" He wears a ragged crew neck AMHERST COLLEGE sweatshirt, maroon, which draws all the color from his sallow, pointed face, a face I can't believe I ever considered attractive.

Charlotte reaches for my shoulder—her fingers are short, fine-boned.

"Tripp, you've had weeks to figure this out," says the passenger, a rotund redhead in LAX sweatpants. "Can't you get it fixed before your dad finds out?"

"It wasn't a problem until I found out my dad is going to visit. And I don't have my credit card anymore," says Tripp, leaning against his car in a sour position of despair. "My dad took it away after spring break last year."

The redhead pries open the trunk and withdraws a lacrosse stick. "I don't know how to help you, man."

He reaches farther into the trunk, his words muffled until he reemerges with a pair of hideous mustard-yellow platform shoes.

I plant my hands over my mouth.

"I didn't ask for your help," Tripp snaps. "I just told you to stay quiet."

The redhead inches toward the makeshift steps up to the house. Tripp follows, reaching into his pocket and removing a red-white-and-blue fidget spinner.

The redhead turns. "Bro, I'm not the one with the vendetta, or whatever."

Tripp claps him on the back, jovial. "What are you talking about?"

"That girl. You shouldn't go after her. It's too risky. Think of that detective who came to our house and Alpha's, asking about Clara Dale. I know you've got *methods* of keeping out of trouble, but—"

Tripp raises his hand, squeezing the fidget spinner. The redhead crumples to his knees, jaw clenched, as if held down by a massive pair of unseen hands.

"Never say that name," Tripp snaps.

Charlotte squeezes my jean-clad knee, which is starting to come into focus. I resist the urge to sneeze, my hand jostling one of the bikes hanging on the wall.

Tripp spins. "Sean? What was that?"

Tripp lets Sean go. Sean raises his lacrosse stick. The fidget spinner flies out of Tripp's hand and starts circling the garage like a drone.

Tripp prowls toward me. I clamber out of the way, cloistering myself in the sliver of space between the trunk and the garage door.

He scans the area and sighs. "Weird."

The fidget spinner flies back to his hand.

Tripp seizes the platform shoes, joins Sean, and slams the door. His voice trails off into the house: "And you're being fucking paranoid, you know—"

The warlocks gone, Charlotte and I leap out from our hiding spots and rub our emerging calves, shoulders, lips, and noses.

"Just take the grimoire," I say. "Sienna told me as long as we take the grimoire away, anything else they've imbued with power will die, in magical terms."

"Thanks for knowing everything," Charlotte mutters, with an eighth grade sort of eye roll. "What a shit invisibility potion. How much of this stuff would you have to take to, like, rob a bank?"

"It was only enough potion for practice," I say, trying to keep my voice from trembling. "Sienna doesn't want us to rob a bank."

"Shame," says Charlotte, tugging at her now-visible denim jacket.

She reaches into the front pocket of her backpack, pulls out two winter hats, a pack of metallic Sharpies, a can of spray paint, and a knife. "Lee, if you put your hair up no one will recognize you," she says, handing me a pom-pom hat with the Yankees logo.

I stare at the hat. "You know I'm from Boston, right?"

"Exactly. Oh, I have ski goggles too. Which double as a disguise."

We place our ski goggles over our eyes. My world turns a faint slime yellow.

Charlotte takes the Sharpies and spray paint, slipping the knife into her boot.

"Just in case," she says.

"Wait, let's get a handle on what we're actually doing," I say. "I'm searching for the grimoire, Luna's our backup, then there's the curse and general intimidation—"

Charlotte indicates her jeans pocket; she's got another potion, but I can't see the inscription. "I'll take care of that," she promises.

We enter the house, the pulsating mass of bodies gyrating half-conscious like a group of rotting corpses animated by strings. I wade through empty pizza boxes and rolling beer cans, sticking to the periphery of the crowd. Someone hands me a drink; I don't dare taste it. All I see are blockish heads fitted with ski masks and hideous neon goggles.

Long hair, blond and brown, brushes the bottoms of crop tops peeking out from Canada Goose puffer jackets. The Sigma boys almost universally chose *Barney*-purple windbreakers.

"Hey!"

I turn. A thick-necked upperclassman in a hockey jersey, red goggles, is staring at me. He's not one of the warlocks, at least the ones we identified from Facebook. "Hey, can I ask you something?"

I step toward him. "What?"

He leans back in his chair. "Lean down, I can't hear you."

I crane down to hear him better.

An invisible hand seizes the zipper on my hoodie and yanks it down to expose my chest.

The warlock sniggers; I take my drink and slosh it across his face.

He blinks, droplets of amber-gold beer hanging off his goggles. I toss the red Solo cup at his broad chest and bolt through the crowd, pushing past grinding couples and swaying stoners, tangles of frat boys breaking apart chopsticks for sake bombs, red-goggled warlocks lifting girls' skirts with the wave of a hand, until I see Charlotte, holding a Solo cup with murky punch.

"Don't drink that!" I reach for the drink, and Charlotte swerves at the same time so the punch spills all over her *On the Banks of Plum Creek* white crochet blouse.

"Sorry! Sorry." I drop the cup.

"S'fine," says Charlotte. She reaches for her phone, checks the time. "I was going to shotgun a beer out back with these kids I just met. Wanna join us?"

I frown. "We have a task here."

Charlotte rolls her eyes. "Who made you the mom?"

"Luna's the mom. I just want to find the grimoire and get out of here."

"Luna's the cool mom who provides a basement where you can drop acid so you don't do it on the beach at night. You're just no fucking fun."

I reach for the tiny backpack slung over her shoulder, where she has the spray paint. "I'll do this," I tell her. "Where's the other potion?"

Charlotte flinches away from me. "Nah, I love vandalism."

"Fine. Get to it."

Charlotte disappears into the crowd, and I start looking for the grimoire, even though I have no expectation of retrieving it in only one night, just getting a sense of where it might be among the empty beer cans and lopsided floorboards.

Parties like this make me feel like I'm drowning in the mistakes of alternative selves from parallel universes; my stomach curdles and my chest is tight and the bass is giving me the sort of sinus headache you might get from having your skull crushed, nose shattered, and ears torn off by one hundred pairs of Ugg- and Sperry-clad feet, soles eroded by sand, yacht floors, and privileged disregard. Beer cans ricochet across the room; warlocks ski down the stairs, avoiding skull-splitting death via timely levitating somersaults; one girl even has her bra and shirt removed with magic, but she's so wasted she just keeps dancing, and her friend has to guide her arms into a borrowed cardigan.

I'm close to leaving, taking an Uber home, calling Luna and telling her I'm not fit to be a witch, to be brave, to do anything that involves large crowds of the sort of kids who used to kick me into thorns and puddles and keep me up at night with rewound fantasies of their cruel brains splattered on the gym floor. Maybe there's no such thing as justice and maybe we're better off erasing all our memories of John Digby Whitaker III and redirecting our girl gang efforts to massive wealth acquisition, but then I see Gabi, arms slung around the shoulders of one of the long-brown-hair girls in Lululemon and heavy contour.

They kiss, sloppily, then Gabi sees me.

"Lee," says Gabi, meeting me at the punch. "You won't tell her, right? Promise?"

"You mean, I won't tell Luna? Your girlfriend?"

"Yeah. I'll talk to her later. It's hard to explain."

"It's complex, sure."

"Thanks." Gabi relaxes. "Everybody makes mistakes."

"Everybody has those days," I reply, but Gabi doesn't get it. We stare at each other, having nothing to say.

I clear my throat. "She loves you."

Gabi frowns. "She called me."

"Luna?"

"Yeah, she told me all about what Sienna's having you do with the grimoire. So I came over to help the coven."

My stomach curls into a knot. "She told you?"

"Yeah, I'm meeting with Sienna next week so she can catch me up. Honestly, I'm pretty pissed none of you told me until now. I mean, the warlocks attacked *me*, not any of you—"

I'm about to pick up my phone and call Luna when we hear a shout, a cry for help.

Three of the frat brothers race up the stairs—stalked by a floating bottle of vodka.

Charlotte races to us, zipping the can of spray paint into her backpack as she runs.

"I'm done. And I stole a dirty sock, for scrying," Charlotte assures us, and Gabi has no time to explain her presence before there's a *crash* upstairs.

We bolt after the noise and arrive upstairs just as a set of NHL-sized brothers wielding lacrosse sticks—muddy Titleist golf balls whizzing around their heads—narrowly prevent Sean, the redhead, from vomiting over the banister (he vomits into a bucket instead). One of the bedroom doors swings open, the doorway soon filled by the upper-classman who unzipped my jacket (his eyes Pepto-Bismol pink, oozing yellow discharge, his blond head shedding like a pine), and John Digby Whitaker III, otherwise known as Tripp, his slim face breaking out in fierce red hives.

Tripp flings a tiny vial in our direction. It lands at my feet (FOR ENEMIES, 100 ML).

"Enchanted lax sticks? Seriously?" Charlotte says, breaking the silence.

Tripp grins, looking straight at me. "*Heidi*, right?"

I lunge forward, seize a lacrosse stick, and knock it over Tripp's head.

He cries out. One massive hockey player steps toward me, hands outstretched, but Charlotte slips between us, sticking her fingers in her mouth.

She whistles, then yells: "FIRE!"

All the warlocks, minus Tripp, and most of the party

downstairs, stop what they're doing, glancing around with disoriented stares. The partygoers start to exit en masse.

I take the lax stick and run, Charlotte and Gabi behind me.

"Don't you bitches come back here again!" Tripp shouts, scratching at his face.

"We're *witches*, you bastards," Charlotte screams back, seizing me by the hand and drawing me into the crowd, which feels like a mass grave, teeming with bones and birds and plague germs, Charlotte's fingers standing in for salvation, the kind that always shows up in movies right before the protagonist dies but in real life doesn't come until your eyes have been chewed up and swallowed by vultures.

The law of mutually assured destruction prevents Gabi from flipping her shit about not being included in the hunt for the grimoire, because if she freaks out at me, blames me, points her sanitized finger solely in my direction like I know she wants to, I'll tell Luna about Gabi acting out every teenage lesbian's fantasy about straight girls, "who are just like pasta, straight till you get 'em wet" (Charlotte, after gin, recounting a Quad party conquest, where there were also a lot of high femmes, so it was impossible to tell who were the straight girls, especially when you consider the bisexuals).

Gabi may overestimate the significance of her insights about Sappho, but she isn't stupid. In tiny actions she makes us even, stacking rocky little sugar cubes one by one until she forms a pyramid that rivals the tower I built to hold her secrets, a tower I could fling her from, live and burning, with the phrase *that one time at Amherst*. The worst moments are when Charlotte is too busy getting stoned to come slurp ramen or hoard crappy naan on Indian nights at Comstock, so I'm alone with Gabi and Luna. After an hour of Gabi *just not being able to hear* me over the din, we wrap up in pea coats and plow through the total dark of early November seven o'clock. New England autumn is immortal only in eighties schoolboy films with heavy homoerotic subtext, or songs about leaves and lost love—in reality, it was eighty degrees most days until last week, when the thermometer plunged and my mom FedExed me a box of wool and the L.A. girl down the hall rejoiced, because soon there would be icicles, and she'd never seen one. This is the single week when the retirement of summer is vibrant orange and smoky and nostalgic, before the world adopts the frozen color of a hospital ward.

It goes like this: Gabi holds Luna's hand, whispers in her ear, kisses her cheek, all the while making it impossible for me to walk next to them, so I follow them like a jester, a true third wheel, Gabi always unable to hear me, always out of earshot, until Sienna's formal lecture when Gabi makes a point of viciously deconstructing my painstakingly rehearsed comment about witchcraft, Calvinist predestination, and Beyoncé. Sienna looks up from her notes and agrees.

"I just think it's a stretch, Leisl," Sienna tells me when I confront her after class. "And Beyoncé as a subject of academic inquiry is so overdone."

At magic practice that night, my mind is brimming with

revenge. So when we're practicing making potions and Charlotte comes up with a bad batch, takes the whole cauldron and goes to pour it down the drain, I stop her, insist that she's a great potion maker and I'm sure her current concoction will turn me invisible, no reason to waste all that effort. And when Gabi is too busy engaging in obnoxious PDA with Luna to notice me switching her cauldron with the fishy brew I just acquired from Charlotte, and when Gabi tastes it and vomits, I can't say there isn't a part of me that doesn't enjoy watching her retch, her face drawn, chest heaving, glazed eyes reflecting an atrocity.

Pierce with the olive undertones ends up on the Huffington Post, upside down, reporters across the nation proclaiming him the AMHERST HANGED MAN after police discovered the Rider-Waite Hanged Man tarot card we left behind for the warlocks. "*1 IN 5* was scrawled on Mr. Ellis's forehead, a statistic believed to be a reference to the number of American women estimated to have been sexually assaulted in their lives." The headline prompts Sienna to send us a curt group email, imploring us to visit her office, nine A.M., bright and early, for a "discussion" about the "daring turn in our coursework."

Sun floods through the skylight of Sienna's office; we take our usual seats. Only Luna is brave enough to ask Sienna how her morning is.

"Lee, you wanted chamomile, right?" Sienna flicks through a small tin of tea.

"I prefer jasmine," I say. "Gabi likes chamomile."

Sienna pours and distributes the tea before taking a seat behind her desk. She takes too long to fold her hands, clear her throat. I lose any thirst or appetite; my hands shaking too much to safely hold the cup and saucer, I slam the tea back down.

Sienna opens a yellowing scrapbook left on the edge of her desk, pulling out an old Polaroid.

"Lee," she says, handing the picture to me, "show this to everyone."

I pass around the photo, which depicts a college-aged Sienna, her wardrobe largely unchanged, lingering in the middle of two girls in extraordinarily short collared minidresses, hair parted down the middle. One of them wears a pointed witch's hat, the other holds a carved pumpkin.

"Halloween, 1971," says Sienna. "This was the night before a particularly visible Samhain celebration on the Quad that triggered a response from the administration resulting in the firing of our faculty adviser. Both of those girls left Smith the following semester, and I have been without a coven ever since." She looks at me pointedly. "I cannot emphasize enough how deeply afraid the public is of anything to do with the craft. You would think women would be thrilled to find out about their magic—it's not that simple. Magic scares women as much as men. Women are raised to deny their power. When it comes, most of them don't want it."

"Leaving the card behind was my idea," says Charlotte,

fidgeting with her nails. "I just wanted to make sure the warlocks understood the reference, you know?"

"*Char*—" I start, before Sienna stops me.

"I know you were behind the 'Amherst Hanged Man,'" says Sienna. "And, yes, I did give you explicit permission to engage with the warlocks, for the sole purpose of taking back the old grimoire, but crushed ankles? Broken thumbs? *Hanging*? Thank Goddess he didn't actually die."

"I'm sure the three girls he raped would have preferred if we'd hung him by the neck," I snap.

Luna tugs on my sleeve. "Lee—"

I grind my teeth. "We'll be more discreet. But we're not going to stop."

Sienna takes a long sip of tea. "Leisl, you surely understand that actions have consequences. I am not able to give you the same free rein, magically speaking, now that you've chosen to use your magic in irresponsible and potentially disastrous ways. And, if you again attract media attention, I will have to put a stop to your magic altogether."

"What if we're more discreet?" I ask. "What if we leave absolutely no evidence?"

"If your coven is going to continue to engage in reckless use of magic, I will have to take away the *privilege* of using magic. Either way," she says, reaching into her desk drawer, "you are already limited."

Sienna places on her desk an elegant contraption that resembles an hourglass, but rather than the sand dripping from one curving compartment to the other, the fine grains sink through the funnel and vanish.

"Every month, at the full moon, I will refill the hourglass.

The rate at which the sand disappears is determined by the frequency and intensity of your spellcasting. Combat magic is especially costly. You are indeed legal adults, and young witches need some degree of leeway over their magical practice—I'm no babysitter—but you've certainly proven you cannot be trusted with unlimited power. Now you will have to be discerning in what magic you choose to use, and we will still have practice twice weekly, so you'll have to save the majority of your power for those sessions."

Luna keeps her hand on my arm, squeezes me like an unruly child.

Gabi takes her head out of her arms and starts sobbing openly.

"I think we'd better get going," I suggest, numb.

Sienna frowns. "Yes, have a lovely day. The weather's so nice and crisp."

ℰ

It's a Saturday morning, so virtually no one is outside. We settle on the lawn between the library and Seelye Hall, Luna laying her head on a bed of rusty leaves, Charlotte lighting a cigarette.

"I'm shocked, honestly," I say. "I thought she would have been more supportive. She was arrested in the seventies."

Gabi, still sniffling, glares at me. "She has a point, Lee. She has a really good point."

"Seriously? You're going to be *that* person?" I say.

Luna bolts up. "Lee—"

"What, you care more about Sienna's approval than the good we're doing?" I say to Gabi. "You care more about your own comfort than making the world safe for women?"

Luna: "Gabi's just afraid that we could get really hurt—"

"Gabi, if you're not committed to justice, you can leave the coven now. You may not give a fuck; I have a personal stake in this, *your girlfriend* has a personal stake in this, we can't just sit back and forget about—"

Gabi: "Justice? I thought we were at Amherst to get the grimoire back—"

Luna steps between us, reaching out to swaddle Gabi in her arms.

"I don't think we can trust Sienna," I say. "Think about it. Once we get the grimoire back, what use will she have for us? She could take away our magic permanently. Erase our memories, Goddess forbid we get on the news again."

"I trust Sienna," Gabi says.

"I'm taking Gabi back to Cutter Ziskind," says Luna. "We'll see you later."

"Oh, so you don't give a shit that we basically can't use magic now? You're not going to do anything? Just going to give up, go hide under the covers for the rest of your life?"

"Since when do you exclusively call the shots?" Gabi shouts at me over her shoulder.

"Since I fucking know the most about magic?"

I watch them leave; Charlotte asks if I want to go out for ramen. I remind her that you can't get ramen this early, so we settle on macarons at the French bakery.

"Mercury's in retrograde, you know," Charlotte explains

as she extinguishes her cigarette under her heel and scavenges for her sunglasses in her straw basket.

"I only read the good parts of horoscopes," I say.

We take the steep road winding around the front gates of campus, SMITH COLLEGE, 1871, the gates you're not supposed to walk through unless you don't want to graduate.

Charlotte says, "Do you ever think, either Gabi and Luna are going to get married and we'll all be in the wedding, or they're going to break up?"

I shudder. "Do you think they'll break up?"

Charlotte is silent. I don't choose an answer, preferring to listen to our boots slam the leaves, the soft whistle of breeze, the honk of oncoming traffic. Anything but the future, the choices we'll have to make, the friends we'll have to abandon, the relationships we'll bury and leave for the worms.

The bakery is almost empty. I make a comment to Charlotte about how I should become a morning person and have my espresso here while I get work done. Charlotte isn't very talkative. She makes some excuse about a hangover, but I know it's about Sienna.

Once we finish our macarons and coffee, I ask the barista for the bathroom key. My chest feels stomped on, sunken, when I see Charlotte inching toward the door, even though I told her to wait for me. I stay in the bathroom stall for a while, crying, trying to wipe my tears with plain old toilet paper. At one point, I hear the door creak open, see a pair of bland, unidentifiable sneakers enter, but I'm past the point of caring if strangers can hear me crying in bathrooms. I'm a college student, after all. Though I do wonder how the sneakers-wearer got into the bathroom without the key.

I stop waiting for Charlotte to text me back and opt to rinse my face in the sink. I end up getting water everywhere, and, because I'm not actually a bad person, gather up a bunch of paper towels and wipe the sink, the floor, the mirror.

I wipe my eyes, too, and, in the mirror, staring back at me, is Tripp.

He waves. I scream, twist my head over my shoulder and he's not there, there's nothing, I must be going crazy, but it turns out I'm not crazy, I'm exactly right, because as soon as I grip the door handle, there are hands on my neck, hands tugging at my hair, there are hands everywhere and I've been here before, this is exactly how it happened. I'm screaming and no one is coming to get me, no one is here to save me and I can't save myself, there are too many hands, dragging me to the floor, there are the tiles and this is just like it happened, his fist at the nape of my neck, pulling out my hair, cheek and nose slammed against the tiles, I'm surprised my nose doesn't break, but I'm bleeding, just like I bled then, just like that one time, this is exactly the same, there's no music but he's providing the soundtrack, *There's a freedom in your arms* . . .

It turns out he's got henchmen cowering in the corners, in-visibility falling off their skin like an explosion of powdered sugar over golden dough—when he puts me on my back, when he seizes my arms, when his buddy with the LAX pants starts fumbling with my vintage 501 buttons with a duti-ful, needle-and-thread attention to detail (and his scrawny, greasy friend, decked out in Amherst gear, lifts my shirt like a plaid tablecloth splayed over a piece of furniture), it's true that sharks go still, sharks become immobile, sharks can't bite.

It's true, this time I have magic, this time I have the power, this time I have fire and lightning and broken glass on my side and soon the potion is wearing off, he's squirming on the floor, knife in hand, little cuts all over his body, this time I love myself enough to destroy anyone who treats my body like an unchained bicycle with parts you can sell at the repair shop, I know I'm a person, I'm powerful, I am the image of God, except I'm the honestly-way-cooler Old Testament God who turns rivers to blood when you fuck with me or my people, I don't do forgiveness.

"Let's go one more time," says Tripp, grinning, wiping a string of terrible vermillion from under his nose. "All the way. You don't want to die a virgin, do you?"

One of the buddies—the brawnier lax one—loosens his grip slightly. "Tripp, we can't kill her here."

Tripp frowns. "You want to take it up the ass too, Rocky?"

He takes his hand from his belt, covering his mouth as he sneezes; from between his fingers, dripping, comes blood, thick red second-day-of-a-heavy-period blood rushing down his wrists, his arms, flowing like a stream, like a fucking waterfall.

I blink, and Charlotte has his throat between her hands.

She's taller than him, able to shove his face with her elbows, position him against the stall and punch him twice. He crunches forward, nosebleed like a faucet all over his khakis.

Tripp's two henchmen cower by the sinks; my wits coming

back to me, I take my scissors from my pocket and drive the blades into the wall.

At once, the brothers start to vomit.

"We have to kill him," I shout, hazy glance at Charlotte through tears. "Fucking kill all of them."

One of Tripp's hands escapes Charlotte's grasp, slipping into his pocket.

"Lee, we have to go," Charlotte says, releasing Tripp.

I pull my scissors from the wall. "I'm not finished—"

Charlotte grabs me by the waist, tugging me from my birthright, my revenge; the door swings shut behind us, and I'm crying, screaming, I don't care what the espresso-drinking bakery-goers have to say, I wasn't finished and I'm worried I'm never going to be.

We tell Luna everything (she thanks us for not including Gabi, who has a huge paper and already had two panic attacks today).

"Why would they want to kill you?" Luna asks at the end of my story.

"I'm a threat. We're all a threat. And now that our magic is limited—"

We enchant Chapin and Hubbard, make it impossible for any man to enter without a crusty, pus-filled rash swaddling his entire body (Charlotte: "What about trans guys? Shit, magic is so cisheteronormative"). Around ten, after two rewatches of *Mulan*, Charlotte leaves. I decide to keep my scissors tucked into the waistband of my sweats; it's better to have a weapon on me, even if I roll over the wrong way and stab myself while sleeping.

I have the dream again, with the broomsticks, the chase, but this time there's music playing, from some invisible stereo in the sky (you know what song), and I wake with a knotted, about-to-vomit stomach and run straight to the bathroom, and it turns out I fell asleep so early, it's only one A.M., the girls next door are playing LeAnn Rimes and *singing along*, and laughing, like he did, he was laughing for most of it (I told you he's a monster, indecipherable, a creature of nightmares come to haunt the day).

I return to bed, slam my head under my pillow, breathe in fistfuls of sheet before I realize that, you know, you shouldn't suffocate *yourself*, and there's an alternative to being my own worst enemy. There's still something I can do. That I have to do, if he's going to keep coming after me, if he's going to do *it* again, if I'm going to lose my magic, suddenly, like your phone going dead while you're stuck in the metal limbs of a primary school desk, school shooter prowling the hall outside.

It isn't murder if it's self-defense. It's just like hunting for rabbits the weekend after the apocalypse—it's *survival*.

I call Luna, tell her what we have to do. She hangs up, shuffles down the hall—we meet in the giant closet Rachel and I share.

Luna asks me to repeat what I said.

She gulps audibly.

"Remember the first time we hung out," says Luna, "when

I told you I wished I had some kind of magic potion that could erase my memories of him, so I could just be done with all of this? So I could move on, live my life?"

She catches my glare, applies a coat of lip balm from the hemp store, and shakes her head. "I'll help you fortify Chapin against him. But go after him, after what he did to you just now? Fuck no, Lee."

I lock the door behind her, try and fail to go back to sleep, but all I see is the vision of his belt, his grin, seemingly stamped on the inner skin of my eyes—and I know one thing: Death won't be the end of this.

CHAPTER NINE

SINGIN' IN THE RAIN

CHARLOTTE'S SWISS ARMY KNIFE THAT somehow got through airport security (which Charlotte assures me isn't that hard): the how.

John Digby Whitaker III of Cos Cob, Connecticut, five foot nine, handicap of two: the who.

Vipers you mistook for garter snakes, deadly hair, and the laws of feminism: the why.

The Hotel Northampton: the where.

Revenge (a dish best served room temperature, Thai spicy, topped with dollar-store wontons): the obvious.

How to cut off a dick, a guide for lesbians and virgins who don't yet know they are lesbians:

The penis is composed of two parts, sort of like if you arranged your box of crystals so your obsidian point is attached to two rose quartz spheres (a wand of negative energy, that's a good way to think about a dick), the long part being the shaft (a term I learned from L/Light Livejournal lemons circa 2008) which is fused to the balls, which, if you'll believe it, are the root of the innate masculine drive to explain how the world works to ill-informed chicks who lack a proper understanding of classic rock (classic rock being a genre limited to Led Zeppelin, Metallica, and maybe the Stones or the Beatles).

Now, most of my knowledge of castration comes from Zara's live-tweeting of this novel about harems, which was really critically acclaimed but she said was absolutely terrible. It was mostly about the main character having sex with this really feminine eunuch. At least that's the part she read to me at a sleepover February sophomore year, when the fisher cats were midnight prowling and we were really into Saint-Saëns and Michael Chabon and Zara denied ever having cried in front of me at four A.M., and our relationship started to ruin itself from there.

So I know how to make a eunuch, you just slice off the balls. (If you do it young enough, you'll preserve that pristine spoon-clanging-porcelain little-boy singing voice, which is what the church used to do for the Vatican choirs until, I don't know, probably not enough centuries ago.)

But when you're blinded by rage, revenge, Rohypnol dreams, you're not so precise, you're not so thoughtful, you seize the thing and you take the knife and you cut, you *slice*, you take the weapon apart like a nasty splinter you're prying from under your skin, pulling, pulling, pulling until it's separate and you feel something close to satisfaction.

)(

Kill and *murder* are absent from the choice words I use the night I confront Charlotte about the problem of Tripp. I reserve one of those study rooms in the Campus Center, the day we get back to campus, Pioneer Valley local news still reporting the pre-Thanksgiving story of the AMHERST HANGED MAN, the man of honor himself even doing an interview and identifying the perpetrators as "a bunch of ugly-ass bitches," a description that fails to incite the Hampshire County police to round up all the people who bleed and bake them under the fry-hot fluorescence of interrogation lamps only to discover that, indeed, most of the bitches in the world would really like to fuck the patriarchy, doggy style, with a crystal dildo and a smoking bundle of sage.

I don't say *murder*, not once, door locked, Charlotte splayed across the foamy orange love seat—I don't even think of death. Instead, I propose a spell from one of our lessons with Sienna, one of the "gentle methods" of ensuring that no unfortunate eavesdropper would ever reveal the existence of magic to the wider world.

"You want to trap his consciousness in a doll?" Charlotte pauses. "He'll be your puppet?"

"Yeah. That's exactly what I want to do." I gulp. "Goddess forbid he figures out Sienna's put a lock on our magic."

Charlotte's into it. She reports she found two of the warlocks on OkCupid; she messaged them and they didn't recognize her. (She also got a message from this dad, who sent her pictures of his two kids, four and seven, respectively, to prove that he's really a dad and really a safe person to tie up and whip at the Hotel Northampton for ninety dollars.)

Charlotte suggests the whipping idea to the warlocks, who are happy to oblige, and they're going to meet her at the hotel on Thursday night.

She's upped her rate: two hundred dollars. (She's wearing stilettos and a corset.)

Her condition: John Digby Whitaker III, otherwise known as Tripp, has to attend as well.

Charlotte changes her profile to reflect that she is "bisexual," in case they had any doubts.

I know you're wondering, and yes, we keep our plans from Luna and Gabi to prevent them from noticing that we are indeed about to use up the entire month's paltry allotment of magic in a single night. We brew something of a persuasive potion for them, dump it in their extra-large bubble teas, extra sweetener (Charlotte, the whole time, is on the verge of tears; I worry she's going to back out).

☽

The trouble is not getting to the Hotel Northampton, Charlotte's fishnets peeking out from under the totally-not-subtle oversize trench coat I lent her. I mean, with me hauling a backpack stuffed with tarot decks, pendulums (the pointy kind, in case we lose the knife), and a *Grey's Anatomy* DVD box set, with the actual murder weapon encased in a Ziploc bag at the bottom, my other arm slung with Charlotte's straw basket stocked with rubber gloves, Sudafed, and bleach, we look like we're about to at least rob the hotel, or perform some kind of *Eyes Wide Shut* Satanic ritual with masks and collars and the like.

The problem is not calling the two warlocks to come up to the room, nor convincing them to take off their clothes and close their eyes while two OkCupid bisexuals tie them to the bed, Charlotte drawing from her rich-people boating experiences and securing them to the headboard with military sailor knots. By this point they've texted Tripp the room number, so we're able to gag and blindfold them, which they don't like, but no one can hear them screaming.

The trouble is not lending Charlotte the key so she can run downstairs and knock the lone receptionist out with magic, just before Tripp arrives and becomes a victim of the same spell. The cool thing about double standards is that a pair of cult-outfitted girls can drag an unconscious twenty-something guy through the long stretch of Northampton's

Main Street and not face a single obstruction. In fact, we get some approving nods, townie offers to help us.

"Rough night for your boyfriend?" asks a burly lumberjack type ambling out of a bar.

"My brother," I respond, and we laugh together.

Yes, we were about to become murderers (though we only knew it the way you know you just got your period for the first time even though your conscious mind tries to convince you it's a cut from your overlong nails), but the truth is, we were the brethren of all those sixteen-year-old girls you see on Tumblr who are sentenced to nineteen years in prison because they killed their forty-year-old rapist and captor and father of their rape baby. Those cases that make you want to break the justice system open and suck out the inhumane unsympathy of juries like a vacuum scraping up shards of invisible glass from the kitchen floor.

Why were we different just because we were *organized*?

Would you like it better if we hadn't been so damn self-determining? If someone else had called us to our mission, Hero's Journey, no-agency-Skywalker style? The truth is, people don't get chosen by big destinies, they choose big destinies. We weren't special. Just bold.

But even if we'd been Chosen, even if we'd been a few years younger, shackled to a heatless Ozark shed all winter by a bearded cult leader, you might have still hated us. Do we remind you of unpleasant things? Like those suburban whites who don't want to watch *The Wire* because they don't want to think about black people or the shitty things that go on in families?

To you we were born monsters, immortal Gorgon sisters and not snake-heads forged by circumstances. Didn't you know Medusa's venom was defensive? Pepper spray doesn't cut it, not in the face of a core Pavlovian need for male approval, tonic immobility, and sea gods who will watch your drink, who know exactly what they're doing, who have six-hundred-dollar-an-hour Westchester lawyers on call on the off chance that one of those maidens dares to bring forth evidence.

Might you see that, in order to be safe among the untamed wild of streets and bars, subway platforms five minutes past midnight, we must grow snakes from our scalps and learn to turn men to stone—*just to go outside*?

That's the truth. Medusa was an Everygirl. Her venom comes from necessity. Her earbuds, shades, and frown are shields, encasing her in noise of her own choosing. The slamming of her Timberlands on concrete emits a fragrant *Don't talk to me*, her short hair shuts up the sea gods lurking in shallow pools of loitering male privilege, scares them as bad as snakes, reminds men of their mothers' vaginas or something. But you don't need psychoanalysis to recognize a girl like that. Next time you see her, know she is Medusa and she is strong as fuck. And if you come after her again, she'll summon her magic, her *real* magic, and cut off your dick before you cut off her head.

Because that's how it happens in most stories. You behead

the survivors and cheer. Behead the Everygirl who dares not to erase herself as soon as *it* happens to her. You'd better make sure girls like that don't survive, because they failed their number one task, which is to not get raped in the first place.

But, for the Medusa who can't shed the past—

Maybe you don't want us outside, because if you were really to look us in the eye—if you were to understand—it would kill you.

The true sight of us will kill you.

The trouble is, once we get to the woods behind Chapin, pull his pants down, take out the knife, snap some rubber gloves on, suddenly Charlotte starts to sob hysterically, drops the knife, and I snatch the flashlight from the bed of leaves and start to sob too.

"I can't use my scissors," I explain, when Charlotte wants her knife back. "Think of the stains."

"You're buying me a new Swiss Army after this," Charlotte says through her tears.

I look at the khakis and dog boxers pooled around his ankles. He's drooling. A few hours ago, I would have done it already—my fingers would be sticky with blood—but now, in the moment of truth, all my sleepless hatred for him, those nights walking home, chest a rip current, drowning in memory, my head aching against that bathroom floor, dissolves into a sort of passivity that feels like a trance—a high, the first dawn, too much vodka, apathy. Maybe this is the *niceness* people back home always talk about, where nothing is raw, nothing hurts because you live inside a personal bubble of antiseptic fluid and numb indifference, 2.5-Lexus-induced enlightenment.

Charlotte clutches the only doll she had in her room— her preschool one-eyed Cabbage Patch Kid in a urine-tinged, stolen-from–American Girl apron—and shuts her eyes. "I'm willing to help you, Lee, but I just realized I'm going to pass out if I see all that blood. Can't I just throw the doll into the fire while you handle the castration?"

I pivot the flashlight so the light cups Tripp's head, shadow cutting a sharp line across his exposed neck.

"Blood is life," I say. "Blood makes you feel alive. I know when we see him, after we do it—you know, how when you wake up in the middle of the night with cramps that feel like *I Didn't Know I Was Pregnant* and you hate your uterus and you hate being female and you question feminism because you're in so much fucking pain like how can you go to work and become president? But ultimately, bleeding that much, you feel really *present* and once the cramps die down, you feel this immense relief and you really appreciate things like your sheets and the heating pad and the feeling of not being in immense pain even though five minutes before you didn't appreciate your painless equilibrium whatsoever? Blood is here and now. Blood is the opposite of stillness, the opposite of death."

Charlotte: "I always wonder, since it's so fucking hard to find the right shade of red lipstick, if you could take your period blood and make lipstick and nail polish out of it? Like how the Warden makes rattlesnake-venom nail polish in *Holes* and threatens to kill men with her nails."

"It would be the correct undertone," I agree.

I hand the flashlight to Charlotte and pick up the knife. The hilt is cold, like the sturdy root of an icicle.

"I'll tell you when," I promise. "So you don't have to look."

"Look at what?"

I swerve, just in time for an overflowing cup of passion fruit black tea and jelly boba to drench my face.

I blink away the tea, jaw dropping. "Luna?"

Luna emerges from the trees, drops the plastic cup into a bed of leaves ("*Litterer!*" Charlotte calls), and takes out her phone.

"I'm calling Sienna," says Luna.

Behind her, Gabi waits with rope.

Luna types in her passcode. "I'm calling Sienna and telling her you tried to drug us."

"You don't even know what we're doing," I say, eyeing Charlotte, whose gaze is fixed on Tripp's drooling head. "You don't even know—"

"Lee," Charlotte says, gripping the doll. "Lee—"

I glance down. Tripp starts to stir.

I reach out, seize Luna's phone, knock her to the ground, end the call, and toss her phone into the dark unknown of the forest. "Char!"

I race to Tripp's side, knife in hand. "Char, get Gabi!"

The knife hovers above his neck, flesh splayed out, twisted and white, like Christ, or a swan.

"Char, shut Gabi up, will you?" I repeat, lowering the knife.

"Do it!" Charlotte shouts, restraining Gabi in a headlock.

I bring the knife down to his chest, his stomach, lower, grazing his skin, ready for it.

Tripp seizes me by the neck.

His fingers press into my throat, and I'm lost, I'm done, I can't breathe, the knife is out of my hand, I'm falling, defenseless, I have nothing, I'm *dead*, I feel it, the blood, my blood, it's thin, watery, painless, metallic, splattering everywhere, but I'm not really in pain, maybe this is what it feels like to rest in peace.

His nails leave my neck, and I collapse to the ground.

Above me, clutching the knife, is Luna. Below her, Tripp's throat is split open.

"No," I shout. "You weren't—we didn't mean to kill—"

Blood leaks through the gaps in Luna's fingers, and Gabi starts to scream.

Luna really starts to cry, her mucus spilling onto Tripp's upturned nose, pooling around his eyes. I'm crying too, and Luna helps me up, raises her hand to wipe my face. Her thumb smears blood over my lips, and I learn that love is red, and tastes like a bite of gold.

I'm the one who volunteers my scarf (Charlotte-knitted, an early Christmas present in scratchy cyan) when Luna and Charlotte agree we have to gag Gabi.

Gabi, slobbering into my scarf, hands bound behind her

back with Charlotte's fringed macramé belt, still earns the attention of Luna. She stoops down and hugs Gabi, holds her tight, tells her everything will be fine and we're not going to prison, nor to hell; I've never been more jealous.

We share a quick snack (Pocky) and start to get rid of the body.

His ear sticks through a hole in the basket, and Charlotte goes to poke it back inside with her knitting needles and I scream at her, *That's got our DNA*, and Luna keeps slathering her gloved hands in Purell, and Gabi, scarf pushed down to her chin, keeps sobbing, and asking when we're going to give back her phone so she can call her aunt.

"If we're lucky, he'll sink," I say, and Charlotte is in the middle of a response about how we're kind of past the point of pretending he committed suicide or went drunk sledding down the hill behind Chapin when Gabi's phone rings, and Luna picks it up.

"Oh, hello, Ms. Avery," says Luna to Aunt Kristin on the receiving line, nodding. "Yes, of course, I'm with her now—she's just gone to the bathroom."

U

"I don't know what the fuck to do with murder gloves," says Luna, shaking like a plastic Jesus swinging from the rearview mirror of a flipped-over SUV.

"We have to bury him," says Charlotte, remarkably nonchalant. "If we burn the body, someone could see the light. If we drown his parts, he'll wash up on shore."

"But we should mark the place we bury him," Luna says. "Runes on the nearest tree. Invisible to anyone but the four of us."

Charlotte passes out rubber gloves and we each take a severed part of him—head, arm, thumb, dick—until we're left with a mannequin-like torso, no head, no limbs, anatomically incorrect. Charlotte and I grab him from either bleeding side, *one, two, three*, and as soon as we lift his remains, a large black block *clunks* to the ground, slipping out from his back like a wallet escaping a bra with broken underwires.

We drop his torso and lean down to examine what appears to be a book, obscured by guts and plasma.

"It's the grimoire," says Luna.

Luna, around three A.M., gets mad. "You're afraid to Google 'how to hide a body'?"

"They keep track of those things," I say.

"*They*?"

"The government. Russia. NASA. You know."

"I don't know," says Luna.

Charlotte pulls her cigarette from her mouth and coughs.

"Who hasn't looked up how to hide a body?" says Charlotte. "First off, no one leaves their wallet at the scene."

♀

We bury everything—our clothes, the body, the penis, the head, the basket—and escape with nothing but our phones, our IDs, the grimoire, and ourselves, hair and lashes dripping, feet caked in silt, through the older hours of the night.

☾

I heard once that back pain comes from repressed rage, but I go to sleep that dawn with a sore neck, knots behind my shoulders, fitfully tossing and turning, unable to really access the landscape of dreams due to the sting of skin overexfoliated by apricot scrub, unable to get the taste of the lake from my mouth, the color red from my lips.

Instead, I keep thinking about Luna taking the shovel and staring down at the bluish visage of John Digby Whitaker III, otherwise known as Tripp, watching him dissolve into the earth, soil coating his skull. She took his ring off his right hand, the last part of him we buried, and then started taking her clothes off, insisted we needed to wash ourselves before we went back to campus. I watched her walk with the ring into the lake, watched her standing there, half-submerged, while we all prepared ourselves for the shock of December water, and Charlotte poured bleach over the leaves.

We cleansed ourselves, but instead of letting his legacy sink, Luna slid his ring onto her thumb and walked away with it, her hand still curled into a fist.

CHAPTER TEN

GHOSTING

THE WORST PART IS, I kind of want to do it again. Aside from the cleanup, the process of wrangling the life from John Digby Whitaker III, otherwise known as Tripp, had been my closest personal approximation of the state of *flow* you're supposed to experience on a regular basis if you want to be happy like Danish interviewees in minimalism documentaries. In the midst of Googling imperfect tenses on my French final (an easy feat, considering Smith's honor code mandates that there are no proctors for final exams; they just open Seelye and you go in and take your test and you can go to the bathroom at any time, you can even *bring* the test to the bathroom if you really want to experience the power of now), and Charlotte shoplifting another straw basket from Urban Outfitters the night before her flight, I feel like I'm watching my life from a treehouse tower, never really *here*, always back *there*, inhaling pine needles, damp from the melt of the first snow, the metallic, menstrual scent of his blood, all over my hands, smeared across my lips.

I sleep about two hours each night. Rachel leaves at the beginning of the week because her finals are all take-home. At the end of the week, on the eve of handing in Sienna's paper, I finally get a call from the Counseling office (I tried to make an appointment like six times in September and October), saying that the psychiatrist, Dr. Applebaum, has an open appointment right before dinner. I go, tell her everything that isn't the magic or the murder, so really nothing at all. She agrees I probably have PTSD, depression, anxiety, the works, and prescribes me Wellbutrin, this antidepressant that's supposed to work immediately, and Ativan, after I tell her how Xanax made me throw up the morning of my AP exam and Valium doesn't even do shit when I go to the dentist.

My mom comes to pick me up after Sienna's final. I slice one Ativan in half with my sticky-bladed pair of scissors and swallow it with not enough water. We pile laundry and sweaters I never wear into the trunk, and she opens up a brown paper bag of gift shop delicacies, including maple butter, which I eat right out the jar, which runs down my chin, leaves a sticky residue even after I wipe it away with a couple of Kleenex. For dinner, we end up at the French bistro in Amherst with the exterior drenched in rooster motifs, BOUILLABAISSE scrawled across the chalkboard in the foyer. The decor is all crimson and espresso; the soundtrack is Van Halen. We sit at the bar and my mom gives me several sips of Bordeaux, and once the night has completely risen, total black and blinking red traffic sinking through the window, the bartender pours me my own glass.

The whole conversation, I'm shifting my hips so I can feel the bottle of Ativan in the front pocket of my jeans, while my mom tells me how her friend's son, the one who was home-schooled and is really into *musical theater*, has just come out as gay, and she's going on about how it would break her heart to have a child like that, to think what he would go through. Yes, what *he* would go through. When your parents think about having a Gay Child they're always thinking about a boy, whom they will accept with open arms after several years of bottling up their own homophobia and locking it into his bones. Lesbians—they basically don't exist.

When I bring them up—*my friends at Smith*—my mom frowns, not with hate but with low-key pity, the way you react to someone who complains of having *battled* seasonal allergies. Lesbians are surely nothing more than gnats on the hairy arm of humanity, apparitions who cling together and adopt Haitian children and eat spirulina-flavored tempeh and maybe make some far-flung contribution to higher culture in the form of flannel shirts and Birkenstocks.

The bartender returns and pours me another glass. We order, *bouillabaisse pour moi, s'il vous plaît, steak au poivre pour Maman.*

My mom asks me how my French final went.

This is too much. I bump my fork against my wineglass, hard enough to make a *clang*, and ask the bartender for water.

He wipes the sweat from his face with a dripping white hand towel. "Just a glass of water?"

"Water," I repeat.

His face hits the deep end of shadow as he reaches for a clean glass and fills it with ice. When he twists to give me my drink, I see *him*, for the first time, it seems. Upturned nose neatly freckled, deep eyes, pointed chin, a sneer, lips sealed in terror. Blood streaming from the broad cut on his neck. Platform shoes between his fists, dangling from the strap.

Of course I know him. Of course I know his face.

The bartender blinks. His eyes turn blue, flush returning to his cheeks. "Water, ma'am?"

He reaches for my empty glass, and I fish in my pocket.

"I just need a stronger dose," I mutter, and drop the second half of the Ativan down my throat, then another pill, whole.

The food arrives. My mom eats her steak and I suck soup through my teeth like cough medicine, the red sticky kind you're not supposed to enjoy but that you always looked forward to because it came with a mother's pat on the back, a bowl of ice cream or ramen. The soup burns the top of my mouth, but I don't care, because I'm drowning, and death is deep and reeks of shellfish.

My mom pulls my face out of the soup and wipes me clean. I still feel an anchor pulling me under; I lean forward again, tipping toward the broth, but my mom catches my hair in her fist this time, keeps my head level, forces me to stare into the old face the bartender is wearing, the same freckles and scar and blood as before, the kind of shark face contained behind too-thin aquarium glass.

I want to speak, I want to say: *I'm not crazy, I saw what I saw, I'm right, I was right.*

But he's reaching for the soda hose with one hand and peeling back his skin with the other, discarding his death on the newly mopped floor and smiling straight at me, fresh sunglass tan and bright eyes, *alive.*

"Hello, Leisl," says John Digby Whitaker III, otherwise known as Tripp.

"Leisl." My mom pulls me from the barstool. "We're going."

She slings my arms around her neck and carries me out, unable to get my arms into my coat. Amherst slaps my sleeveless skin cold.

Christmas Eve: We sit at the counter and mold dough into stars and deformed snowmen and my mom is going on about Christmas cards and implying I'm not a writer because my cards don't glitter with cleverness. "You know who's such a great writer?" she says of this acquaintance who does fundraising for the diocese and favors purple ink.

Christmas morning, among slashed ribbons and butchered skins of reindeer-printed wrapping paper, I see blood transubstantiated from red velour, severed fingers ornamenting the plastic branches of the fake tree. My little cousin knocks into the piano after breakfast, and, reflected in cragged shards of snow globe, I see his parted mouth, his glassy eyes.

In the bathroom, drunk, because that's the only way I can tolerate my relatives, I'm washing my hands and there he is, in the mirror, where my own face should be. I raise a dripping finger—*his* finger—and tap the mirror, but he doesn't go away.

Instead, he *winks*.

I make New Year's resolutions I can't keep and spend the frozen birth of January cocooned in the finished basement, nodding off to the intermittent roar of the new vacuum, the habitual creaking floorboards. In the deepest ditch of night, two A.M., I wake up to the wailing radiator and piercing, unmistakable laughter. The sleep timer's gone off, it's totally dark, but I know that laugh, that nasal pitch.

When I say to him, "*SHUT UP*," (stupid, *stupid* girl, the number one rule of séances and Ouija boards is you never invite the spirits to talk to you) he stops laughing and clears his throat.

Has anyone ever told you you look like Taylor Swift?

I turn on the lights. The basement is empty. I rub the goose bumps down, turn Netflix back on. The Wi-Fi's broken, *fuck*, so I go back to cable. Of course, *We're having trouble connecting to the Xfinity platform*, so I have to watch the local news channel that's already on, coverage of AMHERST COLLEGE DISAPPEARANCE. His yearbook photo eats up the screen, and I cover my eyes, grapple for the remote, press the POWER button repeatedly, but it won't turn off. I throw the remote across the room and scramble to the TV, yank the plug from the wall.

On the couch—tossing the remote up and down—rests John Digby Whitaker III, otherwise known as Tripp, fresh as a crimson bouquet, his only injury the gaping wound where his penis used to be, blood wetting the cushions.

"We could have been a real power couple," he says, approaching me, closer, closer, and I can't move, I can't do anything. "Still can." He scratches his neck. A thick wound opens up, his head shifting from side to side on top of his shoulders like a detached cake layer, a rogue cup of tea skirting perilously close to the edge of its saucer. "Just to offer up some constructive criticism—you didn't do it very well, when you beheaded me. Sorry, when *Luna* beheaded me, because you turned out to be a wimp in what could have been your finest hour. You're supposed to hit the jugular. You made the cut a bit too low. Right through the vocal cords. Real unpleasant."

"We wanted it to be unpleasant," I say under my breath, legs frozen, arms frozen, all of me packed up in ice.

Then I realize I'm talking back to a vision, and I shut my eyes, willing him to disappear.

I blink. He's closer, dripping blood in a trail from the couch to my feet.

"Not to mention *this*," he says, indicating his lower wound. "A bit gratuitous, don't you think? Insisting on *genital mutilation* when you could have gotten away with a bullet through the chest?" He scratches his shoulder. His arm detaches from its socket, hangs from a stringy tendon. "And cutting off my limbs? Tearing my fingers off? Was all of that strictly *necessary?*"

I can't breathe. "You're here to haunt me, aren't you?"

All he does is laugh.

I race up the stairs, go to my room, unlock the window, survey the twenty-foot drop to the dead backyard rosebush, winter's bed. Rash, perhaps, but right now this seems like the only option, the only way to *make it stop*, to just end everything if he's going to be back in my life again. It's not like I didn't try to save myself. We fucking *murdered* the kid, slashed his throat and sliced off his dick, watched the life bleed out of him while I waited for my own nightmare to die with him.

The door creaks open, and there he is, a trail of blood following him down the hall.

He enters, grinning, sits down on my bed. I can see his lashes, his opaque sweating-glass skin. "Lucid decapitation— that shit's real. You really hurt me, Leisl. There was a good thirteen seconds when I was totally aware. I could see all of you. Luna with her knife, the rest of you going at my body like a flock of vultures. Actually, did you know a group of vultures is called a *wake*?" Tripp laughs. "Watching your neck stump, seeing everything inside of you, all the bones and yellow and red and green that's inside a human body— it's not a good way to die."

"You're lying," I say. "You're a fucking figment of my imagination. You're lying and I want you to stop. I command you to stop. I command you to not exist anymore."

I shut my eyes tight.

When I open them, his hands are around my neck.

Tripp opens his mouth. "I'm sure you know this, but there's this whole genre of beheading porn—"

"How would I *fucking* know that—"

"I mean, most of it's animated, but if you know where to go on the dark web..." He rubs his thumb over my collarbones. "First law of the Internet, right? There's porn for everything. What if there was porn for us? That would be a

172

first. A human girl—sorry, a *witch*—and a ghost. Don't you want to try? Don't you want to see if I'll turn up on your camera?"

"Take your hands off me," I say in a small voice, knowing it's futile. "Now."

He squeezes, my breath going short. I push against him, get my nails under the window, wonder how I'll look dead. Tripp didn't look good, but we cut him up. Will the thorns cut me up? Will the fall break my neck? In the last moment, flying, will I feel alive? Free?

"Why would you give up so soon? There is help, you know." Tripp reaches into my pocket, takes out my cell phone. "Do you want me to dial for you?"

I force the window open. The wind slaps my face, I remember I should leave a note, but I don't have time. I have to *get out*, escape, make it end, any way I can. Ugly corpse or otherwise.

I feel my scissors knocking into my hip, inside my sweatpants pocket—a promise, a temptation dangling over the split-apart leaking red corpse of me that is about to exist twenty seconds from now.

I close the window, take the scissors from my pocket and fold them between my hands—I don't know what I'm going to do but I have to do *something*—

"Leisl?"

My mom's voice, her slippered feet ambling down the hall.

I tell her my room was too stuffy. She suggests I sleep in the basement.

☽

The rest of break, I hang out with high school friends I don't really like, go for midnight rides down 3A, the road flanked by coarse woods where everyone swears they shot *Blair Witch Project*, autumn's last seagulls cawing in sweeping ellipses above the Honda and pines. When I have to go home, I either take extra NyQuil or Skype with Luna, who always offers to stay online when we go to sleep, so all our conversations clock in at fourteen hours.

He's still with me. When I'm eating stale cereal, in the shower, in my bed. And I never get *used* to him.

The week after Christmas—when he splays across the back seat of Beth's dad's Range Rover while Beth confides to me that she was raped at college—I come to my senses, the cold water of motivation slapping me back to reality, a reality in which I have *magic* and three witch-sisters to help me banish his ghost to nothingness for good. I'm sure this is totally normal, in witch terms. I'm sure Sienna could help us, in an utmost emergency (of course, she would definitely take our magic away if she found out we killed someone, even my rapist).

When Beth stops short over a patch of ice in the Starbucks parking lot, his fingers slip under my sweater, clamber down my collarbones, chest, breasts.

The next day, I text the coven, *Come back to campus before J-term actually starts. Witch business.* The day after, I pull my mom aside and tell her I can't be here anymore, I have to go back to Smith.

She puts down the spatula, sets the stove to simmer. "What?"

I start to cry, and repeat myself.

"It's normal to want to be with your friends," she says, smiling, like I'm five years old and a lollipop is sticking out the corner of my mouth.

My mom slips on a pair of oven mitts. "Now, your friend Beth—do you think she's *really* bisexual?"

When I get back to campus, Luna's room is empty, because the coven has gone out to shoplift crystals—which actually really hurts crystal sellers and witch store owners, it's kind of an epidemic. Gabi brings back a tiny shard of smoky quartz for me, which she places in my hand and tells me is good for depression and anxiety. The holidays have turned the coven from blood to blankets; we sit around Luna's bed, swathed in Charlotte's knits, footie pajamas, *Twilight* Snuggies, chrysanthemum tea in our fists, speaking softly over the lull of *Adventure Time*, murder an impossibility, aside from Luna still wearing Tripp's ring, on her thumb because her other fingers are too small. We deliberately keep the conversation in cats-and–Joann Fabrics, mac-and-cheese comfort-lesbian territory; Charlotte, who stayed on campus during Christmas, says she redid her wardrobe, which Luna describes as "if Laura Ingalls were a queer girl who did drag sometimes."

The only magic issue we bring up is *who's going to keep*

the grimoire in her room. (Over break, Luna had it in Seattle, but we need a location at Smith that Sienna will never discover, which seriously limits our options.) We draw straws; Charlotte agrees to take the grimoire for the night.

I think I feel better, but the sight of the ring, gleaming on Luna's thumb, inspires me to tighten my scarf to the point where I can't breathe. Part of me, the Pollyanna snippet of little-girl soul that's never aligned with the truth in my gut, believes Tripp is specifically haunting *my house*, and he won't find me here at Smith. Then I remember the bistro in Amherst, the bartender, blood sweating down my glass, and realize it's hopeless, but I'm not going to kill myself just because I'm exhausted and he should already be dead. What if I too became a ghost, cursed to haunt alongside him for eternity? I can't afford to die. I have to live, prove him wrong, destroy his afterlife as I cut out his life, seize him by the balls and introduce him to my own weapon, my rage, the blades of my scissors, ready to slice.

Besides, I have my sisters with me under the covers, the chosen family who love me, affirm me, *believe* me, who would do anything for me, who already have.

I reach for Luna's hand, under the blanket.

"What if I told you something crazy?" I say, mostly to Luna. "Like, the reason I wanted you to stay on Skype with me for fourteen hours last week."

Gabi shifts to get a better view of the screen, and spills half her tea on her chest, soaking the blanket.

"Gabi, are you okay?" Luna's focus abandons me.

We hang the sopping blanket over Luna's closet door, give Gabi a change of clothes. While she's cramming herself into one of Luna's vintage mohair sweaters, I try to tell them, again. "So the reason I needed you to Skype with me for so long—"

"This is so fucking itchy," says Gabi. "I can't wear this."

"I didn't do laundry yet, babe," says Luna. "That's the only other shirt I have."

Gabi frowns. Luna sighs and takes off her own shirt, exchanging it for the sweater.

I clear my throat. "Anyway, over break, what happened was—"

"I have a headache," says Gabi. "Do you have Advil?"

"*Luna.*" I clap my hands together. "This is really important."

Luna tears her gaze from Gabi. "What's important?"

I look from Luna to Gabi and, like an alligator surfacing from water you thought was benign, lily pads and minnow fish and the perfect setting for a picnic, the coven appears suddenly to be *not on my side*, in my camp, on my team of fellow believers. At once, I realize I can't trust them, not with what I'm about to say. I must stay sharp, gleaming. If I break myself before their eyes I will have nothing. If they don't respect me, they'll discard me, it was fucking *crazy* (that's what I am: *fucking crazy*) to imagine otherwise. I know now, staring into Luna's pair of firefly eyes, that if I tell them the truth, they'll never respect me again.

I'll be worse than dead.

"It's just—" I gulp. "I just want to tell you—"

Gabi shuts her laptop, slams her empty cup on Luna's desk, and runs to the bathroom.

Luna rushes after her. "Gabi!"

Of course, because my life is a cheap horror movie now, *this* is the moment Tripp chooses to reappear, well rested, clean-shaven, clothes pressed. The only thing missing is, again, the thing between his legs.

I wait for Charlotte to notice.

"I thought Luna locked her door," I say, as he goes to sit at Luna's desk, blood leaking onto her notebook.

"Weird, yeah," says Charlotte, disinterested.

"A poltergeist," I say.

Charlotte frowns. *He* stares straight at me, grinning.

"Lee, do you seriously need some help?" says Charlotte.

I shut my eyes. "I think we all do."

"I was on Prozac for a while," the ghost is saying. "After my parents got divorced. And—*would you believe it*—I almost went back on Prozac my freshman year. After my girlfriend accused me, you know, of assaulting her. It was really hard for me. Being accused of something *criminal*." He reaches into his pocket. "You do know sex is a fantastic method of stress relief?" In his hand is his phone, which he starts tossing up and down. "Your friends might believe I'm here, if you filmed us."

"How did you get your phone? We buried it with you."

"What?" Charlotte frowns. "Lee, are you seriously okay?"

I shake my head. "I'm fine. Ignore me."

At one point, I actually have to pee, and I take the risk of going to the second-floor bathroom, assuming Luna and Gabi will be talking in an empty shower—instead, they're in the stall right next to me. Over the flush, I hear Gabi, entangled in Luna on the floor, sobbing, and when they finally come back to the room, nothing helps, not Thai takeout, nor

Charlotte's confession of having stuck incense up her vag on New Year's.

"Was it burning?" Luna wonders.

I keep thinking shit like, *He won't touch me again, ghosts have boundaries*, but that's utterly wishful, delusional, my trauma brain trying to cope by pretending he's some Casper who plays by the rules. The truth is, he raped me once. There's nothing stopping him from doing it again. And now that no one can see him, there can't be any evidence.

I go to the bathroom, throw up, then ask if I can sleep in Charlotte's room—"Bad nightmares," I offer as an excuse—because I know Gabi will flip if I try to stay with Luna. Charlotte and I go back to Hubbard and I take her roommate's bed. He leaves me alone until three-ish, when he starts going through Charlotte's books and whistling, some midcentury racist elevator anthem, "Zip-a-Dee-Doo-Dah," and I keep trying to do dream things like grow a third arm and breathe fire, asking, *Am I dreaming, is this real life?*, but of course it's real life, the dickless ghost of my rapist is five feet away, flipping through yuri manga and tapping his reanimated foot to a tempo-less beat.

Eventually I grab Charlotte's econ textbook off her nightstand and fling it at his head.

Charlotte stirs; he doesn't flinch.

I grab the grimoire from my backpack. Hubbard, famously, is one of the only Smith houses with a bathtub, in this single bathroom on the fourth floor. I take the grimoire, a set of matches, a bundle of sage, Charlotte's towel (still damp, with a mysterious stain, but whatever) and my scissors, and pray no one is taking a bath at four A.M. The bathroom is empty—

and, like all Smith facilities, remarkably clean, Clorox-scented, quaint old woodwork and a broad window open to the waning moonlight.

I spread the towel on the floor and start to draw the bath. I open the grimoire, read the spell (*How to Banish an Unwelcome Guest*), read it again, then light the sage, take the scissors and cut a lock of my hair.

"Come and get it," I say as I drop the hair into the steaming bath, watch the individual strands separate, bob and float.

It works, all right. He's waist-deep in the bath, tinting the water pink, blood spiraling out in tornado tendrils. He grins; his teeth are black and rotting. Other parts of him start to spoil. His skin adopts a yellow, jaundiced glow, and his hair starts to thin, shedding over the uneasy surface of the water.

I stick my hand into the water, pulling out the drain.

He seizes my wrist.

I struggle, try to pry his fingers off. The water drains, but he doesn't. I reach again for the drain—if I can keep him in the bath, I can get Charlotte, grab reinforcements—but he seizes my other hand, climbs out of the bath, pins me to the floor. I'm screaming, I don't care who hears, he has my arms and he's holding me down, he's on top of me, dripping and bleeding, his face too close to mine, his smile, the scent of mud and disintegrating flesh.

He lets go of me, dries himself off with the towel, opens the grimoire. "You sure you don't want to take a bath together?"

"Fuck you," I'm able to say.

He leaves the bathroom. I hear his steps creaking down the stairs, then another set of feet approaching.

Charlotte bursts through the door. I realize my feet are wet—there's this huge puddle leaking out from under the bathtub. Charlotte helps me clean up the water with magic. After, I break down crying. Charlotte holds me and doesn't ask questions.

"I lost the grimoire," I tell her. "It was taken from me."

Charlotte doesn't respond. She just strokes my hair, keeps me against her chest, doesn't notice the blood splattering the white bathtub, the brown hairs sticking to the sides.

CHAPTER ELEVEN

EEL DONBURI

TECHNICALLY, WE'RE ALL SUPPOSED TO be taking a one-credit medieval studies seminar over January term, but the entire coven skips the first day of class in favor of bingeing movies that make us feel nostalgic for eras we never experienced, like Prohibition and grunge. I feel guilty and go to the afternoon half of the lecture. When I get back to Luna's room, the coven is topless and Luna has decided, officially, to major in history and do her thesis on the Avignon Papacy. Charlotte might major in religion; I suggest she consider a thesis on liturgical dance.

We succumb to denial, distractions, wasting the week on aborted experiments; we try to make cocktails, but no one likes the taste of gin except for Charlotte, and we try to host a party for the rest of Chapin, but we're an odd entity, *that group of three first-years all from different houses and a Chapin sophomore in Sienna Weiss's witchcraft seminar.* The only person who gives us something in exchange for our shitty lavender gimlets is that junior across the hall who's majoring in Chinese, who brings a clunky wooden box filled with the decrepit remains of a board game called Cowgirls Ride the Trail of Truth. It's basically Monopoly meets group therapy meets sorority hazing; you advance through the cardboard Wild West by confessing how many "stallions" you've ridden in your life.

"I'm more a pony girl myself," says Luna, finishing the gin straight rather than forcing herself to endure our precarious mixture of alcohol, unblended Splenda, and lavender essential oil.

At night, back in my room, shaking, sweating, all the lights on, while Tripp sings, spins in midair, takes out my camcorder, lets me know that if I want the grimoire back, easy peasy, I just have to take off my clothes.

Early Friday evening Luna texts me about the new Greek restaurant opening in downtown Noho, and we decide to go, but don't invite Gabi because she's allergic and doesn't like Greek food anyway. Getting ready in Luna's room—Luna asking my opinion on which bra she should wear, and then whether or not she should wear a bra—I get a text from Charlotte about grabbing dinner at Cutter Ziskind, and I tell her we're going to get Greek food, and Charlotte says she wants to come along. "Come On Eileen" blaring from Luna's phone, jumbo bags of Cheetos splayed across the bed, Luna's smile and toplessness and tall tales of the origins of her cranberry suede trench coat, I can almost ignore the persistent rap of ghost-Tripp's fist on the wall, his humming, you know what song.

Charlotte arrives. We're just about ready—Charlotte with her knitting bag and Luna with her thrift store ushanka and I, pea coat boring, but my hair gold and wild—when Gabi bursts into the room and demands to know why we didn't invite her to dinner.

"Because you hate Greek food and are allergic," I say.

Gabi says she'll come anyway.

We get to the Greek restaurant and there aren't any tables, a twenty-five-minute wait. Luna and I want to wait, because we've been dying for Greek food since the sign went up in November (we walked by the half-finished shopfront when we killed Tripp, the ghost reminds me), and Charlotte reveals that she's high and has the munchies, so she's cool with anything.

Gabi finagles Xanax from her coat pocket. "You know, I can't eat Greek food anyway."

Even Luna frowns.

"That's why we didn't invite you," I say. "We're not trying to exclude you or anything, but the whole point of this excursion was to eat spanakopita, not necessarily to have everyone along and have to compromise."

"That's really unfair and mean," Gabi says. "I mean, I'm part of this coven, you think you'd consider me in more decisions—"

"We're not *not* considering you, we just wanted to eat Greek food—"

"You know I'm allergic to olives—"

"I know, and that's why we didn't invite you because we literally just wanted to *eat Greek food*—"

"You know I don't even like Greek food and you're

making me wait twenty-five minutes to eat something I can't even eat—"

"Fuck, we weren't going *for you*—"

"You know there's two things I can't do, I can't eat olives and if I accidentally ate olives I would have to get a needle in my arm and I have trypanophobia so—"

"*Not everything is about you!*"

Gabi takes her phone out and calls her aunt. Luna puts her hand on Gabi's arm; Gabi hangs up, folds into Luna, and gazes out at me from the shelf of Luna's shoulder.

"Fine, we can get Korean," I say.

Gabi pushes for SooRa, and I say absolutely not, so we end up at the other Asian fusion restaurant instead (three and a half stars on Yelp as opposed to SooRa's four). I'm walking slightly behind Gabi and Luna, texting Charlotte about how Gabi *won't stop playing the victim to get what she wants* but I don't send it, because I really want to have this conversation with Luna but I can't because Gabi is Luna's girlfriend.

Charlotte once said something about how Gabi and Luna are either going to break up or get married, and the thought of me in some kind of iridescent purple bridesperson suit, breast pocket stocked with safety pins and benzos, legs itchy from mosquito bites after several days of hiking because Gabi makes Luna have the wedding in Western Mass and not in Seattle, makes me feel defeated, like a punctured blow-up castle, but I guess at this point it's inevitable, like death and taxes.

We sit at one of the hot pot tables in front, because Gabi wants hot pot, but then she decides she doesn't really want hot pot, so we just have this giant stove in the middle of the table that's completely purposeless, taking up arm and drink space.

Charlotte is getting cucumber maki. Luna wants bibimbap. Gabi isn't sure yet, I need to *stop rushing her*, and I announce that I'm getting eel donburi.

Gabi makes a sickened face, and Luna frowns.

"Gabi doesn't like fish," Luna reminds me.

Tripp pulls up a chair directly beside me, muttering, "Who doesn't like fish?"

"She doesn't have to order it," I say.

"I can't sit next to fish," says Gabi.

"Fine, switch places with Charlotte."

Gabi sits diagonally from me, as far away as she can without leaving the table. When our food arrives, Gabi barely picks at her soppy udon, glaring at my dish, my chopsticks, my lips.

"Do you want to bring it home?" Luna asks Gabi, when the waitress comes to clear our dishes and notices that neither Charlotte nor Gabi has eaten anything. Charlotte immediately declines a doggy bag whereas Gabi just stares down at her winding collection of noodles, and Luna ultimately has to say yes, we'll bring them home, maybe she'll eat later, her arm around Gabi the entire time. The whole exchange makes me sick (sicker than Tripp's hand on my shoulder as I'm signing the check).

Back at Chapin, we can't unlock Luna's door.

Luna fishes a crystal from her pocket. "I don't remember locking it."

We open the door with a simple incantation and step inside warily.

The room is the same—the unmade bed, the crooked moon chart—but there's an oversize straw basket in the center of the rug, overflowing with large pink vibrators. Charlotte, the most daring, steps forward, picks up a single vibrator, and hardly has time to duck before the vibrators transfigure into steak knives with sharp, gleaming blades, spring into the air, and begin to spin in a tornado, expanding outward with every rotation.

We race from the room and slam the door. Gabi suggests calling Sienna, but Charlotte's confident she can stop the knives.

"Frat boy warlocks have got some of the worst energy around," she says, pulling a bundle of sage from her bag, and a lighter. "We'll just smudge it away."

"*Sage*," Luna says. "*Smudge* is appropriating Native American ceremonial customs."

"Do you really think a sage stick is going to be enough to stop a bunch of flying knives?" I ask.

Gabi, starting to panic, glances up at the fire alarm. "You can't use a lighter in the hall," she says.

"Um, this isn't the first time," says Charlotte, lighting up the sage and slipping into Luna's room.

"It worked," she calls, seconds later, and we crack open the door. The knives are scattered on the floor, innocuous as fallen leaves.

We start to pick them up. "How did the warlocks get into Chapin?" I wonder aloud, the answer pricking the back of my neck.

"The same way the pizza delivery always comes directly to the room?" Luna responds. "Nothing is ever locked at Smith. People have sex in Neilson in the middle of the night, like, every night."

Or the ghost did it, I almost say, but I still value the perception that I am sane.

Gabi is sobbing, her back against Luna's door.

"Gabi, what's wrong?" says Luna.

"I don't think you all understand how serious this is," says Gabi, searching for a tissue in her backpack, slobbering mucus all over her sleeve. Her voice is soft: "We *killed* one of them. And they know." She sinks to the floor, holding her knees, chest heaving. "This is really fucking serious. I don't get why the rest of you don't see this. This is so fucking serious, this is a really big deal, we *killed* one of them and they know—"

"Well, if their counterattack is going to be this unsophisticated," Charlotte says, inspecting a knife, "then—"

"This is not their counterattack!" Gabi is screaming now, attracting the arms of Luna, who strokes her hair, tries to hush her, reminds her that other people live in Chapin. "This is only a warning, they're going to come after us, they're going to do the same thing to us, they know, they *know* and they want us dead—"

Charlotte and I finish picking up the knives and exchange a glance.

"Gabi isn't wrong," says Luna. "And I didn't want to tell you this, but this morning—before you were awake,

Lee—there was a police officer in Chapin's common room, asking girls about the boy missing at Amherst. If anyone had seen him."

"We destroyed the evidence," I say, with so little confidence that Gabi cries louder.

"We did," says Luna. "And the police were headed to a bunch of Smith houses, I saw them all over campus. But the last person who saw a boy fitting the description of Tripp—brunette kid, five foot nine, Amherst sweatshirt—told the police he was unconscious, with a couple of girls in downtown Noho. Being carried home drunk, or something."

"*Fuck*," Gabi repeats, head sunk into Luna's shoulder.

"Yeah," Charlotte agrees.

I stand. "So we're not going to do anything? We're just going to sit here and talk about everything working against us?" I steeple my hands, hoping to gain a smidgen of authority. "There are thousands of relatively short boys with brown hair who wear Amherst sweatshirts in this part of Mass. There's nothing pointing to us."

Charlotte raises her hand. "We could go to New Zealand."

"Fuck you," Gabi says.

"We can cast a spell on the authorities, if it comes to that," I say. "But it won't. As far as they know, Tripp fell off a mountain while drunk skiing and got eaten, by wolves, or bears, or—"

Gabi sinks her face into Luna's chest, Luna putting a finger to her lips.

"Charlotte," says Luna. "You brought the grimoire back to your room, right?"

Charlotte purses her lips. "Well," she says.

"Well *what*?" Gabi demands.

"Well, the grimoire—"

"The grimoire *what*?"

"It's not Charlotte," I say. I shut my eyes; it's the only way I can make this confession. "I lost the grimoire. The warlocks stole it when I was asleep."

I open my eyes.

Gabi's mouth hangs open. Luna smacks her lips together, not meeting my gaze. Charlotte hangs her head.

"The grimoire was in my room," Charlotte says. "Lee took it to the bathroom in Hubbard, and I found her sobbing around four in the morning. Without the grimoire."

"So Lee lost it," says Gabi. "And that's how the warlocks attacked us tonight. We were safe, then Lee returned their only source of power. *Fuck*."

I begin to stalk forward, raising my fist, knowing exactly what I'm going to do and not regretting it in the least—when Charlotte's arms close around my chest, my waist, restraining me, her voice in my ear.

"Lee," Charlotte says, quiet. "Come on."

We leave, taking the knives with us.

"Wait, we can't carry a basket of knives through Chapin," I say as we move down the hall.

"You ever heard of a glamour?" Charlotte says, reaching for her menstrual cup, and soon enough the knives glimmer and morph into a collection of used-up smoothie cups, complete with the rotting brown remains of green juice and bent, chewed-on straws.

"Why don't you stay in Chapin tonight?" I suggest. "Rachel is still in Boston. You can sleep in her bed."

"Sure," says Charlotte. If she knows I'm asking for my own sake, she isn't letting on.

Halfway down the stairs, the glamour suddenly lifts. Charlotte tries to cast the spell again—but the knives remain knives, and even my participation accomplishes nothing.

"So we used up all our magic for the month," I say, stomach churning.

Charlotte tosses her sweatshirt over the basket, and says nothing.

At the edge of the woods, Charlotte—parting the icy ground with a shovel stolen from the boathouse—says: "Honestly, I wonder if we're all better off transferring."

I stare at her. "Transferring?"

"I've been missing Mexico anyway," says Charlotte. "Universidad Nacional Autónoma de México—the application process is really easy, you just need a certain test score, and the tuition is really cheap."

"Oh." I frown. "You're seriously going to transfer?"

"Well, I've been looking into it, at least," she says.

We finish burying the knives and head back to my room.

"Hey, Charlotte," I say as we approach the steps. "You know, if you need somewhere to come during Easter, I live two hours away."

Charlotte holds the door open for me. "I actually was going to go back to Aunt Kristin's house with Gabi. Thanks, though."

Why it seems to me that Gabi is consolidating her forces, stockpiling flour for a siege, I'm not sure. We're all one coven, and the threat is from without, not within. And Charlotte is a person—she can't be stolen. Still, unease trickles down my spine and seeps into my stomach; I can taste fish in my mouth, the sweet-and-freshwater umami of eel sauce, ready to surge back up my esophagus and choke me to death in a bed of vomit, snow, and knives.

"Lee, watch out!"

I stumble, my foot hitting the plastic hilt of another vibrator, that same blushing, ontological pink, and all my certainty rushes from me as quickly as my dinner splatters the mahogany edge of Chapin's doorframe.

Charlotte catches me. "Lee—"

She holds me as I vomit twice more, and hands me a tissue before I collapse, my ass hitting a patch of snow on the front stoop.

"I feel like"—I lean into the banister—"I'm not done throwing up."

"Just stick your fingers into your throat until you feel your tonsils," says Charlotte. "Works every time."

I shake my head. "I'll ride it out." I wipe my mouth. "Do you have any water? I can't taste eel any longer."

Charlotte searches her bag, shakes her head. "I'll grab some inside." She glances at the door, furtive, at the vomit dripping onto the slick chunk of black ice. "We have to get rid of this, we can't have Gabi seeing and wondering if you might have to go to the hospital—"

"You're worried about Gabi's fucking trypanophobia when *I'm* sick?" My head lolls back against the wood, and my gaze flickers up at the infrequent stars. "I need water. Now."

Charlotte runs inside, grabs a bottle from the vending machine on the first floor. My stomach starts to settle, especially when Charlotte offers to take the lone vibrator and chuck it into the lake.

We clean up, go back to my room, and Charlotte brings me ginger ale in bed.

"When's the full moon?" I ask.

"Two weeks. January thirtieth," says Charlotte. "It's in Leo."

"Maybe we should all go home," I say. "Maybe we really should transfer." What I don't say is, *He came home with me, he was sitting in my basement, he watched me sleep every night, home won't expel him, there's nowhere I can be rid of him.*

Charlotte gets me a second ginger ale. She settles on Rachel's bed, takes her makeup off with these Korean face wipes she has in her bag, and frowns at Netflix on my laptop. "Holocaust documentaries are not comforting."

"I disagree. They remind you that it could always be worse."

I reach for the light, tell Charlotte to lock the door.

Charlotte's heels meet the rug just as the knob twists and Luna, red-cheeked, eyes shot with veins, bursts into the room, not bothering to shut the door behind her.

"Luna?" I say, raising myself from my pillows. "What's wrong—"

"She hit me," Luna says, her voice cracking open as she starts to cry deep, unbelieving tears, shielding her face with her hands.

Charlotte and I swallow her up in our arms and stay there for a long time.

"She hit you?" I say, Luna's nose brushing my collarbone, her breath on my chest. "*Gabi*, your girlfriend, hit you?"

We sit Luna on my bed between us, not letting go.

"What happened?" Charlotte is able to ask without seeming like she's questioning Luna's take on events.

"We were watching *Adventure Time*," Luna says, curling into herself, hands folded between her breasts like she's trying to pray but can't quite get the signal of divinity, like she's protecting her heart from a sacrificial knife. "And Gabi started to have a panic attack, and I had to go to the bathroom, and I was trying to leave for a couple of minutes, but she kept saying *No, no, you can't leave*, and I started to get up and, it was a hit, she raised her hand and slapped me"—Luna imitates the motion, a firm, focused slap—"right across the face."

Luna shows off her left cheek: pink-tinged, a bit irritated.

"She was having a panic attack," Luna says, taking my tissue.

"It doesn't matter," I say. "She hit you. She *intended* to hit you."

I start to stand—all my suspicions, all the pointed fingers of my gut, validated—when Luna tugs me back.

"Don't," says Luna. She glances out the door—which starts to creak open, gradually enough that Luna and Charlotte would never suspect that Tripp is opening it himself, squeezing his reedy ghost form into my room, leaning his head against the wall, against my Cranach poster, his ghastly hair resting against Judith's silver plate.

Luna: "I should go back to her, I'm worried—"

"She hit you," I repeat. "Gabi hit you. You can't go back to her. She doesn't deserve it."

"I should at least call her aunt—"

"I'll make sure she's okay," says Charlotte, slipping through the door, leaving Luna in my arms, her tears soaking my shirt, her fingers curling into my shoulder blades.

Why I feel suddenly, remarkably *happy*, I don't want to know—but the feeling dissipates as soon as I see Tripp perched on Rachel's bed, smiling at me, giving every indication that he's staying the night.

"Shame you can't punish Gabi with magic until the full moon." The ghost coughs into his sleeve. "In the meantime, shouldn't you hear her out? There's two sides to every story, you know."

CHAPTER TWELVE

IMMORTALITY

I CONVINCE LUNA WE SHOULD go back to her room. She goes to sleep around three. I fold the comforter over her chest, her neck, and slip downstairs to Chapin's basement, where Charlotte and Gabi are splayed out on the worn tartan couch with the broad tracks of duct tape holding together the cushions, Gabi's head in Charlotte's lap, Charlotte's red jeans wet with tears.

Charlotte reaches into her backpack for Pocky and an orange soda; Gabi is crying and won't shut up.

"I love her," Gabi keeps saying, in a mousy tone intended to cleanse her of all sins, the vocal equivalent of putting on footie pajamas after watching porn. "I can't lose her, I love her."

I say hello; Gabi looks at me. She doesn't know I know.

"We can't break up, I love h er," Gabi spits out, sinking her hands over her scarlet eyes, blowing little snot bubbles out of her nose, gulping down pockets of air like she's breathing through a broken snorkel.

"There's lots of fish in the sea," I say.

Gabi covers her face and emits a sound halfway between a sob and a scream; I glance at Charlotte, she's muttering to Gabi, *Your aunt is coming tomorrow, you can go back to her house in South Hadley and figure things out, your aunt is coming.*

I say goodbye and go back upstairs. They don't notice me leaving.

Luna stirs when I close the door to leave and asks me to stay; I offer to sleep on her nonexistent roommate's empty mattress, but ask for a blanket and one of her pillows.

She opens the covers and beckons me. "Just sleep here."

I join her, unable to avoid us touching at all points of our bodies, ankles to breasts, in the coffin's width of the twin XL. She places her hand on my shoulder, and I wonder why she's holding me when she's the one who needs to be taken care of.

"Are you okay?" I ask, turning my back to her.

"I'll be fine tomorrow," says Luna, slipping her arm over my stomach and letting it hang there, heavy as meat, but warm.

Luna falls asleep, and my legs tingle with pins and needles. I shift, slowly, turning myself around so we're face-to-face, so she's breathing on my neck and her fingers drape down my chest like willowy strings of pearls. I reach out, touch her hair—then feel really bad about touching her without explicitly asking, staring at her like a work of art, forever asleep in a fixed container of marble.

I shut my eyes, breathe as she does, and think about how you can't survive if you don't have one major area of joy in your life, someone or something to shred your pain and rearrange it. For so long, my joy was Zara (joy need not be healthy—you can slap your joy, kick your joy, bury your joy alive without one of those live-burial-prevention bells circa the mortality-obsessed nineteenth century). I wonder if Gabi was Luna's joy, until tonight, when everything Luna already knew about Gabi, how she's desperate and manipulative and malevolent, surged into a hand and struck Luna red.

The sky shifts from ink to charcoal, the first intuitive punch of morning. I reach out, touch her again, keep my hand on her hair; the truth is, I will do anything for her. I will take any compromise, I will bend myself, I will keep the peace. Because I need her in a marrow-deep, survival-instinct way, but I'm not sure she needs me.

How to lose your lesbian virginity, a three-step program:

Tell her you've got a secret. "I'm not really blond." (After the two of you have spent three days sleeping in the same bed, glancing at Zillow's Fresno County listings while Spotify shuffles Indigo Girls and you wonder if a farm can sustain itself on weekly farmers market hawking of goat milk products and cherry tomatoes. Talking about buying a house together must come first, in all proper gay girl courtships. *Luna and*

Leisl sitting in a tree, K-I-S-S-I-N-G, first comes U-Haul, then comes livestock—)

She's shocked by your secret. "You look so natural."

I take off my underwear—we're already braless—and show her. That's how it starts: like a naked party, where the bras clip off like dominos and you're relieved the lights are dim so no one will notice that your breasts are uneven, how your nipples get hard in the slightly-below-room-temp chill. In those moments you really sympathize with that artist's model at the weekend figure drawing class you took with Zara at the Art Institute of Boston, that stringy Asian guy who got an erection during one of his sitting poses but came back for the summer session and asked to see our drawings during breaks, his chiseled knees peeking out of the pink silk robe they give the models to wear when they're not working.

Luna takes off Tripp's ring and settles back against her pillows, ass resting on her faux-shearling throw, ankles crossed, toes flexed.

I should mention, I'm pretty drunk. Or else I'd have kept my secret.

"Do you think the warlocks are finished with J-term?" In other words, *How much time do we have?*

Luna frowns. "You're really no good at compartmentaliz-ing." Her gaze lingers on my chest. That was Zara's excuse for *just the way I treat people*, every time I tried to confront her about calling me unfuckable and naive: She *compartmen-talized* like it was a pro tennis match, folded up her dad's car-totaled night in jail in a Ziploc bag inside the band of her pleated white skirt, cut high on her thighs, boxy flesh storing all the vulnerability she drowned with vodka-spiked Red Bull and witty insults hurled in my direction.

I sit on the bed.

"You know Gabi cheated on you."

Luna is unperturbed. "When?"

"The party at Amherst."

She sits up, core shaking, and kisses me.

"So you've never had an orgasm?" I ask her.

I remember that time when I was a sophomore in high school, it was February and my mom was picking me up from school in my dad's naked-color Saab. I liked the Saab better than the other convertible, the VW one that my mom said was useless because you couldn't cover it for winter, because the Volkswagen was the car my mom picked me up in the night I quit swimming, when she screamed at me so much that I sank to the floor, my seat belt unbuckled, stretched around my neck like rope, and the whole stop-and-go highway could see us, could probably hear my mom accusing me of all sorts of suburban crimes, like having a serious interest in art (*Who knows if you can even write?*) and hanging out with gay theater kids (*Honey, actresses don't come in your size*) and going over to Zara's house on Thursday nights sometimes instead of, I don't know, spending five hours at a swim meet followed by five hours of homework, dinner optional, depending on whether or not I dropped my times.

My mom told me how lucky I was, but I didn't see it. Anything that made me smile, she screamed about. It almost seemed that she *wanted* me to be on the brink of suicide all the time, her emphasis on filling the days exclusively with activities that felt like medieval torture. *It will prepare you for the Real World*, she would say, not knowing I was plotting my escape into a dollhouse universe of cauldrons and Baudelaire and the red-hot nails of other girls.

February sophomore year, *that* car ride, the Saab with the heated seats that swaddled my whole lower back and butt, my too-wide hips, my too-soft thighs, we were talking about my body, how I was no longer daughter-of-a-model skinny, how I looked like a fifty-year-old woman, daring to have thighs that chafed together at the ripe age of fifteen, and how did I expect to find "companionship," looking like I did?

This, of course, was why I went out with Tripp. Because even though I know in a feminist sense it wasn't my fault, I will always feel, somewhere in the padded upper layer of my thighs, that *it was entirely my fault*; on a shockingly similar continuum, it's why I sleep with Luna, even though I know Gabi is still her joy.

I wonder if I'm going to end up sleeping with everyone who looks at my ugly face and my fat thighs and still manages to think about sex.

When it comes to sex, straight people follow a script more than instinct, which is why most senior-year-of-high-school accounts of first times include scary campfire stories about him sticking it in you when you're totally dry, which hurts like hell and makes you bleed like the no-agency protagonist of an anachronistic period film where the writer is under the impression that in the olden days you had to procure a bloody sheet after the wedding night to prove the marriage was consummated, which is totally gross and sounds a bit like what the Mormon girl at Catholic school said about getting married as a Mormon, you have to marry within the church and before your wedding you have to go and tell your father everything sexual you've ever done with a guy, which is supposed to dissuade girls from doing sexual things before marriage. Except it didn't work for that Mormon girl because apparently, according to Zara and like five other people at the public high school, when she was a freshman she had sex with a senior in the hallway next to the auditorium and her parents put her in all-girls school as a result.

"That was the problem with my upbringing, I had plenty of free time to be sinful," says Luna, voice in my ear. "This Mormon girl, was she hot?"

Two girls, in effect, have to write their own script, even down to dental dams. (Luna and I agree that safe queer sex is super important but we also agree that we don't feel like putting clothes on and going to get a dental dam from the bathroom dispenser.)

"I've literally slept with one other person," Luna says, which almost ruins the moment.

At first, it feels like fumbling with a container of expired

Play-Doh, trying to make a castle without knowing what a castle looks like, doomed to fail by ignorance. But it's also exactly what everyone says, about people having had sex for thousands of years and it being innate, and eventually we fall into the trance, into the routine practiced by cave gays and Neolithic lesbians and pioneer dykes in calico and bonnets who weren't committing a crime, even in Utah, because, legally speaking, in the nineteenth century gay girls didn't exist.

Fucking another girl is sort of like scribbling in a diary that you're going to burn five years from now, never read by anyone, never even revisited by your own eyes. To the culture, you're an afterthought—and, tangled in her, together in a vacuum of blank space, of eraser waste, you're free to make art that isn't going to survive, art that's just for you, that's just for the experience of art alone, for this exact moment, for the *here and now*.

Lesbian sex is the true little death, making for making's sake, not to procreate but just because she's beautiful and you are here and feelings are good for themselves. If you ever want to escape from the productivity quotas of late capitalism, strike a match, light a hunk of sage, and sleep with the girl whose bra is crumpled on the floor of your mind, and know that, between your fingers and her skin, this is the end. And look forward to death, the only other moment where the fireworks burn down to your toes and vanish without a witness; the greatest art is never known.

ᴕ

I enjoyed it, but the whole time I imagined myself to be a man, and close to the end, my ears submerged in her thighs, I started to remember who I was, how you're not supposed to fuck other girls because other girls are supposed to be sisters, confidantes, and there's something just icky and incestuous about having sex with someone so close to yourself, with touching the slick floral secrets of your mirror image. In our world, where men have weapons and women have forgotten theirs, other female bodies are supposed to be the spaces where you're safe, where you don't have to be productive, and by the time her hands knead my scalp, breath and body squirming, I'm totally out of it, and I start to go back *there*, my head smashing the tiles, lemon soap and toilet water, the scar on his brow, and there he is, legs dangling off Luna's headboard. I bet he's been watching us the whole time, he's had the REC button of the camcorder under his thumb the entire fucking time.

She holds me while I cry, and complains about how nothing is open past eleven in Noho. "Back home you can get Thai at three A.M."

I break from her, stumble to the microwave. "There's Trader Joe's peanut noodles."

"That works."

♀

Then comes Leisl drinking alcohol, two cans of hard lemonade from the bottom of Luna's backpack, and finally putting clothes on and going to the bathroom so you don't get UTIs, and Luna repeating that she believes in God and her head on your chest, wearing your sweatshirt, and your last thought before your dreams, walking up to your parents and saying, *I'm gay and I don't want to straighten my hair anymore.*

Of course, he's there, he's always there, but for brief moments, when she's touching you, you can ignore the spiders occupying the dusty corners of your room; sometimes an experience is so sweet that you don't need to kill the ghosts; sometimes, her hair between your fingertips, she's all there is. There's nothing else, not even him.

CHAPTER THIRTEEN

WEEHAWKEN

TRIPP RUINS IT, AS ALWAYS. One aside about how "she's 'only slept with one other person'—silly little slut, acting like *I* don't count, of course," and I go back to sleeping in my own room. Luna doesn't seem to know anything's gone wrong; maybe after you sleep with someone who isn't technically your girlfriend, you're not supposed to immediately move in with her, spend twenty hours a day with her, show her your Pinterest board with potential engagement rings, try to get a sense of the cut of diamond she prefers.

The ghost, too, brings up the central question. "Are you a *lesbian* now? I don't feel so offended. You just hate dick, I guess."

I go back and forth, digging deep into erotic Tumblr and trying to precisely monitor my reaction to both hunky guys with nice butts and, incidentally, wispy Asian girls with choppy chin-length hair. Between the J-term class I'm supposed to be taking and Charlotte, a good sport, assisting me with stockpiling sage and potions for the tough semester ahead, every waking thought that isn't consumed by the warlocks murdering me in my sleep, or the ghost acquiring such power (power he already possesses, he reminds me every morning when he dangles the grimoire in my swollen eyes), is thus: Am I gay, am I straight, or do I really just fucking hate Gabrielle Avery?

Charlotte gets wind of Luna and I having slept together when she discovers me throwing my phone across my room for the third time, shattering the already-broken screen into a lightning mosaic, sobbing about how she *won't fucking reply*.

"Tell me what's going on," Charlotte urges.

I summarize my conundrum—gay, straight, or vindictive. "And, after we fucking *did it*, Luna's suddenly become, like, a stone-cold bitch who takes two hours and forty-three minutes to respond to Tumblr memes I send her."

"You know, there's such a thing as bisexuality," Charlotte points out.

I swipe my thumb across my cracked phone, pull up a picture of Luna I took when we went to play in the snow the morning after, and stare at her newly purple-tipped hair and the single rainbow feather earring brushing her scarf, her rosebud smirk and the sun in her eyes. I think about Luna visiting over the summer, next to me in a rocky compartment of the dilapidated Ferris wheel at the county fair, holding me as I start to get scared, how she's smaller than me, how her arms are short and slim, how it doesn't compute, us together, going for lobster once my stomach's settled and getting invited to go on the neighbors' boat. But, like salt and chocolate, Luna next to me, surrounding me, holding my neck and kissing me as we reach the top, hidden from view, *works*, and if she would just respond to the meme I sent her I could believe in us and preemptively invite her to join me in August, make plans to take the convertible down to Provincetown for a weekend and swallow clams and take pictures of sand sculptures, mermaids rising out of the dunes and shark-tipped Atlantic.

"No," I tell Charlotte. "I think I'm totally straight."

"And yet you're calling Luna a stone-cold bitch because she took an hour to reply to your text?"

"Two hours and *fifty minutes*, and she still hasn't responded."

That night, after Charlotte leaves to get high, I think of calling Dr. Applebaum about getting more Ativan because I've set up a bunch of blankets and pillows in the walk-in closet because I think the warlocks are less likely to kill me if I sleep in there. But there's a spider in the closet (and Tripp, of course), so I run, sobbing, into the hallway, and fish my phone from my bra to call Luna.

She says she's coming over, five minutes.

Five minutes pass. I go back to my actual bed, lock the door, text Luna and tell her to text me before she knocks or else I'll probably hex her.

I call her again. She doesn't respond. I call twice more, then text her, then I watch *Mamma Mia!*, which strikes me as a musical interpretation of matriarchal prehistory, back in the good old days of no one knowing who their father was, when everyone had three or four Colin Firths for potential dads.

It's midnight, Luna's not here, and before I go to sleep I fling my phone across the room again, for emphasis.

Tripp catches it. "You need to make the call?"

I fling my pillow at him and slip under my covers.

The phone, vibrating under Rachel's bed, jolts me awake the next morning, and I pick it up.

"Lee? Wassup." Charlotte sounds not-too-delirious, and panic starts to pulse through my stomach. "Is there any way I could come over, like, right now?"

"What happened?" I demand. "Is anyone dead? Did they attack—"

"No, *no*, this isn't about that. Seriously." She coughs into the receiver. "I'm coming over, okay?"

"Okay."

I scroll through my phone; no calls or texts from Luna, but multiple messages from Charlotte. *can i come over? we need to talk.*

Charlotte arrives. "Seriously?"

I put down the ceremonial dagger we ordered from Amazon before finals. "Just trying to remain cautious. Who knows, the warlocks could have brainwashed you."

Charlotte shuts the door and slams herself and her new basket down on my bed. "Well, they did show up again. Outside Hubbard. But that's not what I want to talk about," she says, withdrawing another long pink vibrator from her basket.

"Give me that." I zip the vibrator into my backpack.

"So none of them showed up? Just another random vibrator?"

"Yeah."

"Don't you think we should confront this immediately? Meet with the whole coven—like, tonight?"

"Yeah, but there's something else I need to tell you."

"What?"

"Luna slept over at Gabi's last night."

My hand inches toward the dagger. "Oh?" Instead, I get my phone and call Luna, and keep calling her until she actually answers.

"Hey," says Luna, sounding remarkably detached and mildly condescending, or maybe that's just because I know the truth.

"Hey," I say back. "So you spent the night at Gabi's?"

"I slept on her floor. She was having a panic attack."

"And you didn't think to tell me?"

"I don't need to tell you everything."

I take a deep breath. "Are you in Chapin?"

"Yeah, I just took a shower."

I hang up, toss my phone on my bed, and bolt for the bathroom, barefoot, gunk in my eyes, but ready.

She's spitting out toothpaste. I wait by the shower caddies.

"What?" Luna says, cheeks full of water.

"You *slept over at Gabi's*?"

"Holy shit—" Luna wipes her mouth, turns off the sink. "You and Charlotte are, like, kind of controlling everything I do."

"Because we care about you." In a smaller voice: "I care about you."

Luna adjusts the towel at her chest. "I care about Gabi."

"Gabi hit you," I say. "Gabi is abusive. You need to stay away from her."

Luna's hands go to her hips. "I can do whatever I want."

"Abused women often go back to their abusers," I say. "Or seek out similar partners—"

"I'm not a fucking battered woman!" Luna shouts, seizing her shower caddy and throwing it back on the shelf.

I reach for her. "Luna—"

"Don't touch me," she says, holding her towel up as she runs.

"*Luna!*" I scream, sobs flooding my mouth, but she's gone, and there's only one thing left to do.

X

Incidentally, Gabi and I were both signed up to audition for this all-female production of *Antigone* with original songs by one of the drama seniors, set during the Cold War, today at noon, so I go to the theater with a backpack full of malevolent herbs, hastily brewed fuck-you elixirs (the only magic available to me with Sienna's limit on our powers), and Charlotte's lighter, plus Tripp's ring, which Luna left on my desk the morning after, when we came back to my room to grab additional chicken ramen packets because shrimp flavor is gross, and I was naive enough to fall in love.

On the way to the theater, Tripp won't stop trailing me,

tapping me on the shoulder, singing. Not wanting to waste any of my potions on a supernatural entity, I zip off my snow-covered boot and fling it at his head.

The boot passes through him like a plane's nozzle breaking the clouds; I hobble through the snow on one foot to retrieve it.

"An eye for an eye makes the whole world blind," he says behind me as I jog toward the theater.

I find Gabi inside, at the center of a perky assortment of Tegan and Sara lookalikes, reciting her same old comments on mythology and exchanging numbers. That's the thing about abusive exes you just can't shake off, cult leaders, and Leo ascendants. If part of the message wasn't totally spot-on, if there wasn't a truly captivating element of the delivery, they'd just be lone raving hitters-of-girlfriends and dispensers of quasi-accurate Tumblr facts about underappreciated goddesses. Unfortunately, Gabi's vocal-fry intellectualism, her insights on Norse goddesses and *Autobiography of Red*, are beaming and springtime enough to keep drawing frosh hordes and gullible professors and other people's should-be girlfriends to her most-expensive-aisle-of-the-craft-store plastic bouquet, but you can cut your hands on roses, you can get stained black knuckles from wet gold.

The assistant director starts calling Gabi's new disciples into the theater for their monologues, and Gabi goes to the bathroom. I follow her, find her leaning over the sink, massaging soap onto her squat, short-nailed hands, refusing to look at herself in the mirror.

I shut the door, cough into my elbow. Gabi's head twists toward me. She wipes her hands, says nothing.

"We need to talk," I say.

"Yeah. Maybe we do," says Gabi, tossing the wet paper towel and remaining perched, static, several feet away from me, like a seagull that eats all your chips but won't get closer.

I take out the vibrator. Gabi settles, her shoulders easing. "Charlotte found this outside Hubbard. I don't know if the warlocks' aim is to, like, disarm us by just throwing vibrators everywhere and making us think they don't have any real offensive planned, but we need to talk as a group. Obviously something bad is coming when the warlocks are all back at Amherst next semester."

"They put out an article in the local newspaper. Saying he disappeared, that it was probably a suicide," Gabi says, so hushed I have to inch closer, so there's only about the space of another person between us, not enough room for the Holy Ghost (or Tripp's).

"The police aren't my concern." I look her up and down, the greenish veins peeking out from under her eyes, a couple of hives dotting her brows, the ramen-malnourished complexion, the dandruff. "If we don't take them out—*all* of the warlocks—they'll come for us, eventually."

"I'm not doing that again," Gabi snaps.

"That's not what I meant. I think we need to expose them. Force them into a situation where other people realize they have magic—other people who aren't drunk college kids, who actually care—so they have to stop using it. Make them think they're crazy." I pause. "And we need to get the grimoire back, anyway." I purse my lips like I'm telling the truth.

"I think we should ask Sienna," says Gabi.

I pause. "Did you tell Sienna?"

"I just think you're clearly not qualified to deal with this," Gabi continues. "I mean, I agree we're in deep shit, but you're the one who lost the grimoire in the first place. Maybe you *gave* it to the warlocks?"

"And you're dealing with it better?" I set the vibrator down on the counter. "Right now I'm the only one in the entire coven who seems to think we need to do something instead of sitting on our asses and brewing crystal chrysanthemum tea."

Gabi rubs her red eyes, sneezes. "You know what, Lee? This is *your* problem. I'm not careless, I'm not a fucking criminal, I didn't participate in you-know-what—"

"Well, Tripp didn't rape you, you don't know what it's like, and Goddess knows you don't give a shit about your girlfriend's psychological wellbeing, you don't want to give her any peace of mind—"

"Luna never wanted to go after him—"

"And even though it made *your girlfriend* feel better, you didn't give a fucking shit, you don't give a shit about her and never did—"

"You fucking coerced me into something that literally every single person on the planet agrees is horrible and—"

"Luna doesn't matter to you, you don't care about her, you only care about yourself and putting on fucking shows with your panic attacks or trypanophobia or whatever—"

"Most people would have fought you, I'm a second-degree black belt—"

"I bet your own fucking family hates having to trail after

you like a five-year-old because you can't fucking function and you just go around hitting—"

"*FUCK YOU, LEE!*"

We stand apart, both crying—Gabi shaking, teeth chattering, my tears running down my neck and slipping through my collar.

"You need to stay away from Luna," I say.

Gabi wipes her mouth. "It's not like I was abusive or anything."

I put my hand on the edge of the sink, otherwise I'd fall. "You need to stay away from her."

"She can make her own choices," says Gabi.

"I think she needs some time away from you. I mean, you didn't break up for *no* reason."

Gabi shakes her head, distorts her mouth into a shape I'd call a *smirk* if we weren't both sobbing. "I don't need relationship advice from straight girls."

I look from Gabi, to the vibrator, to Gabi again.

"Gabi, there's something I need to tell you," I say.

I reach down, grab the vibrator, and fling it at her head.

She stumbles; I lunge for the vibrator, rolling on the bathroom tile, by the pipes. Gabi steps toward the door, but we're not done. I seize her by the hoodie, take the vibrator, and smack her again, across the other cheek.

She screams. I hold her up against the stalls, cover her mouth, and strike her again—and keep bringing the vibrator to her face, keep my fingers over her mouth, even as she tries to bite my thumb, my nails digging under her chin, her jaw, the vibrator hitting all points of her skull, no aim, just rage, resentment, jealousy, every seventh deadly sin, poor impulse control and PTSD, even though that's no excuse unless you're a thirty-something photogenic war veteran who has "seen things," but you know by now that I never take responsibility for anything.

There's a moment when, anger still moving my hands, I look at Gabi, bleeding profusely from her nose, blood thinner and redder than menstrual blood but with the same sterling scent, and feel I should let go of her, confront the real problem here, take the vibrator and somehow, even though it's not designed to be able to do this, jam it through my eye socket, reach my brain case, make it all stop, make Gabi and the memory and myself all go away, all take wing and descend to the Underworld, to black and cold and the empty vacuum, the forgotten territory of the collective's dark imagination. Here lies the difference between hypothetical guilt and disease, between normalcy and the distorted set of eyes gifted by trauma. You want this, you feel the same rage I do, but your body obeys the tabernacle, you have *control*, you're not going to stumble back from the stall and hit your bum on the sink and look down at Gabi, her blood, her gaping mouth, and wonder how bad it was, how much you did, because you can't tell, all you can see is blood, and your own guilt, forever written into her eyes like paper cuts, scars that paper towels and a sore apology can't erase.

When I look at the mirror, Tripp's head peers over my shoulder.

He says, his voice streaming from my mouth: "What is it about bathrooms?"

I touch my hair, make sure it belongs to me. There's blood on my fingers that darkens the strands.

"Don't call the police," I say to Gabi, after I wash my hands and grab my bag. "I'll tell them about Tripp. I'll tell them you did it."

I get her more paper towels. Once I'm outside, I go to a garbage bin surrounded by a pedestal of snow; I hold my hair up, wipe the tears from my grin, and vomit.

I get back to Chapin and I call my mom. "I'm transferring."

He sits on Rachel's bed the whole time. When my mom hangs up, says she can't talk about this right now, I fling the phone at him. The screen cracks, again, on the windowsill.

CHAPTER FOURTEEN

SALT

GABI AND LUNA DON'T CONTACT me. Charlotte texts me some kind of tag-yourself astrology meme right after I leave the theater, but I don't hear from her again. And Sienna, of course, wants us to die, or else she'd restore our magic to full capacity. All I hear, three weeks later, is that they were all naked in the woods under the moonlight—no surprises there—and that around two A.M. they ran across campus clutching their clothes across their butts and got into the library, went to the fourth floor, where they were all having an orgy until Campus Police busted them and forced them to leave.

I wonder if they really did have an orgy, or if they were just naked for witchcraft reasons and people can't resist sexualizing the female body in any and all circumstances.

Not that it matters. Whatever they were doing, I wasn't invited.

Dreams:
1. It happened like it happened.
2. It's a curling iron, not a vibrator, peeling layers of skin from her face like the sanitary liners that come with swimsuit bottoms. Until Gabi is nothing but skull, muscle, and Venus Verticordia curls coiling past her rib cage, like the child mummy that made my half sister tear up when we passed by the Egypt wing of the MFA to get to the Goya exhibit, and I made fun of her and she claimed I was just like our mother, unsentimental as the plague that robbed that poor mummy child of puberty, regretful first sexual experiences, and the BCE equivalent of staring at your bottle of psych meds before you go to bed every night and wondering if you should take them all, how much that kind of death would hurt.
3. Sex dreams. You know the sort.

☽

Living with the ghost of your dismembered rapist—with absolutely no friends to distract you—is like trying to sleep on a freezing tower-cell floor the night before your impending execution: It's really fucking clear you're not going to be saved and you're grappling with the notion that God actually wants you to suffer, there's some bullshit Earth lesson you're supposed to be memorizing prior to joining your Adventist needle-prick blood siblings in a cyanide-fireworks mass suicide. On the rare occasion that I can focus, that I'm able to feel his presence like the minor subsequent vomiting following a virus rather than the terrible first eruption of stomach acid and day-old falafel, I start reading this book on representations of Anne Boleyn that Luna lent me, and I think too much about Luna, then I think about how Anne Boleyn lived with ghosts, just like me, ghosts of her own split brain stem and neck stump, just like how Tripp appears to me at night, dangling his own head over the quilt-stacked foot of Rachel's bed.

I think about dropping three of my classes, but then I'd only be a part-time student. I think about how to get rid of him with magic, but none of the hexes I have screenshotted on my phone do a damn thing to the ghost (he just laughs at me, sits on my bed, and grins). And I still have no idea where the grimoire is. But my previous understanding of how death works has been obliterated, so I don't hurry to kill myself. Maybe I'm already dead—this is purgatory, this is a preview of hell, this is what I deserve, for being unhappy and getting raped and trying to have a constructive response but only ending up worse than at the beginning, friendless and haunted and probably antifulfilling Luna's prophetic statement about me being unable to fail a class. Studying with him, no matter where I go, the library or Chapin's common room or the new tea shop downtown where you don't have to wear shoes, there's a constant background stream like a long-as-fuck medical center message some robosecretary is reading off on your answering machine and it won't fucking stop even though there's no actual information being relayed. All night, all day, Tripp whistles, sings, taps my shoulder—and always follows me to the bathroom.

I try to confront him. "If you don't stop singing LeAnn Rimes, I'll pass out, hit my head on the toilet, crack my skull, and die. Not that you care."

The ghost, peering over the stall, grins. "I could give the grimoire to someone else. Luna, maybe." He whistles. "Would you prefer a different soundtrack? What about from when Luna and I went on our date last year? It was at Sigma, we couldn't really hear the music downstairs but I think it was Spice Girls. *If you wanna be my lover*—"

"Fuck you—"

He follows me out of the bathroom. "Clara and I, we were in the back seat of my car, she had this little skirt on. She ended up staying the whole night!"

As soon as we're in my room, I charge at him, reaching for his bloody neck, but I just end up slamming into the wall.

There should be solutions coursing through my brain, I should fucking stick up for myself, I should try to get the grimoire back because the coven apparently isn't doing fucking anything, even if all I do is give the grimoire back to the warlocks so they'll leave us alone, I should should should should should *should*, but every effort seems futile, and I just keep thinking about how I failed when I *really* tried to get rid of him, how he wouldn't go down the drain. And I'm terrified of trying anything else, especially after the next night, when Rachel's at her envi sci lab so I'm all alone. I drink a glass of water and as soon as I swallow the last drop, there are fingertips on the back of my tongue, nails scratching my tonsils, and it's really true what Charlotte mentioned about sticking your fingers down your throat, it really works if you want to vomit up all the pho you ate for dinner—plus one of his arms, his toes, and, of course, his dick.

My chest seizes. I'm moving, but not of my own accord.

"Fuck you!" I scream. He doesn't have my voice yet. I don't care if the girls next door can hear; I don't care if Rachel gets back early. "Get the fuck out of me! Get out! Get *out*!"

I start to laugh, then sneeze, and he materializes in front of me, picking up his arm and forcing it back into its empty socket. I stumble to the floor, limp, closing my eyes, sobbing, the wood splintery and cold, slick like wet tiles.

I touch my bedskirt, hoist myself up. He's still laughing. That's all he does, laugh.

"Let's end this," I say. "Too afraid to fight me? I dare you! *I dare you!*"

He steps over the vomit, settles onto my desk.

"Why?" I start to scream. "Why me? Why was it ever me?" I stare at his lolling gray face. "Why did you do it? Why did you decide to destroy my life? Why me? Why?"

He stops laughing, shrugs, which is the best answer he could possibly give.

His mouth starts to move. "You want to settle this?" His voice slaps me, takes me back, but I keep looking straight at him.

My door creaks open.

"Lee?" Rachel says, eyeing the vomit.

"I'll clean it up," I shout as she leaves.

Rachel tells me, the next day, that Ayesha's roommate left for study abroad and their room is Super Big so she's going to move there instead, and I smile and nod, and she grabs a box and I help her pack, carry her *I'd rather be at the Cape* poster and her framed seashells and two pairs of North Face boots up to the third floor, and I let her know that if she forgot anything, she can knock anytime. We hug, she thanks me, and I get what I want. No one, nothing, total solitude. Just me, the ghost, and my medication.

I keep having that dream again. The broomstick, the chase. In this version, a cloud descends over Tripp, trapping him, encasing him. When the cloud parts, he reaches out to grab me, dangles me from the stratospheric sky by my throat.

In his other hand is the grimoire, always a few inches out of my reach.

When I get my first B+ on a paper, I march immediately to Sienna's office hours, because there has to be something she can give me, some magic tranquilizer or enchanted earbuds, so I can at least sleep and bide my time until I definitively figure out how to get fucking rid of Tripp, and stop mistaking every creak of the floorboards for a fratlock's clumsy stomp.

Sienna's office door is open. I knock, then enter, expecting to see her languid as a famished dragon in her wingback chair. Instead, her office is silent, but for the cats and Tripp's ghastly steps behind me.

On her desk is a ninth-circle array of mismatched papers, an open laptop.

"Why don't you go see what it is?" says the ghost.

"Because it's private."

"Never stopped me," says Tripp. He floats over to her desk and begins further dismembering the papers.

I rush to his side. "She's going to notice it's out of order—"

I seize the paper in Tripp's hand. It flies across the room. I race to retrieve it, the ghost continuing to cackle.

Just as I pick up the rogue sheet, catching a glimpse of the heading—GENDER, POWER, AND WITCHCRAFT, FALL 2012, AMHERST COLLEGE—Sienna's pointed snakeskin boot kicks open the door.

"There was a breeze," I say, to justify my possession of the paper. "It flew off your desk."

"The windows are all closed," says Sienna, grabbing the paper from me and returning to her desk.

I sit across from her. "So you did teach at Amherst last year?"

Sienna holds the page up for me to see. "This says Smith, Leisl."

I read the heading again—it's the exact same syllabus we got in the fall (SMITH COLLEGE clearly emblazoned under the course title), but with *2012* and different due dates.

Sienna asks me how I am—no mention of her attempt to render us defenseless, lambs in leather jackets, vulnerable young meat fooling no one into believing we're not helpless—and I wonder how I'm going to tell her: that I just don't care anymore, that I just feel so dejected, like a deflated blow-up doll, the world's saddest excuse for a witch. Maybe I shouldn't have been entrusted with any power at all, if it was all going to turn to shit. If I would just want to give up, like I always do. Right now I would do anything to unkill him; I just want to rest; I just want this all to end, but I'm sure I'll find a way to botch my own suicide the way I've fucked up every other area of my life.

I try to summarize. "Awful, to be frank."

Sienna folds her hands and frowns. "Why is that, Leisl?"

He kneads my shoulders; I start to cry. He scoffs. "Is she always this clinical?"

Sienna grabs a box of tissues and hands them to me. "Is this about your sisters?"

I shake my head. "Not entirely."

"What is it, then?"

The ghost of my rapist is currently standing behind me? He's got his hands on me? Gabi Avery is an abusive cunt, and even though I know that word is misogynistic I'm going to use it anyway because I hate her? She's a stealer and a liar and a cheat and she hit Luna and Goddess knows what else they haven't talked about? *You*, Sienna Weiss, robbed us of full use of our powers at our most vulnerable moment, and any day now the warlocks are going to invade Chapin and slit our throats? John Digby Whitaker III is a ghost? But I can't tell anyone because my reputation is already strung up by the ankles, ready for the butcher, and no one would believe me anyway? No one fucking believes anything I say even when it's really fucking true and I can prove it, I can prove it with DNA and body parts and dismembered dicks and, least of all, my own fucking word?

"We found the grimoire back in December. But we don't have it anymore," I blurt out.

Poker face. "What happened to it?"

"I can't tell you."

"Does this have to do with the trouble with the rest of the coven?"

"No. Yes. It's complicated." I pause, look her over, frown and arched brow and faux-concern, and it occurs to me that she really does hate me. I clear my throat. "That kid who disappeared at Amherst? We killed him."

Sienna stares at me for a long time. "Leisl, why would you tell me that?"

"I'm not sure," I admit. "You know, I'm not exactly like you. I'm not going to do what you would have done. I'm my own person and I get to make my own choices."

"Leisl, if you need counseling, I can help you get an appointment—"

"I'm not like you. I do what's right for me. And we killed him. Oh, we definitely killed him. We knocked him out and cut him up and buried his parts in the woods behind Chapin. I could bring you to his body, if you don't believe me. No one believes me, but I'm telling the truth. We did it. We killed him. We were responsible. I was responsible. It's real. It's true. I'm telling the truth."

Tripp cackles, claps. "Keep going, Leisl, you're doing a great job."

Sienna: "I never said you weren't being truthful—"

I clamber out of the chair, sling my bag over my shoulder. "It's true. No one believes me but it's true. I killed him. I really did, I killed him. That's why he's haunting me. That's why he's always screaming commentary in my ear and always singing LeAnn Rimes. He stole the grimoire, I'm not irresponsible, I'm not careless, *a fucking supernatural entity* stole the grimoire and that is not an excuse."

I turn, and there's Tripp, laughing, his mouth inching close to mine, his bloody nails reaching for my shoulders.

I step around him, toward the door, finally knowing where I'm going, what I have to say, what I have to do, what's my purpose, my point, my ending.

I'm about to turn the knob when a firm gust of wind knocks me to my knees.

Sienna stands in front of her desk, hand outstretched. "Leisl, you're in no state to be alone."

I try to stand. She keeps me down.

"What are you going to do, turn me in?" I say. "It wasn't just me. It was actually Luna who killed him; she held the knife. I just orchestrated it, you could say. I'll take credit, sure. But Luna was technically the one who really did it."

Sienna approaches me, passing through Tripp like she's hitting a patch of sun beaming through stained glass. "As I've tried to tell you before, magic is a privilege."

"Is life a privilege?" I try to raise my arms, can't. "Is a sense of basic safety a *privilege*? You brought us into this world, then you changed the rules as soon as we got into the exact trouble you asked us to get into—"

"You actively ignored my orders by attacking the warlocks in a manner that attracted media attention and potential legal consequences," Sienna spits back.

Tripp cackles. "Even your professor thinks you've gone off the deep end. I could have told you that *months* ago, for free. Before you committed a murder, lost all your friends, turned your one faculty supporter against you—"

I talk over him. "Oh, so you were *ordering* us the whole time? We were just your lackeys, you were just using us to get the grimoire back—"

"Leisl, your current mental state prevents you from responsibly practicing the craft—"

I try to rise again; she's still holding me. "Right, call me crazy. Talk about how unhinged I am. What are you, afraid of me? Is everyone *afraid* of me? Is that why they keep hurting me and taking things from me? I don't have a lot to take. If you strip me of magic, I'll have absolutely nothing. If you take it away—"

The spell lifts.

I leap from the ground, reach for the door. As I'm forcing open the dry old wood, I see Tripp, holding Sienna's hand, perhaps unbeknownst to her. But the shock, the indignation, the *how-dare-you* on her face is clear.

First, I go back to my room. I robe myself like a priest of the night: black turtleneck, black coat, black scarf to complete my midnight habit; cross and snake necklaces intermingling over my collarbones, pendants dripping into the space between my breasts, scissors in my pocket; I can feel the twin blades on my skin and bones. I charge my phone, repeatedly try to turn off a pesky series of nature recordings that sound like the drowning, bubbling deep—but that's just Tripp's ghost pretending to drink, bottle after bottle of Poland Spring coursing over his body, cracking and splashing onto the sheen-lit hardwood.

"You might be the only college kid who doesn't have any alcohol in your room," he says, squeezing the plastic. "Guess that sake really was too much for you."

I glance in the mirror—even though I'm a witch and he's a ghost, I can see us both—and make the phone call.

There's a couple of German shepherds, off-leash, congregating officers and cars and silent flashing lights, local reporter, no cameras, they already don't take me seriously. But they don't need to take me seriously, because I have real fucking evidence, I'll make them touch his body, watch the coroner inject formaldehyde up in the rotten remains of his brain; they'll put me in jail overnight, which is fine, I didn't wear any makeup today so I wouldn't have to take it off, jail is going to suck but they won't have a choice, even though I'm a little girl and you can't help but take pity on me, they won't have a choice because I have evidence and I'm telling the truth and I'm right, I'm a survivor but I'm more than that, I'm a murderer.

I lead the procession into the woods, down the path we took with Tripp's unconscious body that night, over the snow-covered branches and booby-trap patches of frost and ice. I can hear the doubt in their congested winter breath but don't they know, I'm no Jane Doe, no cardboard-cutout Mary Sue victim, I'm a witch, I'm Medusa in a superior version where she beheads Perseus instead of being killed for defending herself. You can doubt me, question me, laugh at me like one of those looked-the-other-way-in-1930s-Germany types, *I see the problems with both sides*, but don't you know, justice is obvious, one of the simplest things, the Babylonians had it right, burn the red tape and if he hurts you, cut out his eye.

We come to the burial site, in view of the lake's thin ice; the dogs are circling, digging for leaves caught under the snow.

I point to the tree, the ground beneath. "That's where I buried him."

The officers exchange a glance, then start to dig, the dogs crowding around the pile of dirt.

Five minutes in: "How deep did you bury him?"

"Three, four feet," I estimate.

The dogs go to the lake, pawing the ice.

"And this is definitely where you buried him?"

I look to the tree, see the runes inscribed above the lowest branch. "Yes. Absolutely positive."

A gruff, quiet exchange between the officers. The taller,

broader one, freckles blended into a tan, emerges from the hole in the ground, shaking his head.

"There's nothing, miss," he says. "No body. No bones."

I shake my head. "No, there's definitely a body. I know there is."

"There's nothing," he insists as I look down into the earth.

"There's nothing, miss," says the other officer, looking up at me, hair dusted with snow.

I look to the runes again; I stare down into the hole. My stomach churns; I hear laughter, *his* laughter, but I ignore the ghost.

"There has to be some mistake," I'm saying, not totally cognizant of my own voice. "There's something wrong. I definitely killed him and I definitely buried him here."

When I start to cry, the taller officer puts his arm around me and tries to move me back down the path.

"Don't touch me!" I reach for my phone. "Here, we can call my friends, I have witnesses, I really did it, I really killed him—"

The other officer seizes me from behind. I scream, kick, resist, try to punch the officer when he takes my phone, keep screaming, tell them I'm some kind of superhero, five feet eight inches of divine retribution, apostle of all the little girls who got anally fingered in the second grade and hereafter describe it as a "childhood sexual experience" because shit like that is totally normal, I'm that version of Jesus in the Gospel of Luke when he quits being all turn-the-other-cheek and he's like *I don't bring peace, I split up families when only half of them believe, fuck the Pharisees*, which I read as, *You can love your enemies after they're dead*, so long as they don't come back to haunt you, and I'm also going to raise a bunch of fucking fish from the lake but I'm not going to feed you, I'm going to smite you, I'm going to destroy you, I killed John Digby Whitaker III and I can kill you too, just watch me, just lie back and think of all the little girls like me and how you thought you trained them to play dead and nice but I'm not nice, the last thing I am is fucking *nice*.

Tripp's voice in my ear: "This whole God complex—not as intriguing as you think it is."

I'm about to light the fucking officers on *fire*, even if it takes the whole of my magic, when my hands go still and cold. Ahead of me, racing down the path, is Sienna. The dogs run to greet her, wagging their tails.

One of the officers, behind me: "Yes, I'd like to request an ambulance. Psychiatric emergency."

Sienna offers to take me.

"I'm not lying," I say to her shoulder. "I'm not lying, I killed him, I really killed him."

She comes with me in the ambulance. All I can see, strapped to the gurney, is her rings, the black tourmaline encased in her palm, the EMT untwisting a series of corded IVs.

The next day, Sienna walks through the hulking gray psych-ward doors that shudder and open with a top-secret-passcode button, like a spaceship. She comes into my no-door sorry excuse for a room, sits on the edge of my bed, and asks me how I am—then immediately takes it back, asks me how I'm being treated, if I have everything I need.

I shrug, give a vague *sort of*. The hospital blankets are thin and flimsy, inadequate for Western Mass winter, and the staff won't give me my phone back.

Sienna lays a small box of chocolates on the foot of my bed and snaps her fingers. The curtains draw closed, and the sound on the other side grows low and fuzzy.

"I made sure the police will only remember your breakdown, not your murder claim," she says. "And, if you agree to cooperate, we can get you out of the hospital tonight."

"Cooperate how?" I ask.

Sienna sighs. "Leisl, did you really kill him?"

"I should have," I say. "I should have been the one to stab him."

Sienna's head collapses into her hands. "Why did you tell me that, Leisl?"

Maybe because I just don't care anymore, I am so beyond caring and planning and strategizing and considering myself from another person's brain-view that I decided to honor the shadow that I'm sure everyone hates, to be my worst self, to set fire to everything I've fixed.

I glance to her and have some idea of what she's going to say. I gulp, reach into my pocket for my scissors, and eye Tripp's ghost across the room.

I hurl my scissors at him, even though I know it won't do jack shit, even though I know, as soon as I feel for the magic that the scissors will simply clatter to the floor a few inches away, mundane, dead, powerless.

"Can't you give me back my magic?" I ask.

"Leisl," says Sienna. "I need to know you're mentally well enough to appreciate the responsibility we bear as witches. And, right now, I don't know that. I don't know if I can trust you."

"What would make you trust me?"

"You used your powers to commit a murder."

I'm crying. "He raped me."

"The future and protection of the craft is more pertinent than your individual concerns."

I wipe my face with my sleeve. "Everything that's done to you, it makes you crazy, but when you act crazy, when you act like the circumstances, people say you're the one at fault. They say you're looking for attention. You're overreacting. But it's just like, you reach this breaking point. You get mad and you don't want to take it anymore, you can't take it, if you have to take more you'll die, so you fight back. And, then, suddenly, you're evil. You're bad. You're the problem." My eyes sting with tears. "Sienna, don't you realize, if you take my magic away, you condemn me to death?"

"The future of the craft is paramount," says Sienna, impassive as a frozen bottle of Poland Spring left in your car during a blizzard.

I sink to the floor and wail.

Sienna rises but doesn't lift the spell on the curtain. "I'm assuming you'll want to keep the privacy."

I point to the box of chocolates. "Is this actually crystals, or herb sachets—"

"No. Just chocolate."

Sienna smiles and leaves.

ꙮ

My bed, basically a stretcher, inhibits my usual sleeping posture, how I typically sprawl my limbs across the mattress, frog-like. Instead I have to sleep on my back, which is better for your spine, skin, facial symmetry, but this enables the ghost, in the middle of the night, to seize me by the shoulders, open his mouth, but instead of his voice it's LeAnn Rimes, needing me like a martyr, like air, like rain.

I start to scream. The nurse on call gives me an Ativan with not enough water to wash it down.

The hospital therapists tell me their *conclusions*: that I'm obsessed with him, that he was my boyfriend, that I'm having a maladaptive grief response, and that's why I made the police go searching for his body. (Sienna's spell works; no one remembers my claim that I murdered him.) When the counselor tries to force tears out of me and gets screams instead, Tripp is there, hanging from the pebbly hospital ceiling, still singing, still freezing my blood like an ice-cold hose washing away any first-spring buds of hope, serenity, healing.

The next day they bring in a psychopharmacologist. We talk a bit about my treatment, how Ativan was crap and Wellbutrin was even more crap and Zoloft, so far, isn't worse, but isn't especially better.

Her eyes flick from me to the clock, over and over, as I tell her how I feel like I should die because I cannot be bragged about, how I don't need to be perfect (just more perfect than other people), how I don't think there could be anything worse than being judged, which makes me want to die, and every few minutes she makes a sort of *mm-hm* noise in addition to nodding.

Tripp, the whole time, makes broad circles of the room in the therapist's spinny desk chair, but she doesn't seem to notice, even when he crashes into her bamboo plant.

"Odd," the therapist says, noting the fallen plant limbs, the broken vase, the puddle, and not doing anything in response.

At the end, I mention that I was raped and she says we'll talk about that next time.

When the staff therapist first suggests a day program at McLean Hospital, I ask, *From the movies?*, imagining myself the hospital roomie of young Winona, realizing upon encounters with the other patients that, in the scheme of serious mental illness, I'm not all that seriously mentally ill, I'm just fixated on destroying the body and reputation of this little girl named Leisl Davis, because maybe reincarnation is real and when I kill myself I'll be gifted a more beautiful body with no trauma and a fighting chance. I wonder if they still have horseback riding at McLean, like in *The Bell Jar*, or if that's something they suspended when the hospital stopped being a psychiatric vacation for the hysterical wives and daughters of the Boston Brahmin class.

"No, McLean SouthEast," the therapist says, the new location that just opened, near Plymouth. They have a zen room, designed by a feng shui expert. Bigger windows, more light.

My parents come to see me. My mom brings an old SpongeBob blanket, energy bars, and silence. My father encourages me to *paint* or take up some kind of *creative outlet*, didn't I paint when I was younger? He thought I was very talented. The therapist finally arrives to tell them about McLean SouthEast, the zen room, the group therapy model she believes could solve me like a jigsaw puzzle—but the insurance company, back and forth with my dad over the shitty Western Mass reception, only wants to give me three days out of the recommended eight, and I can tell by the way my mother's shoulders tense that it's a nonstarter.

My parents agree to come get me the next day, and the staff, shrugging, say I'm no longer dangerous enough to occupy one of the few narrow beds. Dinner, rubber-chicken teriyaki and a Diet Coke, then lights off. I shiver beneath the SpongeBob blanket, bury my face in the rough cotton pillow, and try to escape the white walls in my dreams, but all I feel is his hands on my skin, my shoulder blades, his feet tangled in mine under the sheets.

I rip back the covers.

"Get the fuck out of my bed," I demand.

"Ah." Tripp clutches the sheets, stained with his blood like pink watercolor. "You really don't understand, do you?"

"No. I don't understand." I gulp. "Well, actually, I *do* understand. You're a fucking monster. You're beyond comprehension. You ruined my life, all these girls' lives, and you just laughed it off. What you are is *evil*—"

"Don't you want to know?" Tripp says. "Why? Why I did it? Why I chose you?"

"Don't fucking pretend you chose me for any reason other than convenience."

"Actually, I thought you were pretty, Leisl. Haven't I told

you you look like Taylor Swift? Same hair, eyes, lips. Bit of a stronger nose, but I like that you've got *character*."

I toss my only weapon—an illustrated Shel Silverstein volume from the hospital's tiny library of books—at his head. It sinks through his skull, bouncing up against the pillow. "I said *get out of my bed.*"

Tripp grins. "The truth is, Leisl, all those girls—they'll remember me." He wipes the blood dripping down his neck with the SpongeBob blanket. "Better to be famous than infamous, but better infamous than forgotten, amirite? So many women will never forget me, as long as they live. I was your first. We've shared so many *firsts* together, haven't we? Sex. Magic. Murder. It sounds positively romantic, I think. We're a bit star-crossed, aren't we?"

"Shut up," I say. "Shut up now."

"I wanted you to remember me," he repeats. "And you will. I'll be with you until you die. And, judging by this arrangement"—he sticks a ghastly hand through his stomach and pulls it out again—"perhaps beyond."

"You're fucking sick," I insist.

"And you aren't? You're a murderer, Leisl. You knocked me unconscious, kidnapped me, and killed me. You're a murderer. That's the truth." He rises. I stagger back, hit the cold plaster wall.

"What do you want?" I demand. "What's the purpose of continuing to do this to me? What does it accomplish? Do you want me to fucking kill myself? Do you want me to suffer until I work up the guts to overdose on my medication? Or do you want to keep me around—am I terribly *entertaining* to you?"

He laughs. "There's a solution, you know."

"What is it?"

"I know where my body is," he says. "My brothers moved it shortly after I was buried. I could tell you where to find me."

"Why?"

"So we can settle this."

"You're already dead," I say.

Tripp continues toward me; I raise my hand.

"Don't touch me," I say.

Tripp laughs and starts to float. "You think I've come back because you killed me, but you didn't kill me. Luna killed me." He somersaults over to the corner-mounted TV, pings the screen with his pointer finger—the channels begin to shuffle, producing a kaleidoscope of sound that the night nurse will hear, no doubt. "What's between us isn't settled. I couldn't come back to you if you had killed me. If I was truly dead to you. If you had moved on. If you had really won."

"What are you saying?"

"Bring me back," he says, face lit from below, shadows tugging at the nascent lines around his nose, below his eyes. "Bring me back so you can face me. So we can settle this like we were *destined* to. Don't you want to kill me? Don't you want to end this?"

"I don't know how to resurrect a dead body. I don't have a spell for that."

He opens up his chest cavity, pulls out the grimoire, slick with a film of blood and plasma. "I do."

The door shudders open.

"Miss Davis, there is no television past nine." The nurse seizes the remote from my nightstand and brings the room back into oblivion.

By the next day, the Zoloft starts working, and the possibility of suicide isn't so engine red, even if the ghost keeps up his nonsense about bringing his body back to life. (*I don't think you'd actually go away*, I keep repeating to him, *I don't think you're ever going to go away, you're lying, you'll be here forever*.) My parents are late getting me, so I spend my lunch with Tripp as my companion, sitting in the empty seat across from me and repeating how the solution is where the magic is, and the magic is at Smith. "You need to go back to school, face my bones."

I have no desire to return—to Smith, to life. But the sight of Tripp, detailing how his ghost eyes enable him to see "everything" beneath the black-bobbed psychiatric resident's white coat and Theory trousers (*"She's a thong girl, can you believe it?"*), how he can see every part of me too, how he can't wait for me to get out of the hospital and take a real shower, makes me *feel* something, and *feeling* is not what I'm going to get in the McLean zen room, or in my little attic bedroom at home.

My parents arrive, finally. The staff give me back my clothes and belongings at discharge; it's easy enough to duck into a bathroom at the highway rest stop, throw together a sachet with the random herbs I have sprinkled through my bag's innermost pockets. I don't know if it will work, if Sienna's October lesson on "emergency talisman-free magic" applies to psych-ward witches on power probation, but I don't have another option, so I strike a match and state my intention (that my parents will comply with whatever I tell them).

In the car, I tell my parents I'm going back to Smith.

"You want to be with your friends, of course," says my mom, nodding understandingly and telling my dad to reroute the GPS.

CHAPTER FIFTEEN

DEATH OF THE FIRSTBORN

MANY PEOPLE HAVE NOT EXPERIENCED Extreme Social Isolation, particularly not at college, which is supposed to be the Greatest Time of Your Life, but maybe there are more of us than I know, all huddled in our single or newly single rooms, speaking only to the smoothie girl at the Campus Center on nonclass days; the people who show up eagerly to every office hours just to have someone to talk to, even if all the professor does is answer a fake question about Habermas I came up with just so someone would look me in the eye and address me as *Leisl*.

I don't know why I came back to Smith, if the problem just keeps drilling deeper, and there's no solution in sight but the ghost's nightly monologue in favor of my finding his body and bringing him back to life, so I can really kill him, so this can be over.

Luna and I still live on the same floor, so I see her at least a couple of times a week, even though I make a conscious effort to only leave my room when I know she has class, but Luna, of course, doesn't often go to class. Chapin's common room and basement are off-limits, as it would be totally like Luna to bring the whole coven onto the eighties brocade couches while I'm lying there, trying to do my homework in a setting in which social graces mandate I can't randomly start sobbing and researching whether Wellbutrin kills you in a borderline-humane manner, not that I care.

In those weeks, into March, I keep up the habit of painting my nails red, every Sunday after my shower and before my weekly breakdown about not having written a good enough paper; my consistent string of As and praise cannot possibly last. I go through bottles of Essie's Forever Yummy, Geranium, Scarlett O'Hara, even expanding the definition of red to Clambake, not finishing them, never satisfied with the color, vowing in a rare moment of optimism, if I survive this, to invent a really genuinely blood-red drugstore nail polish, because I, of all people, know the color of blood. It needs to match the hands that keep showing up in my dreams, my own hands, the sticky residue of Tripp's blood always stuck under my nails, even though I spent valuable hot-water time that December night cutting my nails short enough to get rid of the caked-under blood, so half my fingers needed bandages, which was, in retrospect, highly suspicious, especially coupled with my brief fixation on wearing gloves inside, even when typing during lectures. *Anemia,* I offered, to anyone wondering why I was so cold.

"You could make me bleed again," says the ghost. "Check the color. Make sure."

Of course, only going to the bathroom when Luna has class is not sustainable, so eventually I start going up to the third floor to pee, but that's when I see her, on the stairs, unable to put as much distance between us as I need, unless one of us leaps over the banister (which I consider). The first couple of times, I shuffle past, eyes down, earbuds in, pretending to be lost in a podcast, but she always waves and says hello, and I, easily startled, always get duped into staring her straight in the face.

She would appear, in the eyes of any objective onlooker, to be taking the high road by smiling and making eye contact, but I know her, and I know how condescending she can be. Everything Luna ever said or did seems colored with deceit, betrayal, and hatred, now that I think about it.

Sometimes, we're both going upstairs at the same time, and she tries to let me go first through the door, but I step aside, and as she passes I feel the urge to slam the door on her fingers, shatter her nails and turn her stupid betrayer's hands to clanging science-classroom bones, held together by tiny metal brackets, her face decaying into two hollow eye sockets that reveal the whole empty inside of her skull, every part of her that ever hated me and made me feel like killing myself because of shame and failure and opening up too much. All her flesh vanished, yet her memory still haunting, somehow, until I too am made of dust and memory, ashes and herstory.

Worse than seeing Luna is the *idea* of seeing Gabi, even though I never see Gabi until the third week of March, at a distance, on the edge of the Campus Center, Burberry scarf and Kånken backpack loaded with books, hurrying across the street to Cutter Ziskind, sucking on a latte, fingerless gloves, alone.

But I know a lot about what Gabi thinks, because I keep going on her "personal LiveJournal" (that I learned the URL of within five days of meeting her), where she writes really candidly, in lowercase text, about her feelings, and I learn that she's deathly afraid of me, like, *the mere idea of me* has been giving her mega panic attacks, to the point that she even conceded to visiting one of those soul-retrieval shamanic healers in Northampton, she was so desperate (and every single benzo stopped really working for her years ago because she takes them multiple times a day). She thinks that if she sees me in a dining hall or something, I'm going to fucking kill her, and I start to believe in telepathy.

And the warlocks? Silence, aside from cryptic anons on Tumblr, until one Wednesday night post–econ seminar, when I take off my snow boots, twist the lock, and see blood dripping down my door. I clean it up, my mind numb as I gather the stained paper towels in a brown Whole Foods bag and lug the trash down to the big garbage bins in Chapin's dining room. Red leaks from the brown paper bag, and I mop the floor with my scarf, which I really should wash anyway. No matter how many times I lather up, my hands are stained.

I take a shower, feeling the whole time like I'm about to face a dagger. The next morning, I compose a text to Charlotte, but don't send it. I know the warlocks are planning something, I know we're not safe, but I'm so close to swallowing my bottle of Zoloft whole, like a snake slurping down a nest of eggs, that I don't care about the mongoose, waiting with claws.

It seems I've done everything I could possibly do, gone to the Title IX officer and talked to therapists and taken psychotropic drugs and joined a coven of witches and killed and smashed and hung more rapists than most judges probably ever sentence, I've tried so many different ways of feeling okay, and none of them has worked. I'm still as lost as ever, but now my compass is shattered, it's dark, and all I do is sit on the edge of my bed, feeling some sense of accomplishment because I'm not under the covers, I have *shoes on* while I'm streaming Netflix and getting through approximately three sentences of the econ paper that's forty percent of our grade. But he's still there. On top of my desk, bleeding all over my stack of notes and textbooks. Talking incessantly—through my headphones, *inside* my mind, it seems—about bringing him back to life, about *settling* this, about the same old fucking thing he's said at every possible moment since that time in my hospital room. "We could settle this. This could be over. You have to face me to get rid of me. If you had killed me, if you had closed the door on me, I couldn't haunt you. You have to kill me yourself. Feel my blood between your fingers. Rip my head from my neck. Slice me up. It's your only chance. It's all you can do. You know you want it."

Every day he says this, every moment I'm awake, I consider it more and more, I wonder if there's a loophole, some fine line I'm missing, if the ghost is trying to trick me. Of course, he probably wants me to bring him back so he can kill *me*. I wonder if I'm capable of beating him in a fight. A magic fight.

With the rest of the coven, sure.

I don't humor him, don't tell him what I'm thinking (though I suspect he knows, that he's been inside me all along). I go back and forth. I could try to get the body back—not a guarantee—and I could try to get the coven to work with me. I'd probably have to apologize to Gabi, to her sick face. Maybe that's worse than just killing myself. I could just kill myself. I could drown in Zoloft, pour the whole bottle into my mouth and suck the pills down like the tapioca at the bottom of a cup of bubble tea. Or I could fucking stick up for myself. I could *try*. Exert *more* effort. Because, obviously, I haven't tried hard enough already.

That's all I can do. *Try harder.* Despite the damp, basement-locker-room feeling that Zoloft doesn't erase, that no amount of ghost talk can unravel. Each day, every cherry-Popsicle dinner, time jogs forward while I sit and stare, my bed my palanquin; eventually I get scared enough to write most of the paper, but doing the bare minimum never feels like enough and never has. The sun rises and falls and I sleep through most of it. Not used to *him*, but used to feeling like I'm about to die, every day, all the time.

In my desperation, I try emailing Sienna, but all I get back is an automatic reply saying she's away at a conference.

I try calling her, but she doesn't pick up.

"I told you," Tripp insists, dangling his severed head over

the quilt at the foot of my bed, the one passed down from some great-aunt I never got to meet. "I told you she hates you. And why wouldn't she? You're trouble. You're bad. You're a disgrace to witches everywhere. You don't even have the balls to fucking settle this."

I take an extra Ativan, shutter the blinds, use a pair of twice-worn underwear as a sleep mask; I haven't done laundry in five weeks.

♀

On Tuesday, always a bad day (the French acknowledge this, *mardi*, Mars day, the planet of war and collisions and violent death and venereal disease), we get an email from the school stating that Professor Sienna Weiss, chair of the History Department, was involved in a fatal car accident in the early hours of the morning and has since passed.

I read through the email several times, trying to talk myself out of it, but there's nothing else that can be done.

"Stop fucking gloating," I tell the ghost. "I know you're responsible. I mean, your *followers* are responsible."

"You'd be surprised by the amount of influence I still have," Tripp remarks.

Before taking the PVTA to Amherst, I stop by the Campus Center for a smoothie, figuring that Gabi won't be awake this early and I should eat a fruit or vegetable or some kind of protein. I order a green smoothie, which tastes awful, and I end up throwing most of it away once I get outside.

I walk down the shallow architectural steps leading up to the Campus Center, catching a whiff of smoke from the congregation of European exchange students huddled at the edge of the green. Some guy in a sweatshirt, a straight girl's boyfriend or prospie's brother, passes on my left; I swerve to examine him.

There's no one, just the preblizzard wind rattling the hinges.

I take out my phone to check the PVTA times.

"Watch out!"

I look up, squinting as the sun reflects off the mounds of cleared snow. The male voice reverberates and my knees buckle and I slip, bouncing down several steps, the impact so hard that the rip in my jeans splits and tiny rocks puncture my skin.

Out of the tight corner of my eye are two big-shouldered guys in Amherst sweatshirts, the tall, lanky one wearing women's mustard-yellow platform shoes over white athletic socks. They sprint for the PVTA station, too fast for my bleary vision to catch.

At the bottom of the steps is some kind of crystal boomerang, obsidian.

A hand on my shoulder.

"Lee?"

I look up to see Luna, tingling capillaries crackling across her cheeks, cigarette cloud bringing out the tears in her eyes.

She helps me, slings my arm over her shoulder.

"I can walk," I insist.

"Weak combat magic, that's all," Luna says. "Let me help you get back to Chapin."

She keeps her arm around me. I fidget, hoping she'll let me go, but I'm glad to have her touch.

"I feel so stupid," I confess as we walk through Chapin's foyer and up the stairs.

Luna brings me to my room but doesn't step inside. "Are you hurt?" She probes my knee, frowning.

"I'm fine." There's blood, but it doesn't hurt yet.

)(

The next day, pus starts to leak from the scratched mess of my knee, the bits of gravel that I never picked out. I call Luna, then hang up before she can answer.

Five minutes later she knocks on my door.

"I have rubbing alcohol," she says. "Come on."

We go to the bathroom and pull back the shower curtains. I sit on the clinical white edge of the accessibility seat in the largest stall, and Luna gets on her knees.

"Thank you," I say.

"It's fine," says Luna. "I mean, you shouldn't have put a bandage on this without cleaning it, but we'll make it better."

I grip the moist edge of the seat. She tears the Band-Aid off and digs into the wound, extracting the gravel and rubbing away the bits of crust.

"Fu-*uck*," I say, the stinging unbearable.

"If you keep moaning like that people are going to think we're having sex," says Luna.

"Stop," I murmur, tears in my eyes. "Stop, please."

Luna takes the cotton pad away and rolls her bubbling

250

San Pellegrino eyes. "It's only going to get worse if you leave it."

"I'm not going to leave it," I protest, "I'm just taking a break because it feels like minor surgery when you do it."

"You left it overnight," Luna says, incredulous, her hand sweeping forward to sting my knee again.

I bite my lip, my fingers. Luna starts to talk, but I can't seem to hear her. I close my eyes—I can't look at her excavating the round bits of sidewalk from my cheesecloth flesh, skinless and mired in pus.

I crack an eye open. "Are you almost done?"

"Not yet," she snaps.

She unwraps a new Band-Aid, presses down, ensures the adhesive sticks to my skin. "You'll want to clean this again, tomorrow or the next day."

I look at the shine on her lips, her folded legs, the strand of hair stuck to her lashes, and I remember what it's like to *feel*, to have a body and not a young adult wasteland of arms, legs, and dead dreams, and when she starts to get up, starts to leave, I put my hand on her, start to cry.

She doesn't move. "What is it?"

I know what I really want to say, but I stop myself. "Luna, I need to tell you something about Sienna's murder."

Luna frowns. "Lee, I think it was actually a freak accident. I called her sister to give my condolences. There was nothing suspicious."

"Not Sienna." I shut my eyes. "Well, *yes* Sienna, but I really need you to *listen* to me and not judge me and not call me fucking crazy. I can't have anyone else call me crazy." I take a deep breath. "Luna, I think Sienna's death had

a supernatural component. Not the warlocks. Another...
entity. I think."

"You think what?"

And even now, after everything, I can't tell her. "I mean,
I think we should go to the wake. Tomorrow night. To
make sure."

"Fine. I'll ask the rest of the coven and text you."

I clear my throat. "Wait."

"What?"

"I miss you."

Luna takes my hand away, slowly, with the ease and
gentleness of an angel. "Lee, what happened between us—
it's over."

"It doesn't have to be," I say, swallowing sobs. "We could
try again."

"No, we can't. We can't be together," she says.

"Why?"

"It didn't work out—"

"Because Gabi's better and more attractive and smarter and
just overall a more worthy human being than I'll ever be?"

"No—"

"Because you were duping me all along? Because I was fool-
ish enough to think someone could be attracted to me—"

"Lee, when we were together, I really felt—"

"I know, I'm ugly and I'm bad in bed and I couldn't
possibly compare to the unparalleled *Gabrielle Avery*—"

"Lee, you're beautiful, it's just—"

"You hate me, you hate me like everyone always hated
me and I should just douse my face in antifreeze, it couldn't
possibly look any worse—"

"You could stick your head in an oven, also," the ghost suggests.

"*Lee*," Luna says, her own voice breaking, her face in her hands. "What we had was real. But I can't be with you."

I wipe my snot with a sleeve and sneeze. "Why not?"

Luna averts her gaze. "Because of what you did to Gabi? Because sleeping together once isn't the same as dating—"

"You're going to take Gabi's word for it?"

"I believe women when they say someone attacked them, yes."

Silence ricochets off the white tile, splattered with layers of shampoo and St. Ives apricot scrub.

I gulp. "She hurt you—"

"I'll be the judge of that."

I scoff. "I was defending you. I was avenging you. I was trying to show you how much I care—"

She shakes her head in frustration. "By putting persuasive potion in bubble tea? By the way you treated Gabi like shit from the beginning? By always escalating everything, the fucking Hanged Man idea, and the hotel—" She stops, stunned, as if her tongue has been seized by metal clamps.

"Please, go on. You haven't even made it past December."

She slams her eyes shut. "I can't. I won't."

"You don't get it."

She laughs, and tears leak down her cheeks. "Yeah. I guess I don't."

"I saved us. I *defended* us."

Luna stands, grabbing the bottle and bandages. "I do not need to be saved."

"No, I guess not." I don't want to go *there*, but looking

up at her, I can't help it, I'm a slave to my worst mind. "You certainly know how to use a knife."

Luna turns around, uncaps the rubbing alcohol, and pours the whole bottle onto my knee.

The raw flesh hisses on contact, and I scream, as if someone is going to come and help me.

The ghost just laughs.

Luna screws the cap back on, and with a low "Fuck you, Leisl," walks out of the bathroom.

The ghost emits a low whistle, then a gloating chuckle. "*What is it about bathrooms?*"

I ignore him, wishing with my whole body that Luna will turn around, swaddle me in her arms, kiss me, and want me so much that all of my mistakes evaporate like stray dew under the naked sun.

I sit there, moaning, sobbing, not strong enough to help myself, full of excuses and hate and exhaustion. Not even the lone sophomore pushing past me to grab her shower caddy bothers to ask me if I'm okay.

☙

Sienna's wake is at a local funeral home, off a commercial stretch of postindustrial New England where people probably sell heroin in the off-hours. Apparently Sienna's mother was a passionate Catholic convert, and the rest of the family followed suit (I heard Sienna's sister, who was previously complaining about the lack of gluten-free Holy Eucharist options at the church where they're holding the funeral, explain to an aunt that Sienna's spiritual convictions were unknown), so the wake is the traditional open-casket, praying-on-each-bead-of-the-rosary deal. I stumble in my job-interview heels, wondering if I should have researched what witches typically do for funerals, if that kind of information is even written down.

I greet several professors I know and a couple of Sienna's older thesis students before joining the line, giving my condolences to Sienna's family, and kneeling before the casket. After an Our Father and a Hail Mary, I rise, willing myself not to look inside the casket, but I can't help it. Sienna lies embalmed, hands over her chest, her many rings going with her to the grave. I still suspect the warlocks, or the ghost, but even I'll admit that Sienna's corpse doesn't have any obvious markers of foul play.

"I would agree," the ghost says in my ear. "She looks pretty damn peaceful for a dead person. Maybe you're just a crazy paranoid bitch—sorry, *witch*—after all?"

I find Luna and Charlotte by the light assortment of cheese, crackers, and beverages; Charlotte sips a Diet Coke and complains about the lack of alcohol.

"You should come to an Irish wake," I tell her.

Sienna's death keeps us talking, without us having to talk about ourselves. We collectively white-out Sienna's faults, her spurning of the coven, the limitations she placed on our magic; Luna in particular is red-eyed and somber, saying she aspires to be just like Sienna when she's teaching English, "Equally intimidating and inspiring, with great shoes."

Luna is still convinced Sienna's death was really an accident.

"Sometimes a cigar is just a cigar. A death is just a death," says Charlotte unhelpfully.

Luna starts talking about ancient Greek funeral customs, and it's almost like old times, until Gabi emerges from the bathroom, posture rigid in a too-small black velvet dress and pointed stilettos. Her pantyhose are ripped down the calf.

Luna and Charlotte surround Gabi and follow her to the door. Gabi takes Luna's hand and, as if to mock me, to say, *She's mine, I won*, pauses in the doorway to kiss Luna openly on the lips, then checks her phone, lights a cigarette with magic before sliding her phone back into a metallic clutch that still has the tags on it.

I lunge forward, seize Gabi by the wrist.

"You do realize, now that she's dead, there will be no renewal at the full moon," I say. *And my magic is gone forever*, I don't say.

Rather than punching my already knotted gut, Gabi tugs her hand away from me, sniggers, and lights Luna's cigarette with a snap of her fingers.

The only person who meets my gaze is Charlotte, though she doesn't say anything either.

It takes all of my willpower to hang back, drink my Sprite, make pleasant conversation with the youngish history professor bemoaning that Sienna didn't finish her last project, on representations of the Goddess in the early Middle Ages during the transition from paganism to Christianity. Between carbonated sips and interjections of "Interesting," I think of Luna's ruby nails, her laugh, her smudged eyeliner, the shape of her dress, even when Professor Whatshername starts sharing the grisly details of Sienna's death, how it was a hit-and-run, some large SUV slammed into the driver's door and Sienna suffered massive head trauma and the ambulance didn't get there in time.

It's a cliché, but, as a typical young queer girl—or whatever you call it when you're in love with another girl but memories of the suspect lesbians on the eighth grade bus having the one-inch hairs plucked from their just-cropped heads, thirteen-year-old boys passing them notes about scissoring, keeps you repeating the same-old-same-old *I'm totally straight*—it's not that I slept with someone, it's that I Slept with Someone. Sex with Luna wasn't a one-time, brush-lint-off-my-jacket event, but an invitation for my mind to ponder how we would choose grad schools in the same city, get an apartment together, get engaged, get married, if we would both wear dresses or both wear suits, which of us would have our child, if we would even bother with pregnancy or just adopt instead. It sounds crazy, it sounds like too much, but once you meet this girl and she Transforms Your World, grabs your hand and pulls you down her rabbit hole, you can't let go, you can't cross her out like a failed experiment.

I glance out the door, catch the faint three-headed outline of the coven waiting at the end of the road for the bus. I turn to the youngish history professor, complain of a sudden headache, and burst through the door before I can get my coat on, silently bemoaning the Western Mass frost of April and how it really should be fucking spring by my almost-birthday.

"Luna!"

They're getting on the PVTA: I get on the bus just as the

doors are about to close and scramble to the back, where the coven, seated, stare up at me, dumbfounded.

"We have to find the hourglass," I blurt out, realizing how out of shape I am, panting from a sprint of a few hundred feet. "I'm going to Sienna's office. Who's coming with me?"

I stare at Luna's blank bobblehead expression, her pretty eyes blinking, unfocused, refusing to *see* me, almost.

"I'll go," says Charlotte. "Lee's right, for once." I bristle. "We really can't let the magic run out. Not with Sigma still active, with them having the grimoire back."

Luna and Gabi reluctantly agree; we get off at the Smith stop, walk to Neilson in fighting silence, use three precious spells to unlock the doors, ascend in the elevator to Sienna's office, and open her locked door.

The search begins at once. Luna flicks the lights on, Gabi dusts Sienna's desk with a tissue and a squirt of hand sanitizer, Charlotte climbs the spiral stairs and explores the upper level (the cats are gone), and I kneel to the lowest reach of Sienna's file cabinet.

"Sienna has a shit ton of stuff," Charlotte shouts from up top. "What color is the hourglass again?"

"Do you think she hid it *with* magic? So we couldn't break into her office and find it?" says Luna.

"Shit, you're probably right," I say, heart sinking. "Wait, let me try something."

I reach into my pocket, grip my scissors; at once, darkness cramps the space. Success; I'm grinning wildly, out of my mind, power back in my fingers. Teeth clenched, I hold the intention, and the light returns—this time with a *meow*. Sienna's young cat paws the broken remains of the hourglass, a stormy assortment of previously obscured papers flooding her desk.

All my relief vanishes, invisible, never there, when I fully process what is arranged in meat-market symmetry on Sienna's back table.

Luna screams. Gabi clings to Sienna's desk. Charlotte chimes in with a single "Fuck!"

Sienna even retrieved his head, severed from his blood-splotched, half-skinned five-month-old corpse, his dead fingers hanging precariously close to the table's edge.

I sink to my knees. "*Fuck*. Fuck fuck fuck fuck fuck fuck fuck fuck *fuck*."

"Thanks for using up even more of our magic," Gabi says pointedly to me.

"I had to use magic to find the hourglass. And *you* were the one who used magic to light up back at the funeral home—"

"Shut *up*, both of you," says Luna, descending into Sienna's oversize desk chair. "Come over here. Look at this."

Luna scoots over to let Gabi share the chair; Gabi smirks at me as she secures her arms around Luna's neck.

"You're going to look through her papers, not at Tripp's dead fucking body?" I say.

"Maybe she left behind something to let us know why she kept him. Research notes, I don't know," says Luna, gaze diagonal to the ground, calm as total denial.

I turn my back on the corpse and go to the desk. A Moleskine notebook, the big expensive leather variety, lies open. Beside it, an old syllabus is torn up.

HIST 313
GENDER, POWER, AND WITCHCRAFT
PROFESSOR SIENNA WEISS
AMHERST COLLEGE
FALL 2012

Next to the heading is the name *Clara Dale*, scribbled in anachronistically perfect parochial cursive.

"Sienna did teach at Amherst," Luna says, refreshingly ignoring her girlfriend's cloying kisses on her cheek.

I seize the Moleskine. "*New Year 2013*," I read. "*He's following me, but it's not him. I got rid of the platforms, took them off campus and buried them, but he's still here—his apparition. I hate to say I'm haunted, and I'm fairly sure I'm not hallucinating. I have no history of mental disturbance. I'm a psychology major, I should know.*"

Across the room, the ghost cartwheels down the stairs, cackling, laughing so hard he drools blood. "April twenty-seventh," he calls, almost inaudible through his laughter.

"I know my birthday," I shout back.

"Lee?" Luna raises an eyebrow.

I cough. "Sorry, I was reading from the diary. I think this is a diary—*April twenty-seventh. Today, Professor Weiss was found dead at the scene of a hit-and-run accident on the highway between Northampton and Hadley.*" I turn back a few pages, looking for a year; my search takes me back to the cover, inscribed with the same lush cursive, *Clara Dale, 2012.*

"Fuck, did Sienna's former students hate her so much they wrote fanfiction about her dying?" Charlotte asks.

Luna and I exchange a long glance.

I start from the first page. "*August twenty-fifth. The special group all moved back to campus early, and we all had to take the PVTA to Smith to meet our professor. There's this cute guy who sat next to me on the bus. His name is Tripp.*"

My voice breaks. I toss the Moleskine at Luna like it's a tissue containing a hornet.

"*November eighth,*" says Luna. "*The coven doesn't believe me. Professor Weiss believes me, but she can't do anything until we get the grimoire back. Today I finally understood— she's scared of Tripp, too. She thought because Tripp and the other guys would be the first men to use magic, ever, that they would be weaker. It's his confidence, she told me, that's the root of his power. But then she started going on about the "magic IRS" and how she had to quit the course and install Professor Higgs as a replacement. How exposing men to magic, much less giving them a grimoire, is expressly forbidden. I wonder if she's just afraid of punishment. If she really intends to help. I won't tell her about the ghost, not until I know her intentions are pure.*"

"The ghost?" Charlotte leans over Luna's shoulder; they don't notice me shaking.

"Sienna literally *gave* the warlocks the grimoire," says Luna, color drained from her face. "For some kind of Amherst coed coven experiment."

"She needed us to retrieve the grimoire to avoid punishment from the magical authorities," says Charlotte. "We were her lackeys. We were used. Fuck."

"Fuck," Luna and I agree.

261

"Luna, can we go get ramen? The place downtown is still open," says Gabi.

I clench my fists. "Gabi, we're literally in the middle of discovering the truth about Sienna and the grimoire. *And Tripp's dead fucking body is on the table over there.* You have Cup Noodles in your room to eat later if you're hungry."

"I have to pee," says Gabi. "Luna, come with me."

"No," I say.

"Don't speak for me," says Luna, rising out of her chair. "Gabi, come on."

"What the fuck?" I block the door. "What the actual fuck?"

"I have to go to the fucking bathroom. Let me through," says Gabi.

I step aside. "So I'm on my own, as always. I'm going to have to figure out how to get the grimoire from Sigma all by myself."

"You're so fucking full of yourself," Gabi shouts from the hall.

"Shit, you just want to leave the body and the notebook?" I reach for my scissors, throw a light glamour over our discoveries, seize my backpack—"*Lee*," Charlotte pleads—and take the next elevator down after Gabi and Luna.

I realize, despite my criticism of Gabi, that I'm starving, head pounding, so I run past Chapin and the Campus Center, hit the convenience store for Pringles and Advil. It takes the cashier an unusually long time to check out due to an issue with the register, so I end up eating the entire sleeve of chips while hunched over the front stoop.

Once I finally pay for my devoured chips and ibuprofen, it's almost an hour later. I stumble back in the direction of Neilson—Tripp behind me, shouting out various dates to look up in the Moleskine—reaching Main Street without my headache resolved.

I cross the deserted street, even though it's a red light. The moon guides me, a bright porthole under a misty film of clouds.

I'm about to reach the sidewalk when a vigorous gust of wind strikes my back, and I lose my footing. My knees hit the pavement, but, instead of reopening the wound still bandaged on my knee, the wind lifts me, my squirming legs parting the air like water, and I'm floating, up up up until my eyes are level with the top of a streetlamp.

I rip out my headphones, glance down to see a red-faced, out-of-breath Charlotte, arms outstretched, menstrual cup in hand.

"Lee!" Charlotte shouts. "Stay calm!"

She starts to lower me, in sharp, rickety motions.

"Just drop me already!" I insist.

A black Escalade zooming toward downtown Noho stops in the middle of the road, makes an illegal U-turn, and speeds down the wrong side of the street, curving toward the curb.

"Charlotte!" I cry as I hit the concrete on my ass.

"Sorry, you had your headphones in and—" Charlotte starts to explain, before the Cadillac leaps over the curb and knocks her square in the back.

I swerve into the fence, Charlotte slides under the hood, and the car brakes.

"*Charlotte!*" I scream as the passenger door swings open, and two reedy warlocks hustle out of the vehicle, each holding a cheap plastic broom. The shorter of the two is wearing the yellow platforms. They mount the brooms, lift into the air, and fly up over the fence, over Neilson and Seelye, fading to black like rolling credits.

I get under the car and pull Charlotte out. Her arms are scratched, she's delirious, and I don't know about internal injuries, but she's breathing, her heart is beating, and for the time being, that's enough.

I call 911, hold her tight, taste tears and exhaust. Luckily, the Cadillac has a license plate. I briefly relay to the police that two Amherst boys were responsible, it was a hit-and-run, I was too shocked to follow them.

I go with Charlotte in the ambulance and, once I'm waiting in a flimsy plastic chair in the hospital, open the group text.

CHAPTER SIXTEEN

KAMAKHYA DEVI (THE BLEEDING GODDESS)

AT THE HOSPITAL, LUNA TELLS me that Charlotte was originally coming after me because the warlocks sent her this horrible message on OkCupid, about how they were going to run me over with the Cadillac as soon as I left the convenience store—a warlock buying Marlboros had seen me.

I'm surprised the coven went out of their way to save me.

"Of course we saved you," says Luna, wrapping her arms around me.

In the absence of Charlotte's family, the doctors tell us Charlotte has two broken ribs and some internal bleeding. In typical nonalarmist MD fashion, the suave young resident proclaims her injuries "mild," considering she got hit by an Escalade—Charlotte credits the quartz point she keeps in her bra.

Charlotte will obviously be staying the night.

"Why don't you girls go back to campus and get some rest," the resident suggests.

We refuse, and he calls the nurse to bring us blankets and a couple of pillows.

"At least my dad will come to see Smith," Charlotte says once we're all in her hospital room—just like old times, aside from the blinking monitors, the stark white fluorescence, the IV sunk into Charlotte's elbow. "Maybe he'll take us all out to dinner. And if he brings Jean-Paul, you'll all really get along."

Gabi and I, as far away from each other as possible, considering the tight dimensions of the room, exchange a rare glance. We may all be together, but the old times are dead, never to be resurrected.

Sometime around four thirty A.M., when Charlotte is going on about her mom's eighth-house stellium ("That's why she's obsessed with watching her own surgery on video, and why she had a frank discussion with me about the location and purpose of the clitoris when I was in the seventh grade"), Luna and I tuck Gabi up in Luna's mohair pea coat (my whole face grimacing, shriveling, when Luna dips forward to lay a kiss on Gabi's cheek, but at this hour, there's nothing to hide) and go to get some peanut M&M's at the vending machine in the lobby, because peanuts have some nutritional value. I watch Luna withdraw a dollar bill and three rusty quarters from her wallet, lovely pale-dawn brightness gripping her face and the bit of neck peeking out from the top of her scarf, and think about how, because I'm always in pain, I can never love another person the way she deserves; that's the truth, I'll never love or be loved, I'm always giving from an empty pot of dead roses and dehydrated soil.

"Lee," says Luna, after I relate this to her, chocolate-saliva uncharacteristically leaking out the corners of her mouth, "we already had this discussion. It's not that I don't care about you. I have a girlfriend."

"A girlfriend hell-bent on wasting the remainder of our magic every time she lights a cigarette or summons her phone from across the room because she's too damn lazy to get off her ass."

Luna swallows her last M&M and fishes in her wallet for more change.

We grab a couple of waters and go back to Charlotte's room, passing a row of long gallery windows trimmed in tabernacle bronze, gift of the millionaire namesake of the maternity ward. Outside, blue police lights flash and burn through the dewy fog; the part of me that's attracted to emergencies wants to stop, investigate, find out what's going on, but ahead of me is the ghost, shadow cast off his hovering body, the crisis that's always dominating my attention, stealing me away from the outside world.

We walk in on Gabi taking down a shopping list for Charlotte on her phone: peach Snapple iced tea, her iPad from her room, Pocky, nail polish.

"Char, I have a confession to make," says Gabi. "When I first met you, when you had the acrylic nails, I thought you were super straight."

"Nah, just super single," says Charlotte, noticing us at the door. "How's the vending machine?"

"Fine. We got some waters," says Luna, settling onto the foot of Charlotte's bed, hanging her head over the side.

After Charlotte and Gabi are asleep, Luna and I devise

a plan in whispers, even send out a message on OkCupid, inviting the warlocks to attend Smith's Take Back the Night event next week, where we hope to settle our dispute once and for all.

"You really think the warlocks will trade the grimoire for the body—or, at least, agree to meet us to do so?" Luna asks me, over Gabi's snores.

I gulp. The ghost sniggers at me. "If they still have the grimoire." The ghost is silent for once.

The warlocks message her back—no mention of the grimoire, but they'll meet us at Take Back the Night.

"And we'll be able to use the body for the spell you have in mind—to take the warlocks' magic away and wipe their memories permanently?" I listen to my voice peak at the end, worry she'll hear my lie—but Luna doesn't catch it.

"If we can defeat the warlocks before they actually take the body," says Luna.

"We need to get rid of the platforms too," I mention. "They're a talisman. One of the warlocks is always wearing them."

"Should we cut off his feet?"

"Surely there are other means of taking his shoes off."

The next day, a short-haired nurse with an octopus tattoo and septum ring comes to express suspicion over Charlotte's refusal to eat even Jell-O, coupled with her reportedly low BMI, and Charlotte somehow manages to flirt with said nurse effectively enough to earn a higher dose of morphine. Charlotte won't be leaving the hospital for at least two nights, and will require a long, strict period of rest.

We tell her about our plans while Gabi is at class. "Shame

I can't be there," says Charlotte, indicating her hospital bed. "Bigger shame we have so little magic left. What can we really do in the meantime? Can I help batch potion ingredients? Make a really good sign for the march?"

The preparations: Luna and I dirty our fingers with playground chalk, inscribing sigils around Chapin House. Charlotte organizes dragon's blood and calendula and tiny locks of our hair into small plastic bags, telling the nurses she's an aspiring herbalist. Luna gently informs Gabi of our scheduled showdown, and Gabi stays out of my way, so I don't really know what she's doing, but the few times Luna brings her up, it has to do with combat magic and Gabi's alleged black belt.

As the protest draws closer, Luna and I see each other almost every night, but she manages to keep the conversation away from sex, intimacy, and the precise details of the passing of John Digby Whitaker III, a real accomplishment, considering there's hardly ever anything else on my mind. All she talks about is Gabi, Gabi's exams, Gabi's new haircut, Gabi's new medication, Gabi's favorite ramen shop, and then she wonders why I've got resting sad face all of a sudden, why I always seem to be on the verge of tears.

April twenty-first, the day of the protest, arrives and we're as ready as we can be. Charlotte won't be attending; she's been discharged from the hospital, but the accident triggered the expression of some unexpected paternal instinct from her father, who is staying with Charlotte in a hotel and insisting on taking her back to Paris early, having her go on medical leave and finish her finals over the summer after such immense trauma (if only he knew).

Luna and I meet in her room, which looks the same as it did

three months ago, only she's got a new Mucha poster above her desk. We wait for Gabi in semisilence, talking about classes and final papers and what we're planning to take next semester, like we're just getting to know each other instead of trying to unknow each other. I expect Gabi either to not show up or to sabotage the mission in some way, forget Charlotte's stockpiled potion ingredients or admit she's erased all our sigils, but she arrives, hair fluffy and clean, remarkably well rested. She plants a kiss on Luna's lips and raises a hand to me in a sort-of wave, without saying hello.

As we file out the door, the ghost starts to cheer, shouts, "I always knew you were using me for my body, Leisl." I want to throw something at him, spit at him, but I stay closed-lipped, placid; I can't give it away, what I'm really going to do.

We march down to the protest, gather among the throngs of Smithies wielding homemade signs (DON'T RAPE, NO MEANS NO, the mildly problematic CONSENT IS SEXY). The seniors have set up a makeshift podium, where a spoken-word poet, Latina, Kate Moennig haircut, recounts her assault (how she can never taste vodka again, even in cream sauce, slathered on penne, her used-to-be-favorite dish). Gabi, color sapped from her face, swallows another two Xanax. We're keeping the various parts of his body back at Sienna's office, swaddled in white garbage bags enchanted to trap the scent of decay (the only premarch magic we permit ourselves), a takeout corpse ready to go, but Gabi's acting like she's got his head zipped into her backpack, her eyes are so unfocused and shifting, guilty.

The organizers distribute a candle to each person marching. The group collectively bow their heads and begin to move through campus, circling the paved walkway around Chapin's green before passing Neilson Library, Seelye Hall, the administrative offices, then emerging into downtown Noho. A long line of traffic halts for us as we cross the street.

We're hardly out of view of campus when, like a stealth tsunami, the hundreds of candles rise into the air, floating, as if by magic.

My own candle lifts into the air—with my own magic—and I tap Luna on the shoulder. "Are you two seriously going to blow our cover—"

Luna swerves around, a finger to her lips.

They emerge from storefronts, bars, coffeehouses, silent but visible, tendrils of burning sage clearing their paths: young witches, old witches, black witches, Latina witches, trans girl witches, witches with two kids and masses of curly hair, witches who own bookshops, professor-sorceresses, dining hall employees with side gigs as enchanters, witches gliding out of grand Victorians on broomsticks, diviners from the street, witches in short skirts, witches with lipstick, witches with nothing on their faces but power. All these witches we didn't know were there, gathering under hundreds of tiny candle flames, under the crescent moon, witches with political lips and political legs and political hands, witches whose bodies are contested territory, whose bodies are ravaged battlefields, a whole army of witches come to face the handful of warlocks with lacrosse sticks crowded under the bridge at the end of town.

The witches come with metal spatulas, cast-iron pans, eyeliner sharp enough to cut, stilettos made to puncture, old bras and lighters. Fifty-four to forty-six on campuses across the nation, the witches outnumber you, the witches made you and we can unmake you. The tree has been rotting slowly for centuries, disease trickling up from the root—and now the intrepid witches charge forward with the spontaneous fury of a hurricane, severing the trunk in one fell swoop. We are the original natural disaster, a storm that lost its courage after millennia of *you* imprisoning our bodies in PTSD oblivion. Yes, there's the internalized corset, misogyny that comes from within, but there's also straight-up ass-grabbing, pussy-grabbing, Rohypnol, and rape, for all unjust regimes are sustained by violence, by intimidating bodies, by inspiring terror, because how else could you rob a whole planet of witches of their power, their Goddess-given right to take a bunch of levitating yarn from the knitting supply store and tie your wrists, tie your ankles, give you what you deserve?

You're afraid of the truth, that there is no nice ending to the patriarchy because endings can only arise out of beginnings, everything is a pattern and a journey and all those thousands of years of holding us down, it's payback time and it's not going to be fun. The patriarchy was a story of violence and it will end in violence, there are no bloodless revolutions that are truly revolutionary, you must eat the blades you used to cut us down, those in power will never give it up and so the oppressor must be cut out, the witches have to take a pair of scissors and snip snip snip like Sanson, like Fates. That's the scariest idea of all, woman unleashed as the God she is, giver of birth but also giver of death, mother and murderer.

All the witches under the candles, all us gay girls, all us angry girls, all us fed-up girls, watch us exist, watch us raise our hands and cast you from the throne. We'll strip you, break your lax sticks in two, bind you with our own chains, Spanx and silicone implants and, you know, the feeling of being physically overpowered by people who have nothing but bad intentions toward you. But these tools themselves aren't evil, they can aid us too, we can break your skin with stiletto heels and secure your arms with corsets, we can fling Naked palettes at your heads like arrows, mark you like William Tells struck in the middle of the forehead, bleeding shimmering taupe. We even stick apples in your mouths, pigs ready to be roasted.

☽

Matriarchy begins with sirens, screams of birth emanating from police cars, the forces of the Empire arriving in minutes to break up the restoration of the divine feminine. They'll say it was a bloody protest, I'm sure; they'll repeat their old lies, that revolution, violent upheaval, transformation at the root never worked and never will. You see, it's all guillotines and gulags and toxic corrupt vanguards and the Founding Fathers were wise for compromising, for postponing abolition to the next century and leaving the work of the national razor to Pickett's Charge and the dry ashy fields at Gettysburg, instead of severing the heads of the genteel planters and inviting Jefferson to water the tree of liberty with his own blood as soon as the doors slammed shut at Independence Hall.

The solution to patriarchy, they'll say, is the sort of choice feminism that elevates individual women to corner offices, their own miniature Mount Olympuses where they can gaze down on cities they rule and strike fear into subordinates just like men, where they will sink so deep into patriarchal power that they will forget they are witches, that they had power of their own all along.

Back to the street: With so many covens, so many arrests, so many red lights and screams and barking German shepherds, the police rounding up witnesses—in such chaos there is opportunity, and Gabi, Luna, and I manage to slip down the side street with the multiple vegetarian restaurants and circle back up to Smith, candleless, Take Back the Night pins ripped off our jackets and tossed into the gutter. We bolt through the college gates, across Seelye's lawn.

"We need to get into Sienna's office first," Luna says with a pointed glance in my direction. "To grab the body."

We clamber into the library, into the special elevator leading to Sienna's office. Luna unlocks Sienna's door with magic, wiping a few tears with her sleeve as she twists the knob. "I really miss Sienna," she mutters.

We file in, turn the lights on, shut the curtains, lock the door. I think I see someone's outline, laying a tall shadow on the hardwood, but it's only Tripp's ghost, perched on top of Sienna's desk, snacking on a stale bag of Quadratini.

Luna sets her tote down on Sienna's desk. "Okay, Lee, do you want the head?"

His body is split between four white garbage bags. We load the sum of his parts into our backpacks and Charlotte's jumbo straw basket.

The whole time, the ghost looks straight at me, cackling, dead mouth full of partially chewed wafers.

I pause, listen to the quiet, the slight creaking of the floorboards.

"Luna." I put a finger to my lips. "Grab the basket."

She cocks her head to the side. "What?"

"Grab the basket. Come on."

She takes the handle.

Gabi: "Lee, what are you—"

"Shut up." I raise my hand, open Sienna's curtains with magic.

Huddled against the windows, carrying lax staffs and enchanted beer, are three of the warlocks, splattered in paint, hair scuffed up, clothes tangled from the protest.

They step forward, the hem of the brawny leader's overlong track pants covering the platforms, and we bolt from the room—into the elevator, out onto the lawn—but the warlocks are just behind us, shoving out of Sienna's window on broomsticks.

Gabi, in a rare moment of appropriate crisis response, lifts her hand, phone in her right fist, and shrouds us in darkness. The shadow grows to encompass the pavement, the library steps, the lawn.

"Good thinking," I shout to Gabi.

As if cursed by my praise, Gabi lifts her arm slightly too high. The shadow shrinks back, omits her, reveals her to the light, and the platforms-wearing warlock swoops down to seize her like a hawk spotting a rodent.

Luna reaches into the straw basket, takes out a thick, dowdy historical novel and her NARS pencil, and flings both in Frisbee orbits at his bullish blond head.

He topples from the broom, onto the lawn. The pencil rebounds back into Luna's outstretched hand.

We race down Chapin's driveway to the forest path. I can still hear the two remaining warlocks, circling above us, cackling, a sound I confuse with the ghost, up in the sky with his brothers.

"You want to get Rocky first," the ghost shouts. "The bigger one."

We follow Luna across the pine needles, squint at the low yellow moon hovering under the branches. Rocky cracks open a can of magic beer and splashes it across a pile of leaves, unleashing a whole host of flames that begin to crackle across the forest.

Luna stays back, puts out the fire, shouting, "You really need to fuck Mother Earth too?"

Rocky hits a branch, narrowly avoids toppling from his broom.

We're at the crux of the lake. The warlocks emerge out of the trees, into the direct rays of the sunset; their shadows break the smooth, dusk-lit surface of the water.

Luna takes my hand. "Ready?"

I look to Gabi. We reach for each other, slowly, until Luna mutters under her breath and we join hands, clasp each other tight.

We take them down like this: Raise the water up to the height of the trees (Tripp's ghost, at the top of the cresting wave, refusing to drown). The warlocks fly up, up, away, until Luna summons a surge of wind and wrangles them into the enveloping towel of water.

I squeeze Luna's hand, and Gabi's, and watch the lake scoop the two warlocks onto the opposite shore and trap them in ice.

When they scream, Luna snaps her fingers to muffle them, shutting their mouths.

We take a collective deep breath.

"GODDESS OF LIGHT, RULER OF TIDES, MOON, SOIL, ENSURE THAT IF ROCKY AND—"

"Brendan," the ghost contributes.

"Brendan," I repeat.

"BRENDAN TRY TO RECALL THEIR FOIL, THEY WILL FOREVER TOIL."

"Well, that wasn't as hard as it could have been," says Luna with a sigh. "When the ice melts, they'll wake up, thinking they rolled up by the lake drunk after a Quad party."

"Everyone's at the protest," Gabi says, for herself, gazing over the lake. "No one will see them, right?"

Luna ignores her, points to the center of the lake.

The grimoire is bobbing up from the water, waves lapping over the black leather; nearby, Tripp's ghost floats on his back, head folded into his hands.

I breathe a sigh of relief.

"The pages won't be ruined?" Gabi asks.

"It's a fucking magic book," I remind her. "I'll go get it. I was a competitive swimmer. Also, we need to get the platforms off Brendan."

Gabi and Luna ignore me.

"The platforms?" I repeat.

"We'll handle those after we get rid of the body," says Luna. "Which we should have done months ago. Damn, we should have burned him."

I take off my shoes, give Luna my phone, wallet, and ID, and wade into the water.

It doesn't take me long to reach the grimoire. I tread

water, seize the leather binding, open the book. The pages, no matter how much water laps over them, stay dry.

The ghost floats over to me. "Page two-fifty."

I glance over the spell.

"Lee!" Luna shouts, disentangling herself from Gabi. "Is the grimoire okay?"

I glance to the shore, don't hesitate.

"You ready?" I say to the ghost.

I take the grimoire to the shore. I lay the book, open to the right page, on the silt, and start to seize the various parts of Tripp's body from our bags.

"Lee," Luna says, watching me, wary. "Lee, what are you doing?"

"Assembling the spell," I say, unzipping his legs from my backpack.

"What spell? You know a spell to get rid of the body?" Luna says.

Once the body is out, I kneel before the grimoire.

Behind me, the ghost: "Tell her. Tell her what you're going to do. Don't you want her to believe in me?"

I take a deep breath, turn to Luna. "I don't think we're going to do the spell you want to do," I say. "If that's okay."

Luna raises an eyebrow. "There's a more effective one?"

I laugh, keep reading the spell. It requires a large body of water, go figure.

I look over the spell again, stand, face Luna. "No. I'm bringing Tripp back to life. So I can kill him. Myself. I deserve that, don't you think?"

Luna rushes forward. "Lee, you can't be serious?" She gets

that I'm serious. "Lee, what the fuck? You're going to put us in danger, you're going to put other people—"

"Other people never fucking cared about me!" I say, smacking her away. I glance to the ghost, the grimoire. "If you'll excuse me, I need to get on with—"

Luna grabs my arms. "Lee, you're not thinking straight—"

"I'm never thinking straight. I'm not straight. I'm not the person I should be. I'm not fucking good. I attacked your girlfriend. But why do I get punished for it? Why am I the bad guy? Gabi started it. Gabi is a bad person too. Gabi—"

I break away. Luna seizes me again. "Lee, this is not about you—"

"It's time I fucking prioritized myself and my needs and stopped letting other people walk all over me. It's time I stood up for myself. It's time I stopped letting you limit my power. Do you know where I'd be, without you, without your fucking deadweight?"

"You were without us for the entire semester—"

"I've been *haunted*. He's been with me the whole time. I couldn't focus. I couldn't do anything. I couldn't use my power. And it's your fault. It's your fault because you killed him. I never had closure—"

"I didn't—"

"It's your fault, it's your fault, and he's been haunting me and following me and looking at me twenty-four hours a day and I'm sick of it! I'm fucking sick of it—"

Gabi races up to me. "Lee—"

"I have to kill him. I need closure. I deserve closure. This is how I'm loving myself. This is how I'm sticking up for me. This is how—"

Gabi and Luna join hands. A fierce gust of wind, with the dexterity of fingers, removes the grimoire from my grip. "You can't—" I say. "You can't take it—I need it—I need this—"

The grimoire is under Gabi's arm. I raise my scissors, summon a fire, maneuver the flames like a puppet snake, circling Gabi in heat. Sweat collects on her face.

Gabi takes her phone out of her pocket and extinguishes the flames.

I grip my scissors, spark another flame, and direct the smoke toward Gabi. The smoke twists into two giant hands, the fingers craning forward to grab her throat, closing off her windpipe as soon as I make a fist.

Luna leaps between us. "Lee, let go!"

I shake my head, nails digging into my palm. "No."

"Lee, you need to stop now," says Luna.

I tighten my grip. Gabi makes little choking noises, her eyes rolling up, limbs shaking.

"I don't think so," I say.

I keep Gabi restrained by the throat, watching the grimoire, which she's almost ready to drop.

"Lee," says Luna, voice cracking. "Don't make me do this."

"Do what?" I unleash another furl of smoke, another pair of hands, reaching for Luna's neck, phantom thumb closing right over the spot where I gave her a hickey back in January, fingers settling into her collarbones.

Luna throws off the smoke, reaches into her back pocket, withdraws her Rider-Waite, and tosses the deck at me. The cards start to spin at a fierce velocity, whacking into me one by one, slicing up my face and arms, dozens of tiny paper cuts. Still, I hold my scissors. Nothing can stop me, nothing can distract me.

"Lee!" Luna screams, watching Gabi. "Lee, you're going to kill her—"

"So you're going to keep hurting me?" I shout, raising my arm to protect my eyes from the onslaught of cards. "You're going to keep doing this to me, who loved you, who stood up for you, who would fucking kill her for you—"

The Four of Pentacles smacks me right in the cheek, slices my skin open and knocks me to the ground.

Luna seizes the grimoire from Gabi, opens it to a page about halfway through the book.

The ghost laughs. This time, his voice comes from the center of my mind. *Fine. If you won't bring me back, I'll take another body. I always wanted to see what it's like to be a girl.*

"Luna," I croak, digging my nails into the soil.

"I'm sorry, Lee," Luna says, face heavy with regret.

She doesn't look at me, doesn't see Tripp's icewater hands reach down my throat, his arms invading my ribs. I let go of Gabi, who shudders to the forest floor, coughing, face a muddy red.

Luna continues to flip through the grimoire.

I open my mouth. A black cloud rises from within me, spirals into a blade of smoke, advances toward my sisters.

Luna finds the page, joins hands with Gabi. They start to chant.

"GODDESS, MAY YOU RECOGNIZE OUR PLIGHT—"

The garbage bags shielding Tripp's remains melt away. His

body parts start to rattle like electric toy trains; his legs, his arms, his head, his fingers, his dick all lift into the air, circle like a tornado, a rainstorm of flesh.

"WITH YOUR GRACE AND MIGHT, TURN OUR MINDS TO THE BLACKEST NIGHT—"

My limbs jerk up and forward, and I'm hurtling into the flesh and bones. Inside my skull, he's laughing, and I can't even cry. This is how I'm going to die. I bet my family will describe me at my funeral as *conscientious*—

"WITH THE LIFE OF ANOTHER I VANQUISH MY FRIGHT—"

I shut my eyes, I shut my eyes and Tripp's laughter climbs to the peak of my mind—

"MAY THAT WHICH HAS HAUNTED ME LOSE FOR-EVER ITS BITE—"

In the dark, there's a kiss, the musty petrochemical whiff of Axe, uncut fingernails marking the back of my neck, tongue forced between my lips.

Tears stream down Luna's face.

"Lee, I'm seriously going to call 911," Luna says. "Lee, if you don't stop it, I'm going to call the police, I'm going to have to let them take you again, I'm sorry, Lee, I'm sorry."

Gabi cradles Luna's head as she cries.

"Tripp is literally right in front of you," Luna shouts through mucus, clogged throat. "Tripp is right here." She leans into Gabi's shoulder, muffles her own words. "Leisl Ann Davis, I'm seriously going to call 911."

"It's okay, Leisl," says Tripp, arms around my waist. My hands rest on the square bones of his shoulders. He is breathing, wholly intact, clean pleats on his grass-stained khakis, whiff of detergent and peppermint two-in-one shampoo. "Don't worry, I'm not going to let the police take you. We're going to calm you down right here, right now, and get you back to bed. Then I'll drive you home to your mom, okay?"

He smiles. His breath is slightly rotten.

I start to wail. Tripp presses my head into his chest.

"Tripp is your boyfriend," Gabi says, sniffling. "Lee, seriously. Tripp is trying to help you. He's the only one who's willing to help you. If you don't stop it, we're going to call the police."

"Tripp's taken care of you all semester," Luna chimes in. "What the fuck, Leisl? Tripp has been so good to you."

Tripp whispers in my ear: "Leave them alone, Leisl. Let them be dykes. You and Luna were never going to work out. I could have told you that back at Christmas."

He presses me tighter.

"Luna," I call.

"You're safe with me," Tripp says, hands dripping down to my ass, and I remember, crisp November, his high school varsity jacket surrounding my shoulders, the gray cashmere leash he wound around my neck at New Year's, telling me in the shower during January term, "You're not a real lesbian, Leisl, you love dick and you know it," pressing his nails into my blue-veined underarm skin, my knees slipping to the drain and banging the tiles, gargling water up my nose.

His blood staining Rachel's headboard—

I look over his shoulder at Gabi and Luna. They're kissing, muttering to each other, cuddling and grinning like I don't exist, like none of us knows the truth. I feel like my chest is a vase shattered by a whirring baseball; the loss I should have felt, the sharp incision of grief, when Sienna got in a car accident and Charlotte overdosed, when the police shut down the march—all those months ago in the bathroom—all that loss swallows me and I don't have a choice.

"You're dead," I tell Tripp.

"You're a crazy bitch," Tripp says, baring his faded teeth.

He forces me into a kiss, fingertips digging into my back, like thorns cutting under my shoulder blades. I'm drowning in him, gargling his words, nothing but a stupid little girl, unable to escape, even when I have my chance between my hands, I can't fucking move. I'm a deer whose internal organs have shut down because a human touched it, capture myopathy. I know what I should be doing. I know what I need. I still need the closing, the ending, *NO*, but beyond the ditch of deep dark frustration in my chest, I'm blocked. I'm a human crossroads and I can't move on.

He spins me, his arm clenching my shoulders.

"I'll never go missing again," he assures me as he escorts me from the woods.

Luna is tangled in Gabi, oblivious.

He buys me these yellow-5-Creamsicle roses at the natural foods store. The hemp shop with the tight red window, neck-down female form in bondage, we stop there too, he shoplifts too, he's the worst kind of person, shoplifting and dying young. Only he'll unscrew his own hands from the cross and land face first in the snow, he'll break his nose but plastic surgery does wonders, sixty-five years old it's a silver dollar toss-up between the Turks and Caicos and the Supreme Court, leisure or power, he was born sucking on a solid gold egg and he'll have both so long as he lives, that's how he was born and how he will die.

He's used to people on their knees, he knows what it is to be the heir to someone. After he buys me a new outfit I kiss the WASP fantastic and think of what Sienna said, her second or third lecture, when we were handing in our first assignment, *All you girls who can't write your papers unless you're under your covers with Pooh Bear and a personal sleeve of Thin Mints, you worry me, how you're going to survive in this world*, and she was right, she was right that we're lollipop-throating pink gingham *girls*, we sin by being who we are, we deserve this, we deserve to hurt and bleed and follow him wherever he insists on taking me.

I complain that the tiles are wet, and hurting my knees.

He drops me off at my room after.

Charlotte doesn't answer her phone. Neither does my mom. My Internet searches turn up quite informative— Zoloft isn't like lithium, one of those psych drugs where you need another drug to effectively keep it down and not just throw up your self-hatred and get chained to a hospital bed by intravenous needle.

I go to the vending machine downstairs to grab some water. Just to be safe, I dig out some old Ativan from the secret pocket of my purse.

The whole time, I'm thinking about her, per usual, how all I ever wanted was for someone to see into my heart, to understand me, to get me, and how Luna did see me, did get me, and she chose to leave me anyway. She saw the wolves and left me anyway. It hurts enough that I'm never going to open myself again; it's enough for me to ruin the temple of my body, surround my corpse with NO TRESPASSING yellow tape, announce to potential looters that all the treasure inside has been stolen, she took it all.

CHAPTER SEVENTEEN

THE SNAKE

IT ENDED WITH AN UNSUCCESSFUL hex and a bottle of pills prescribed to me by Dr. Applebaum, and tiles for a pillow.

(THE DOCTOR SAYS SHE ALSO HAS A TYPE A PERSONALITY.)

Trying to kill yourself with Zoloft is like manually removing the pus from each of your pores with unwashed fingers, ravishing your skin with the imprint of everything your phone has touched. It's clarifying; satisfying. Until the next morning you wake up and see bloody little hovels rising on your chin, cheeks, and the space between your eyes that isn't forehead but isn't nose or eyebrow either. Nothing can cover the last defense of your immunity against your dirty fingers, not NARS or peroxide or Colgate, the bottle swung upside-down like that early Hockney with the lovers and their sixty-nine toothpaste cocks, that piece you saw with Luna when the soft fluorescence of the campus museum convinced you that you loved her.

(MISS, CAN YOU HEAR ME? MISS DAVIS? CAN YOU HEAR ME?)

Here's a little suicide primer: Taking a bunch of psychotropic medication will not kill you. You'll throw it up, the whole bottle. I don't know if the pills all disintegrate, or if digesting the first five pills powers your vomiting and the rest of the bottle comes up whole and draped in stomach acid, white cylindrical horseflies that tried to get a bite and couldn't, because your body and mind aren't on the same page, if they were on the same page you would be a flickering old woman and not Almost Nineteen, you would never be Almost Nineteen for the rest of your life.

(HOW MANY FINGERS AM I HOLDING UP?)

Our world prefers girls dead. In the dead girl, Everygirl sees her *self* for the first time, the self she is when she goes outside, ever since she was little, ever since she went to the playground, ever since she ran, screaming, sprinted as fast as she could, the boys had her Payless sandal, mud stained, white felt flowers, he took a fistful of shirt and she ran, she's running, she's running for the rest of her life.

(MISS DAVIS, CAN YOU HEAR ME—)

She's been a dead girl ever since her mother told her to make up for her lack of a penis by sticking the sharp metal part of the car keys out while she's walking through the parking lot, never go anywhere without that cragged silver phallus sticking out from your fist like a dagger.

NEVER LEAVE YOUR SCISSORS AT HOME.

(MISS DAVIS?)

Every time a girl goes outside she is dead, now and inevitably.

(MISS DAVIS?)

You could say that by taking a bunch of Zoloft I did not actually intend to kill myself, that I was looking for help, attention, making excuses.

(EXCUSES—)

Are you going to tell me I didn't try hard enough?

(EXCUSES—)

It's true that I want to be saved.

I open my eyes and my eyes are surrounding me. I am the witness to all the flaws of my own dead body: the slightly bowed turn of my legs, reclined amid the silken casket, sheathed under black pantyhose, the sausage blocks of my thighs stacked over my too-thick knees, the short dress that highlights the chunky pair of twin fat deposits between my armpits and my breasts, the way my nose curves slightly to the left under hair that is frizzing up from the holy water, brassy under the relic-yellow chapel light, dark roots still growing even though I'm finished with life.

The mortician did a shit job: I'm bloated under the tight dress, and the poorly chosen shade of archangel pink on my cheeks does nothing to offset either my deathly pallor or my acne.

No one is crying, except for Tripp, sobbing in the first

pew, clutching my mother's elbow, face shaking against her collarbone.

Luna is at the pulpit, reading from a gospel I don't recognize. "*I used to dream, you know, about some kind of magic potion that could make me forget him, some sci-fi dystopian innovation that could get inside my mind and get rid of him forever—*"

Luna takes her seat in the pew and a priest in an infinite black cassock starts to read some psalm my grandmother chose, *Happy shall he be, that taketh and dasheth thy little ones against the stones, amen*, and the priest has long lashes and lips that sneer and Tripp's upturned nose, his dusting of freckles, the gaping red hole between his legs, thick and rich and cranberry blood soaking the cassock and dropping ping-pong onto the marble edge of the altar, he's drinking the blood of Praise to You Lord Jesus Christ.

I look to the stained glass, the eaves, watch a flower girl, age three or four, distributing peonies and black dahlias down the aisle. The apocalyptic wardrobe of the funeral crowd catches the midmorning sun coming through the heads of Mary and Joseph and the open-jawed Byzantine apostles; my mother encapsulates Tripp and strokes his tearful face.

A veil shields my corpse's head. The priest reaches down and slips a ring onto my dead finger.

I sit up in the casket, rip off the veil and shake my head.

"No," I say, throwing off the ring, *clink* against the golden bowl of Eucharist, and my sentence is complete.

ʊ

When the fire cools and the night comes and you can see again, the comforting automated blink of artificial lights, wheels down the hall, footsteps, you're deathless, and he's gone.

Gone.

You hold your hands up and see yourself for the first time, new cells, new life. This is not the same body he touched. You are remade, new skin, new feelings; the only magic you need is time.

CHAPTER EIGHTEEN

DOCUMENTING MADNESS

You could say that by taking a bunch of Zoloft and Ativan I did not actually intend to kill myself, that I was looking for help, for *attention*, which is what they say at the hospital, and what they repeat once I get transferred to McLean SouthEast, closer to home, where they upgrade me to group therapy once I'm keeping down solid food again.

The first time they mention the word *psychosis* is when I'm sitting across from the doctor and the resident who's going to overhear my evaluation (it's always really awkward when you think you're going to have a private audience with the doctor and then he informs you his resident is going to *observe* the meeting, like you're a fish fossil, an artifact, a specimen to gawk at). Tongue blurred by benzos, I accidentally let slip something about *flying tarot cards* and the resident gapes for a moment before he starts laughing, and the doctor laughs too.

They can't decide what's causing the psychosis, if it's my PTSD (forty percent of combat veterans with diagnosed PTSD have visual and auditory hallucinations, a nurse tells me), if it was drugs (I insist I never did drugs, and they struggle to believe me), if I'm actually bipolar instead of "just" depressed. The most helpful perspective comes from the staff therapist, a prematurely bald man in a Hawaiian shirt, who explains that, yes, there's chemistry involved, but, like most big problems, *what's wrong with me* is multilayered, multifaceted, a many-legged beast. "You can have trauma and you can have a chemical problem," he explains as we sit on a bench in the hall, watching the nurses guide patients from individual clinicians' offices to the group ward.

"So there isn't one magic solution that's going to fix me," I say.

He shakes his head. "It's not like you're a murderer. You self-harmed. You tried to take your own life. But don't let anyone convince you that your action was selfish. You were trying to escape from very real pain. And we're going to help you manage that pain, so you won't break the hearts of your friends and family by removing yourself from the world."

I wish this were a neat ending, in which I choose to make Daddy proud and become a lawyer after my Hallmark-boxed experience of justice, that it will end in the courtroom and the validation of an old white guy judge can soothe my mind enough to let me know I need not freeze anymore and remember *him* when I'm chopping scallions, when I'm between yellow intersections, when I'm in the shower and the lobby and the fitting room and my front-row business class seat with seventy-five dollars of extra legroom. But I know the truth: The bruises on my knees won't heal at the magic wand of an objective someone else telling me it *really did* occur.

"Leisl, we discussed this already. There is no evidence of rape, dear," the therapist repeats, and *dear* ruins it, though it doesn't rot so much as *sweetheart, Leisl sweetheart, Miss Davis my darling girl,* YOU'RE FUCKING CRAZY, bipolar and too attached to the past, do you take pride in being a victim of a crime that never took place anywhere but your fucked-up Pretty Pretty Princess head?

I should care but all I care for is dusk and blackout curtains. I am too tired to fight for myself. I just want to float into nail salons and other people's motorboats and Bowery bars where I can wear little secondhand designer skirts and feel the hands of some other mind that can confirm real and true for me, so long as I have sex with him whenever he wishes. I only care to be a satiated civilian; if I go to the front lines my stitches will burst and I will be dead soon enough (or back here, with all the other unbaptized trauma babies in marshmallow-walled limbo). Someday I might even get diamond-skinned enough to grow into one of those freeze-dried-astronaut-bananas women who glance up from the laundry and say to you, *She got raped? So what? What's the big deal? Get over it.*

Later, in the zen room, when I topple out of a crane pose and catch the creepy guy from morning tai chi staring at my upturned ass, I excuse myself from the class and walk the halls, nod to passing staff like I know where I'm going, find my way outside and go sit in the courtyard, watch the nascent bees circle the geraniums. There's a broom leaning against the bricks, bristles caked in dust. I hesitate, surveying the windows for onlookers, but I can't resist. I seize the broom, feel the familiar tingle of power coursing through my fingers, straddle the handle and lift into the air.

I stay close, do several rounds of the parking lot and the hospital roof, skirt the edge of the neighborhood, avert the Cape seagulls and, mostly, lift my face to the sun, smile wide, thank the power within me for this one last time, for the confirmation that I'm *not crazy*, that, even if I suit the diagnostic boxes the doctors are trying to cram me into, what I saw was real, I can be sick but that doesn't make me a liar, I didn't imagine anything.

I return to the courtyard, leave the broom where I found it, avoid the creepy guy when I see him in the hall. Back in the zen room, just in time for *savasana* (corpse pose), I lie on the mat and feel some measure of peace, knowing that there is no peace but at least I can trust myself.

When my mom comes to visit over the weekend, I beg her to let me sleep at home; I can complete the last few days of group therapy commuting back and forth, the doctors confirm. Wading through the adolescent ward—middle schoolers with teddy bears and hospital bracelets, grim boys with Power Rangers blankets—she relents, tears in her eyes.

We wait for my discharge; she brings *OK!* magazine from

the foyer and we gossip about people we will never know. Finally free, around nine P.M., we load everything into the car and drive off. She reminds me, once we're on the highway, that we'll have to go back to get my stuff at Smith before finals week. Did I email all my professors about making up my exams? Oh, right, I didn't have phone access.

I yell at her about her choice of topics, complain that all I really need is quiet and a long shower. She shuts up; close to home, one exit away, I see that she's crying.

"When your cousin was in the anorexia facility, she took her exams," my mom says, almost inaudibly, and that's the thing. We love the oh-so-secret melancholic who lives under the top dermal layers of the outwardly flawless Class President type, who might strangle herself beneath the slanted ceiling of her Cape Cod bedroom following her valedictorian address, whose parents will appear on the local news, shocked, heartbroken, unable to grip the rope-burn truth, that their tumble-proof baby had the manners to kill herself after cleaning up the kitchen and taking down the party banners and folding her laundry and leaving it perfectly arranged in her dustless bureau. We don't love the girl who can't hide her issues, who succumbs to her demons' ideas and cruel suggestions at every turn, who dares to have a visible breakdown, who dares to *allow* her life to be disrupted by such an innocuous event as *rape*.

I guess that's my goal now: to numb and freeze myself to the right subzero degree to ensure that I never get visibly *fucked up* ever again, that my trauma stays chained to my stomach lining and never steers my hands or mouth, that my issues remain unresolved in the subconscious backdrop of my pristine suburban existence and instead of going to therapy, like a weak, attention-seeking, *damaged* person, I just take my neuroses out on my future children, like all good respectable people.

Only I'm so far beyond the possibility of cutting my past out by the umbilical cord, it seems a more realistic strategy to wear my mistakes like a regrettable tattoo, a good story even if it's embarrassing and ugly. The truth is, there will always be coffee stains on the edges of perfect white bedspreads, there will always be chips in bridal manicures, there will always be forest fires tormenting the gated community of your immaculate life plan. It's true, I'm not one of the perfect people, but I'm interesting, and I deserve to heal. Maybe even go to L.A. and discover if I still want to follow my dreams, because once you're damaged, you're not afraid of spilling milk. Once you've fucked up, you're *free*.

"That's great for cousin Jenna," I reply, proud of myself for daring to be weak.

We swerve off the highway, back to the Puritan-haunted suburbs, back to the beginning, and my mom complains that the car is stuffy and rolls the windows down. I get hair in my face, yell at her again, start to roll my window up.

My mom stops at a light.

"What's that?"

She points to a broomstick, moving of its own accord, bouncing across the road like tumbleweed.

"Strong wind, I guess," she says as the broom shoots up into the pines and disappears.

NEXT FALL

In October 2014, I get an email from Gabrielle M. Avery, asking if this is still my email. I stop there, mark it unread, leave it trembling at the top of my inbox during the train ride into Boston, the boarding of the bus, the stranding at the Springfield Peter Pan station and the Uber tour of New England postindustrial decay, ending in the comparative vibrancy of autumn Noho, Smithies and UMass adventurers clutching non-Starbucks maple caramel lattes to their pea coats (infinity scarves are still de rigueur).

The driver lets me off at Thornes; I grip the stress ball they gave me at McLean, the yellow foam star with a little face I drew myself in black Sharpie.

Sienna is technically on sabbatical, but it's one of those sabbaticals where she's still in her office all the time so she can advise her thesis students, she's only headed to Croatia for part of January term and then it's back to dictating the manuscript to her research assistant (after her car accident and the injury sustained to her left hand, she can't really type). She told me she would "definitely" be in her office when I arrived, so I head straight for Neilson, shoving boxy vintage sunglasses over a good quarter of my face and keeping my posture bent, my steps rapid.

Sienna is out of her office, no note on the door, no text, so I settle in amid the open boxes of seventies thesis papers and open Gabi's email—which is, simply, a revelation. Not only does she write, *What I did to Luna was wrong*, she informs me that, lo and behold, I was *the only one who knew what was right*. In fact, I was so right that she wants advice on how to act with her new girlfriend, because she doesn't want to repeat what happened with Luna.

I consider never answering the email, but I do write back, tell her some bullshit about forgiveness and recommend she seek psychiatric assistance, if she still can't distinguish right from wrong. But the email does cauterize the grudges still festering in my heart. Maybe all I wanted, all this time, was to know that I was right.

"Leisl?"

Sienna helps me out of the cardboard dust, hugs me (a first).

"How *are* you," she frets, welcoming me into a leather chair across from her desk, handing me tea, Quadratini cookies, and I remember my wounds are still hot, no matter how many ice cubes I melt in my fists (per DBT).

Sienna tugs at the hourglass charm hanging over her chest; she holds her hand to her chest like it's still broken. She still isn't painting her nails. She settles into her old chair and crosses her legs, adjusts the buckle of her mustard-yellow seventies platforms, complains of a blister.

"I'm transferring," I begin.

Sienna nods. "I'm sorry to see you go, Leisl, but I'm happy to help you in any way I can. Where would you be applying to transfer?"

"Boston area, mostly. BU, BC. Maybe Tufts. A big school, definitely."

She nods slowly. "What do you want to do?"

"For a major? History—"

"No, in your life."

"I used to want to go to L.A."

"For what?"

"I wanted to be a filmmaker."

"Do you still want that?"

"I'm not sure."

Sienna raps her right hand, thronged with rings, on the edge of her desk, and the office feels empty without Luna's breath and Charlotte's fidgeting with pins and zippers. "Well, whatever you end up doing, you're an incredibly gifted young person, Leisl. I look forward to hearing about whatever you decide. And if you're still interested in getting that paper published, I'm happy to look at your revisions. You really should think about presenting your work at conferences. A shame you couldn't join me at Columbia back in June. If you were to stay at Smith, I would be able to assist you even more. Next semester—on the off-chance you were to return—I'd be happy to reserve a space for you in my senior seminar. I've only ever had one other sophomore, but you—"

I start to cry.

"I can't come back to Smith," I tell her.

Sienna grabs me a box of tissues.

"Tell me, how are you doing? How is your health?" She sits back down. "It wasn't your fault, Leisl. You've survived. You're stronger, whether you know it or not. We often look back and give thanks for the obstacles we encountered on our paths. Though it doesn't always make sense until later."

"I wish it had never happened," I say, about other things. "There are so many other ways to become strong. I could have grown another way. I'm not even sure I've grown. Actually, I feel exactly the same."

Sienna congratulates me on my recovery, asks me to send her the application due dates so she can know when to submit her recommendation. "The world needs you, Leisl," she calls after me as I walk out of the office, vaguely, like one of those motivational posters that hangs over a school auditorium doorframe, inviting you to value your individuality and never compare yourself to others, right before you're about to take a standardized test.

Yet she is really smiling, and she sounds sincere.

"Thank you," I call from the hall. "Thank you very much."

Stepping into the elevator, I notice a Moleskine note-book, black, pebbled, frayed, but I don't pick it up from the ground.

I step out of Neilson and it's one of those eighty-degree October afternoons all of a sudden. I sling my coat over my arm and cut across the lawn, narrowly missing a garter snake in the grass. My bus doesn't leave until six.

I find a bench, out of view of Chapin's phantom height, and take out my phone.

"Lee! Leisl Davis!"

My stomach makes a fist. I swallow, turn, but we've already joined eyes, and I can almost forgive her, her hair is shorter and lilac and that's a new lipstick (it can't be Train Bleu, must be Cruella, or a heavy application of Dolce Vita), she has a new tattoo on the interior of her wrist, and she sits down without my permission, though my bag stays between us.

"Charlotte's been asking about you all the time," Luna says, hands electric in her lap; she wants to hold me. "We've really missed you."

"I texted her over the summer," I say. "We were supposed to get ramen before my bus leaves, but she never got back to me."

"She lost her phone," Luna says with a frown. "Are you back to get your stuff?"

"No, I had a meeting with Sienna about her writing a recommendation."

"Oh." Luna nods slowly.

She opens her mouth, closes it, swallows; we're both wild rivers, pummeling the dams, but neither of us is willing to spill first, we're content to wait, to search each other's faces like maps and wonder what has changed, if anything has changed, if everything has changed.

"You probably don't need more people asking you about your educational future," Luna says, when it's right.

"No, I don't."

She picks a stray purple hair from her lips.

"Can I touch you?" she says.

My eyes sting. I move my bag to the ground.

"Of course."

She seizes me.

I wrap her tight, her neck in my elbows, she still smells like lavender; she is thinner and older, and I wonder what has changed about me. Hiding in her, I don't have to tell her the truth, I can just keep my secrets a part of me, not say what I mean aloud and let it cut me from the inside, until I become nothing but a dark room of disconnected parts, the sum of my secrets and unrequited unexpressed never-loves.

All I really want to say is, *The six months I didn't see you were the best of my life*, but I am never cruel.

She gives me her new phone number and assures me that I should stay in touch.

"I will," I say, brushing an awkwardly long piece of pixie hair behind her ear.

Her lips part and I can see the pink behind the dark paint.

"Lee," she says, "last semester, have you thought about—"

She gets an idea and rummages inside her rucksack's front pocket.

"Damn," she mutters. "Oh, okay. Here."

A tape-mended, fraying tarot card, the Star.

"Is this from one of your decks?"

I gulp. "No, I think all my decks are complete."

"You sure?"

I nod.

Luna tucks the ragged card back.

"Well, I don't want to keep you," she says.

"Yeah, my, um, my bus is probably going to arrive soon."

Luna stretches her arms out again; I pick up my bag.

"It was nice to see you," I say, standing.

I start to walk away.

"You know he's been expelled," Luna says suddenly.

I turn. Her hand is outstretched, like she's trying to catch a firefly in her net.

"During the investigation about Clara. They were able to expel him. He's totally banned from all the Five College campuses. He's not even in this state anymore."

I gulp.

"I just wanted you to know," Luna insists.

My eyes fall to the gap between us, the pavement, the lonely can of hard lemonade rubbing itself on the gravel to the lull of the breeze, the dingy old pair of craft scissors lying open, sticky-bladed from slicing Twizzlers or tape, spinning, twirling like a compass, hay rolling to my feet.

"Luna," I say. "Don't talk about him ever again."

We part. Student crowds fill the path, and Luna disappears behind a wall of arms and legs. I walk back to the Peter Pan station, stare down at my phone, and try to forget where I am, but I don't have faith that my open wounds will regenerate on their own. Nature to me is still storms and tsunamis and vengeance, and heterosexuality may be the carnal equivalent of choosing to major in engineering and Chinese, but ten years down the road, when you're living in a Shanghai high-rise with Gucci money in the bank, you'll be glad you chose abundant boredom and long hair over starry nights and turpentine and curiosity, because your pussy doesn't have nine lives, only an expiration date.

I reach the end of campus, the teal spiral steeple and the junk drawer of traffic, the air thick as butter; it's like how at the end of the movie, everything is the same, the top of the mountain looks exactly the same as the old world locked in the valley—finally you're trapped in the future, but only you know you've moved on.

Or have you?

I run back to the bench. It's empty, but I can still see, hear, taste Luna's memory. I pick up the scissors from the ground, slip them into my coat pocket. Then I reach for my phone, fingers clammy but sure.

"Luna?" I exhale into the receiver. "I have two hours. Do you want to get ramen?"

ACKNOWLEDGMENTS

Thank you to my agent, Lucy Cleland, for your total dedication, immensely hard work, and belief. Thank you to Maddie Caldwell, my editor, for your enthusiasm, meticulous attention to detail, and commitment to making *Consensual Hex* the best book it could be. Thank you to my UK editor, Poppy Mostyn-Owen, for your insight, dedicated attention, and hard work on behalf of this novel. Thank you to the team at Grand Central Publishing, including Jacqui Young, Tree Abraham, Abby Reilly, Laura Cherkas, and Anjuli Johnson. Thank you to the team at Atlantic Books, including James Roxburgh, Kirsty Doole, Aimee Oliver-Powell, Gemma Davis, and Carmen R. Balit. Thank you to Hope Denekamp and my phenomenal agency Kneerim & Williams. Thank you to my UK agent, Ben Fowler, as well as Sandy Violette and the whole team at Abner Stein. I am also grateful to Heather Baror, at Baror International, for championing the work in translation, and Flora Hackett at WME.

Thank you to Mom and Dad for your unconditional love, support, and encouragement. Thank you to Richie for being an incredible brother and for your promise to read the back of the book. Thank you to Nanny and Grammy for always supporting my dreams—I deeply regret that M and Poppy are not here to read my debut novel.

Thank you to Elizabeth Tammi for years of fantastic feedback; I am so grateful to have your support and insight as my critique partner on this publishing journey. Thank you to Caroline Lengyel for your valuable insight and appreciation for the project. Additional thanks to Weronika Janczuk, Emily Gardner, and, of course, my highest gratitude to you, the reader.